PAPER CLIPS

Short Stories By Writers From
EASTERN ENGLAND

Edited By

SUZI BLAIR

NEW FICTION

To Stella.
With Best Wishes.

Ron Measell

First published in 1993 by
NEW FICTION
4 Hythegate, Werrington
Peterborough,
PE4 7ZP

Printed in Great Britain by Forward Press.

Copyright Contributors 1993

Foreword

The advent of New Fiction signifies the expansion of what has traditionally been, a limited platform for writers of short stories. New Fiction aims to promote new short stories to the widest possible audience.

New Fiction collections represent the wealth of new talent in writing, and provide enjoyable, interesting and readable stories appealing to a diversity of tastes.

Intriguing and entertaining; from sharp character sketches to 'slice of life' situations, the stories have been selected because each one is *a good read*.

This collection of short stories is from the pens of the people of Eastern England. They are new stories, sweeping across the spectrums of style and subject to reflect the richness of character intrinsic to the region, today.

Suzi Blair
Editor.

Contents

The Prisoner

by

Roy Kibbler

He had always thought of her as a perfect circle. Even with his eyes closed he could feel her all-round perfection. She was intelligent, beautiful, and in a kind and shapely way, very well behaved. Or so he had believed.

He had reserved a compartment for her, a neat rectangular affair. Until recently their relationship had been exactly the same shape, but now it had become much more pointed.

For the duration of her stay he requested her to remain within the confines of the allotted compartment.

He expected her to meet his request.

For a while she had.

Occasionally her curiosity, like a stray bubble, caused her to open the door and peer outside. On these occasions he had appeared out of the darkness, speaking calmly, hypnotically , urging her back inside, carefully closing the door behind her.

Tonight she had smashed down the door.

The rectangle had fallen away from her, spinning crazily, over and over, ever diminishing, downwards.

She ran amok, breaking into every compartment she could find.

She filled his mind, flooded his being.

He caught hold of her, held her firmly and pressed her ferocity against his panic.

Her ferocity was wild, it spun around her like a whirlpool. His panic was disguised yet he let himself fall gratefully into her, spinning crazily, over and over, ever diminishing, downwards.

He realised that it would always be like this.

He would never be able to let her go.

She would never let him.

He would never let him.

He got out of bed, dressed quickly and went downstairs.

He was full of her, over flowing with her.

He switched on the TV.

1

Reflections held captive by the blank screen slipped out into the room.

The grained image hardened, formed a confrontation. Face to face.

He turned the sound down.

Deep within him he'd always secretly feared she'd escape. Memories were dangerous.

Especially when they were as clear as those he had of her.

He began to write her a letter.

He unfolded her from himself, smoothed her across the surface of the paper, wrapping his words around her.

In times of stress he used words as a means of defence. Tonight he needed words very badly indeed.

He needed them like a mine needs pit-props, and without them his mind would cave in.

On the screen, expressions flicked like static between the two figures.

He was rejecting her.

His expression slapped her face.

Both her eyes were loaded with resentment.

She calmly let him have it with both barrels.

He'd finished the letter.

Folded neatly, like a pressed flower, he'd sealed her in a white rectangle.

With a sense of relief he'd flipped it on to the carpet, next to the TV set.

It had tumbled through the air, spinning crazily, over and over.

His body began to relax.

It was closing down for the night; like lights in an apartment block, it was systematically switching off.

The face with the smoking eyes seemed to be staring at him. He switched her off.

The unspoken words on her lips folded into themselves. She fell over backwards, a blurred rectangle, spinning crazily, over and over, ever diminishing, downwards.

The screen went blank.

He went back to bed.

A white rectangular reflection was hung on the screen.

It was a prisoner with a suspended sentence.

Hero Worship

by

K D Kenning

The rain drummed heavily on the roof of Jenny's car. As she sat there staring out into the murky streets, she tried to draw comfort from its constant beat.

She folded her still shaking hands into her lap. Try as she might, she could not stop herself quivering. The sight of the blood that had been there only moments before was still etched into her mind, making her dizzy and nauseous.

Still, it was all over now. She'd done it - finally, she'd done it. Now, the only thing that had ever come between her and her husband had been removed - permanently. At last, they could be happy again - just as it had been when she had first married Brian.

Slumping back into her seat, she allowed her mind to wander, remembering the good times. . .

Brian had attracted her from the first instant she saw him. Tall, leanly muscled, with a shock of unruly black hair, he was everything she had ever dreamed of. He had, quite literally, swept her off her feet, and within seven months of their first meeting they were man and wife.

Jenny remembered that time fondly. She had been so happy - everything had seemed so perfect to her, nothing could go wrong.

But it had.

It was barely six months after their wedding day when it began. When *That* program had first come onto prime-time TV. Advertised as the most astounding sci-fi drama in the history of television, 'Star Force' had immediately shot to the top of the ratings. It was as if the entire nation had gone Star Force crazy - books, magazines, posters - everywhere you went, people were talking about it.

Including Brian - especially Brian.

From the very first episode, he had been glued to the set, a look of total fascination in his glazed eyes.

At first Jenny had been a little offended at this interruption of their routine, but after a while, even she had begun to enjoy it. Well, at least tolerate it.

3

Who knows, if things had stayed like that, she would never have been forced to do what she had just done. She would never have considered murder, let alone actually committed it. . .

She sighed deeply, pressing her fingertips to her temples, gently trying to massage away the persistent headache beginning to form there. A migraine was the last thing she needed now.

Closing her eyes, she redoubled her efforts to relax. Once again remembering the events that had led to such a gruesome ending. . .

When the first Star Force fan club started up, Brian had been the first to join. Shortly afterwards, the parcels had arrived - infrequently at first, but soon becoming a daily event.

At first, he only bought the more useful souvenirs from the series - books, TV guides - the usual things. But soon, he had become obsessed with the collecting and bought everything he possibly could which bore the Star Force logo. Slowly the bills began to mount up.

Then, one night, when Jenny returned home from work, exhausted from having to retype her whole report, came the final straw. She stumbled wearily through the doorway, to find Brian slumped in his chair, wearing a Star Force uniform. To make matters worse he was blind drunk.

They had a blazing row, leading to Jenny storming out in floods of tears.

Brian apologised the next day. He promised never to let himself get so carried away again. Jenny believed him, and for a while anyway, things were fine.

But then he started to wear the uniform again. At least he didn't get drunk though - he couldn't afford it with all the souvenirs he had purchased.

Deep down, she knew, Brian felt upset and guilty for allowing this obsession to so completely overwhelm him. Indeed, in his more lucid moments, which became more infrequent as time went on, he broke down and apologised for everything that he had put her through.

He was desperate to rid himself of his mania, but didn't have the force of will that required. He no longer had any control over his life.

It was then that Jenny had decided to take matters into her own hands. Something drastic had to be done - the series had to be stopped.

The hero of the show was a local actor. A rather quiet, usually ignorant, antisocial man, he completely transformed himself to become the dashing hero in front of the cameras. Ever since the show had first aired, he had received sacks of fan mail, and was mobbed by worshipping fans every time he left his house.

4

If he quit the show, it would have to cancel. If he decided to give it all up, Brian would have no-one to idolise. He would return to her again. . .

Jenny shuddered and opened her eyes. She checked herself for the hundredth time. No, there was no trace of blood anywhere on her clothing.

She carefully inserted the ignition key, and set off for home. Brian would have heard the news on TV by the time she returned, and the torment of the past year would be over.

The steady thump of the wiper blades across the windscreen lured her into complacency. Once again, her mind drifted. . .

Entering the actor's house was easy, as he thought she was just another adoring fan. Grimly, she had confronted him, and told him all about Brian. She begged him to quit the show - it was the only hope for her marriage. Surely he could understand her grief.

But, of course, he hadn't. Refusing to entertain the idea of giving up the fame and fortune, he had tried to push her back out the door. He even dared to laugh at her.

And that's when she had snapped. How dare this man, who had caused so much unhappiness, dare to laugh at her?

In a tear-blurred haze, she snatched his hunting rifle down from it's cabinet in the hallway, and fired it point-blank into his face. For a few sickened moments, she couldn't believe what she had done. Wishing desperately to take these last few moments back, she had collapsed to the floor, horror-stricken.

And then, she realised. This was the answer. With him dead, the show would be cancelled, and if she could make everyone believe it was suicide. . . well, no-one could worship someone who took their own life, could they?

She sat down at his typewriter, and hastily prepared a suicide note;

'To whom it may concern. . .'

Okay, so it was a little over-theatrical, but he had been an actor after all. . .

Finally she arrived home. All the lights were out - Brian had probably gone out to get drunk after hearing of his hero's 'suicide'.

She unlocked the front door, flicking on the lights as she entered. She went straight to the drinks cabinet in the lounge, pouring herself a generous amount of brandy to calm her nerves.

As she raised the glass to her lips, she noticed the letter.

5

Stuck to the picture over the fireplace, she could just make out the first few words, written in Brian's characteristic scrawl;

'To whom it may concern. . .'

Indian Love Call

by

W H Elder

Dave pummelled his pillow into something resembling an ethnic neckrest, laid back and reviewed his life so far. As a fully-paid-up member of the mediocrity he was finding it sadly lacking. He hadn't taken a glamorous film-star out for ages; in fact he couldn't even remember the last time he'd seen a film. Funny, when he was a kid the cinema had seemed so real. He had, in his innocence, taken it as a preview of what life would be like. One only had to grow up, he thought, in order to experience it all. Well, he had grown up and life wasn't like that was it?

The week had started badly anyway. Things seemed to go like that: things would gang up on him. Keys would lose themselves or break in the lock, the car battery would die a sudden death. . . What was it about 'things' anyway? People could be bad enough. . . people could change their minds, drop bombs on you, steal your milk bottles. . .

'The animosity of inanimate objects'. . . he must have read that somewhere. Dave was fed up with things. He decided to busy himself with not getting ready for work, but then, perhaps he had better ring the shop, tell them he would not be in today, tomorrow or ever! He reached for the phone and then checked himself. Why should he bother they would know he wasn't going in when he failed to arrive.

He reached across the bed for the little alarm clock and slid it into the silence of the drawer. Forget about time for the moment. And that went for the radio too; the news he could do without. He could do without so many things really; after all, suppose he had been born a Red Indian or an Eskimo or some such? Surely there would be less things to worry about. He made a quick mental toss-up between a wigwam or an igloo and came down very firmly on the side of the Indian. Why freeze to death in the frozen north for goodness sake? Tearing himself away from the comfort of the bed, he pressed his nose against the window pane searching for the sun in order to work out what time it was; he would have to know things like that if he was going to be an Indian!

Toying with his breakfast toast, he thought about all the decisions he would enjoy not having to make that day. This would not do at all; he was being far too negative. It was no good just doing nothing all day; he might as well have stayed in bed. Outside the sky was a brilliant blue - you could actually see quite a bit of it from the back door, that is if you leaned a little to the right, and Mrs Whatsername from number seven hadn't hung her washing all over the place.

Suddenly he realised he would have to do something. For a moment he stood there nonplused. . . this was terrible, he just couldn't think of anything. He recited the alphabet. . . o, p, q, r, s. Sex? Well, not first thing in the morning! After all, there was only Mrs Whatsit next door who had decided to hang her washing out after all. Anyway, there was something decidedly off-putting watching her bloomers billowing about like demented spinnakers in the Admiral's Cup. He decided on a walk for a change. It was ages since he had had a real good walk. In fact, since buying the car he had almost forgotten how, seemingly doing most of his walking round and round the bedroom in the middle of the night. He would frequently wake up firmly locked in the driving position using the bedpost as a gear lever. It could take several circuits of the room to get his legs to reach all the way down to the floor again.

Well, a walk it would be then. Ignoring the fact that he had neither washed nor shaved, he took his old dufflecoat from behind the door and stepped out into the yard letting the door slam shut behind him. The air was crisp; he felt quite excited and he rejoiced at the prospect of the whole day spread out before him. What would an Indian do he wondered: hunt for food he supposed. So a good walk would get him into the spirit of the thing. Whistling as he went he soon made the end of the road, then predictably he stopped, half turned and cursed. Had he locked the front door? Had he turned the gas off? Oh, to hell with it! He always had this feeling, had to protect all his blessed little things. He wasn't going back now, there weren't that many buffaloes roaming about that he could afford to waste good hunting time like this, worrying about things!

How had he accumulated so much junk anyway? Was it some sort of Parkinson's Law - 'Things increase in number in order to fill the space provided for them'. You have to have somewhere to live and then you fill it with things. You have to 'put down roots' as his Mother had been fond of saying. He reasoned that if the woman of his dreams were to come along, then he would at least be able to offer her somewhere to live. He knew he wasn't Britains answer to Robert Redford, but he did have a two-up and two-down in Battersea and a Morris

Minor. Well, he hadn't found the right Squaw person yet, and he would soon be over the hill the way he was going. Stuck in a dead end job living in a dead end street: it was a cul-de-sac as it happened. Anyway, he had made a decision that he would make no more decisions. Planned to make no more plans and would try very hard to stop trying! It was all nonsense, of course, but in his present confused state only the nonsense made sense. He had reached that middle ground, that no-man's-land that lay tempting him just beyond the bounds of sanity, that other dimension into which he could sidestep, and who would notice, who would care? Subconsciously he made for the park and took a straight line across the grass in the general direction of the pond. 'Do not walk on the grass' he read. Well, Indians don't take any notice of things like that.

'Hey you!'

Dave kept walking. . . ignore him, what can they do to you, shoot you?

'Hey, you in the duffle coat!'

Dave reached the edge of the pond and stood next to a little boy who was launching a tiny yacht. The boat bobbed along gamely enough for a little way and then sank for no explicable reason.

'It's your fault!' the boy looked at him accusingly.

'How was it my fault?' Dave spluttered turning to the youngster who had been joined by the now irate Park Warden.

'You should keep to the gravel path, sir.' His eyes were rivetted on the dirty duffle coat and the unshaven chin.

'He sank my boat' the boy accused again.

Dave coloured up but ignored them both, admitting to himself that he did look a bit like an out-of-work submarine commander. The water looked quite shallow; bending down Dave removed his shoes and socks.

'Are you going for my boat mister?'

Dave spoke without looking at him.

'No, I'm not going for your damn boat. I'm going for a paddle.' He turned to the Warden. 'I can't see a notice saying 'Do not paddle' so paddle it is then .... Indians do quite a lot of paddling.'

With his shoes round his neck and a sock in each pocket he set off across the water. The bottom of the pond was a veritable minefield of debris: he could feel the pop bottles and empty tin cans as he made his way gingerly to the other side, emerging like a bedraggled Gulliver to a welcoming party of midgets.

'Is the water cold mister?' All the children gathered round him. 'Are there any frogs?'

9

He dried his feet as best as he could with his handkerchief; they were cold but not unpleasantly so. He felt relieved not to have cut himself. Stretching out on a bench he wriggled his toes to the great amusement of his audience. The sun, which had been hiding behind a tiny puff of cloud suddenly reappeared and his feet started to steam slightly. He felt good although perhaps a little apprehensive. The Warden had disappeared, no doubt to call the police or the Cavalry or somebody. Perhaps he had better make himself scarce. A woman was walking purposefully towards him, she seemed to be walking at him. Dave stood up as she approached as if to defend his position, but at the last moment she bent down, scooped up the scruffiest little kid in the group and shook him.

'I thought I told you to stay away from strange men!'

Dave looked at her and couldn't help smiling.

'Don't start smiling at me, I know your sort!'

'And what sort might I be then?'

'Barmy' she replied 'walking in your bare feet.'

He looked down. All the kids had vanished and so had his shoes and socks; he was stuck in the middle of the park with nothing to walk home in! Well, Indians walked barefoot. . . or was it rode bareback. . . he could never remember which. Anyway, he was sure he could make it to the nearest shops and buy a cheap pair of sandals or something. Making his way across the grass yet again he met the Warden and a Policeman.

'Why do you insist on walking on the grass sir?' the Policeman enquired while the Warden just stood glowering at him.

Dave stared into the middle distance.

'Well, as you can see I have become separated from my footwear.' He lifted a foot and wiggled his toes at the Warden as if to emphasize the point, 'and I have no intention of walking on the gravel path in bare feet.'

The Policeman grunted, 'And I believe you have been paddling in the pond?'

'Yes, I wanted to know how deep it was.' The logic of his answer seemed to scuttle any reprimand the lawman may have had in mind.

'Well, if you have finished your examination of the pond, sir, I would suggest you go home and have a little rest. . . have an early night, and do try and obey the park regulations in future.'

The policeman turned and made off with the now furious Warden.

'He's a nut case I tell you - a real fruit and nut case.'

When Dave reached the pavement again it felt quite warm under his feet; he was sure people would stare and make remarks, but they all seemed far too preoccupied with their own problems, probably all worrying about their precious

10

little things. Only the children noticed his bare feet, pulling on their Mothers' arms and pointing. Tiny babies in prams with eyes like Daleks locked onto him with twin laser beams.

'Look, Mummy, that man's got black feet!' Blackfeet! It was all too much. . . the most famous Indian tribe of all time, or was it Blackfoot? Did it matter?

The first shoe shop he came to hardly looked promising, but he entered and watched a woman of about his own age dusting some shelves. He wiped his feet on the mat and coughed. She turned round and presumably desperate for a customer, appeared to ignore his dishevelled appearance.

'Have you any cheap sandals? Er, I seem to have become separated from my footwear. I'll have to stop saying that. It sounds as if I've lost something half-way up the Orinoko!'

'Oh!' she laughed, 'I've just what you need.' She delved into a basket of reject seconds and pulled out a pair of moccasins. 'They're not much better than slippers really. . . Look, I can see you're in a bit of a mess, I'll get a cloth for your feet, and I've just put the kettle on; you look as if you could do with a cup!'

Dave, quite speechless, nodded gratefully, a lump in his throat. This was the first time in ages he had encountered the female of the species, let alone shared a pot of tea with one. He couldn't help staring at her, she was quite attractive, or could be. Dark hair, slim, not exactly sexy, just sort of 'nice'. 'Nice' seemed inadequate somehow. He noticed a ringless hand.

'I'll take the moccasins, they fit beautifully.' He sipped the tea.

'Would you like them in a bag? Oh, how silly of me, you'll want to put them on.'

Dave walked around the shop; he could have a done a war dance the way he felt. There was something in the atmosphere, he could feel it; they seemed to be striking a bond, kindred spirits. He couldn't let it slip away; what would an Indian do - jump in with both blackfeet? He had reached the door, it would soon be too late!

'Do you live round here?'

She just gave him a blank look. He knew he was making a poor attempt to chat her up. Catching his reflection in a mirror he could see he looked as ridiculous as he felt, so what had he got to lose? Whatever her reaction might be, he could be out on the pavement in two steps and gone forever.

'I just wondered if you lived locally, I don't recall seeing you before. I pass this way in the car, I've got an old Morris Minor.'

'I live above the shop. . .'

'I wondered if you would like a little run out at the weekend?'

'. . . with my Father.'

'Oh!' Their voices had overlapped awkwardly. Had she heard his proposition? Dave looked out into the street: it seemed to be full of women. The glass door was like the side of an aquarium, plenty of other fish out there. Why was he so hooked on this one?'

'It's a green one, isn't it?'

'What is?'

'Your Morris; I see you most mornings. You stop at the lights just here. . .' She looked, at that moment, rather like an Indian Squaw. For the first time he noticed she was wearing some kind of bead necklace.

'How about Southend on Sunday then?'

She smiled eagerly.

'That would be very nice. . . er?'

'Sorry! Dave. . . Dave Walters.'

She held out her hand which he grasped hold of like a lifeline.

'Pamela. . . Pamela Brown.'

He repeated the name under his breath; Pocahontas would have been more appropriate under the circumstances.

'Would you like some more tea?' Dave could only nod.

'I'll need my hand back' she half-whispered.

He released his grip and she disappeared into a cubby-hole at the back of the shop. Dave made the most of a few moments to himself desperate to collect his thoughts. It was the most exquisite irony; the first time he had nearly lost his sanity, and his mad escapade had thrust him headlong into a new relationship. She was all he could have hoped for, prayed for. Just as quickly doubt filled his heart. Perhaps she was just as desperate for a man as she had been for a customer! Did it matter?

Pamela returned with the tea. Their eyes met, searching, reaching out for the truth. She raised her cup to him.

'To Southend on Sunday then!' Her face told him all: her eyes positively sparkled with enthusiasm.

Dave joined in the toast.

'This is a lovely cup of tea.' He paused savouring the moment. 'Tell me it isn't Indian!'

The Judgement of William

by

Frank Webber

The Judgement of Paris resulted in the award of
the Golden Apple. Sir William's choice would win
the Golden Pear.
He too has to choose between three ladies and one
of them is very alluring.

Carlton Associates had had a good year. Sir William, Chairman of the Company, was more than pleased and the staff dinner added even more to his enjoyment. Splendid! It was simply splendid.

'It's time Sir William' murmured the Company Secretary as the waitresses removed the last of the plates. Sir William stood up somewhat unsteadily and banged on the table with a salt pot. The rectangle of tables in front of him transformed themselves into a squadron of white-hulled ships at anchor. The air stilled and crews turned smartly, all sitting at attention.

Sir Willian reviewed his fleet. A smart turn-out. A pity there weren't more wrens. Must do something about that. He beamed at them all and all ears went into 'receive' mode: 'What a pleasure it is to welcome you to this year's dinner and I hope that the pleasure will continue in the dance to follow and, ahem, perhaps even later'. He beamed even more as one or two of the younger frigates transmitted a series of hoots. 'Carlton Associates have enjoyed a successful year and on behalf of the Board I thank you all for your loyalty and damn hard work'.

The Company Secretary clapped and all ships joined in the salute. Sir William heard only a roaring noise in his head and he murmured to himself that the sea was cutting up a little rough. He poured himself a glass of water from a jug that moments before had held sticks of celery. All hands stared, somewhat amused, but none spoke. The Company Secretary concentrated on a chandelier. His expression giving so sign of panic as a patch of damp spread across his trousers. Sir William had spilt some water.

'And now for our Annual Miss Carlton Competition, if 'competition' is the right word because, as we all know, the ladies didn't actually compete. They

13

were entered, as it were, by the votes of our male colleagues. I myself did not have a vote because mine is the pleasure of choosing the winning finalist from the three to be presented this evening. The prize will be our Golden Pear Award. So let us begin. First we have. . .' and the Company Secretary hurriedly handed him a somewhat damp piece of paper. Sir William held it gingerly having noticed the now conspicuous stain on the man's trousers.

'Er ... we have Miss Penelope Goodbody. Come along Miss Goodbody. Is she here ...?' and Sir William searched out his fleet.

Penelope Goodbody whispered to her husband. 'He's a dirty old man. He's drunk. They all are. It's like one of those award things they show on telly.' She rose and stepped up to the top table as Mr Goodbody clapped enthusiastically.

Sir William shook her hand. 'And which department are you my dear?'

'I'm the cleaner' she smiled back, 'and I'm a missus.' Such a reply caused Sir William to stare hard at her before seeking a haven in his list of finalists. The paper itself was beginning to tear across the creases. The Company Secretary concentrated even more on the chandelier.

'Miss Jocelyn Philpott' Sir William announced. 'Now I know this young lady very well. Step forward my dear'.

'How ridiculous' muttered Miss Philpott to her mother sitting beside her. 'And how embarrassing'.

'You must go,' said her mother. 'After all you do have a position to maintain.'

Sir William greeted her warmly. 'We are all indebted to Miss Philpott for her most efficient supervision of the secretariat,' and light applause broke out. She condescended a gracious smile which froze on her face as Mrs Goodbody hissed 'Good luck ducks'.

'And now Miss Leonora Hardy,' announced Sir William which acted as a signal for the fleet to break out in cheers from the male Fletcher Christians, much to the annoyance of their female Captain Blighs who laid into their mates with well aimed kicks on the shins.

Sir William stood transfixed as Miss Hardy cruised to the top table. He saw a sleek, fresh, and gleaming schooner, well turned out both fore and aft. The schooner made way effortlessly towards him and dropped anchor.

'And which department are you my delic. . . my dear?' His voice was a whole tone higher.

Leonora smiled her broadside of a smile. A smile she had soon learned could sink any male vessel within range.

'I'm in reproduction Sir,' she said. 'Photocopying and all that.' Numerous Captain Blighs laid on some more.

14

Sir William raised his hands and the fleet came to order. 'Now it falls to me to choose this year's Miss Carlton. Whom shall it be? It will help, in such a delightful chore, if I question each lady in turn. From their answers I can then judge accordingly. Are we ready. . .?'

He turned to Penelope Goodbody who stood looking as haughty as she could. To be truthful she was annoyed at that secretary woman. Them in the offices thought they were something above a cleaner and that one in particular wasn't friendly at all. But she knew that Mr Goodbody was proud of her. Good lookin' old gal he called her. And she wasn't bad for forty-four. It was the physical hard work that helped her keep such a slim figure.

'Now Miss Goodbody...' Sir William started to say.

'Missus Goodbody if you don't mind'.

'Yes, yes. Mrs Goodbody. Now why do you think I should award you this year's Golden Pear?'

'Well. For a start I'm the cleaner and first impressions make all the difference. I could make your office sparkle like a jewel. Your visitors would think they're in front of royalty.'

Sir William joined in the applause. 'Splendid. Quite Splendid.'

He looked anew at the faded but haughty beauty in front of him. But she was married. Pity that. And that huge chap must be her husband, very much a navigational hazard. Not to be trifled with. Steer well clear. He turned to Miss Philpott and nodded.

'The business world depends on correspondence,' sniffed Miss Philpott looking severely at Mrs Goodbody. 'Very few actually visit the offices. It is the quality of the letter, its presentation and layout that really reflects the efficiency and reliability of the organisation. I would ensure that my girls turn out work of such high standard that success in our business dealings would be well nigh guaranteed.'

'Hear, hear!' Sir William was impressed. She had such a well formed face, such slim silhouette. But oh! So severe. So impregnable.

He turned eagerly to the third of the trio. She stood like a proud figurehead as befitted a queen of ships. The fleet seemed to envelop him as all ships took sights of the same beacon as himself. The beacon intensified its broadside of a smile and its bearing occupied his full field of vision.

'Miss Hardy ...?' he managed to signal.

None would ever know why, at that moment, Leonora Hardy decided to slip off her lambswool cardigan and to stand, so obviously, in view of them all. Most of the Fletcher Christians experienced a broadening of the bruising on their shins; Mrs Goodbody sent a warning shot across the bow of her husband; Miss Philpott sniffed and looked disgusted.

Sir William's face went through the colours of the White Ensign. His head was full of noise. Perspiration ran into his eyes obscuring his view of a well-filled mainsail but with much effort he was able to point and signal to all ships: 'She has the Golden Pear'. The sea took on a mighty swell and he toppled to the heaving deck beneath him...

The following Monday morning found Mrs Goodbody preparing to leave the offices after finishing her stint. She looked up to see Miss Philpott arriving for work. 'Morning ducks. Is he still with us then?'

Miss Philpott looked at her icily. 'I understand that Sir William had a comfortable stay in hospital and was allowed home yesterday.'

'He was drunk if you ask me. Drunk as a Lord. A dirty old Lord.'

'It was overwork and the strain. He demanded too much of himself, which is more than can be said of some.'

'And our miss-you-know-who demanded that little too much. Dirty old man. He deserved all he got.'

'Nothing of the sorts. Besides, Miss Hardy has left the firm for a fresh career. In fashion I believe. She has much to learn. But I must get on. Excuse me.' Miss Philpott swept away leaving the other woman thinking that Miss Hardy had little to learn apart from, perhaps, cleaning a house.

Some miles away, Sir William sat up in bed nibbling at his toast.

'Damn good night that,' he murmured to himself. 'Pity it was so rough. But by gad! That little wren was delicious. Delightful. Leonora Hardy. No wonder Nelson had cried 'Kiss me Hardy' when he was a gonner. But I'm not a gonner, my word no. I feel as fit as a fiddle. My word yes.

There was a light knock as the bedroom door opened.

'You're looking much better this morning darling,' said Leonora. 'I've brought you some more toast to nibble.' She cruised towards him, her pennants streaming behind her.

'Stand by for boarders,' cried Sir William. 'Let's have the old battle flag aloft eh! My gad yes'.

The Caretaker

by

David Lightfoot

'Leave the light on, Mr Robinson, I've a few things to do in here yet,' said Quinn. He half turned awkwardly on the step ladder's narrow platform and looked down at the top of the caretaker's bald head as he leaned in around the doorjamb.

'I've been intending to check on the numbers of these books for weeks now,' he added, partly to reassure himself that Robinson had heard his first request and would not in fact, as he seemed about to do, switch off the light.

The caretaker was well known for his uncommunicative surliness. Indeed, throughout his fourteen years at St. Lawrence's, Aubrey Quinn had found the man impossible to like.

'I'll lock up,' he said, turning again to the column of red textbooks that he had been counting, then 'Damn it all!' as he grabbed at the top shelf and sucked in his breath.

Robinson had switched off the stockroom light and walked off without comment, leaving the door open. Was the man deaf? Or just more thoughtless the nearer he approached retirement? Quinn groped his way backwards down the ladder and to the doorway. By the time he had reached and looked out into the corridor his anger was subsiding. Perhaps he had mumbled. Several of his pupils complained he did. And there was little point in a confrontation with the drab little man; he hadn't the energy at this time of the day and it would only spoil his digestion and with it his evening meal.

He found the light switch annoyingly stiff and a small spark arced beneath his fingertip. Snatching his hand away, he decided to leave it off. He had had just about enough for tonight. He smiled in pleasurable anticipation of their Monday night treat; Beryl and he did so look forward to well cooked fish. At the thought of the better part of a bottle of dry white wine to himself, he felt his stomach contract a little. Kedegree and Muscadet, the latest le Carré in front of a coal fire, Elgar on the CD player, a malt whisky or two . . .

As he started down the corridor, he remembered that he had left his mark-book on his desk in his classroom. Cursing the inconvenience half-heartedly but pleased to have remembered, he turned back down the corridor towards the room that dominated his waking hours.

He blasphemed as he found its door apparently locked. He tried to shift the brass handle but it seemed jammed. Searching in his pockets without avail for his keys, he concluded that he must have left them in his briefcase in the staffroom. Rather than risk more rudeness from Robinson, he decided he would go and find them.

Sunderland was standing in the staffroom doorway, keeping the sprung door open with his foot while speaking to someone inside. From the coarse laughter it sounded like Steadman. As Quinn approached, Sunderland glanced lazily in his direction, rested his arm on the top edge of the door and shifted his foot.

Quinn passed underneath his outstretched arm, squeezing between him and the door. If he had tried to excuse himself it would only have resulted in his being asked in a bad imitation of a German accent to show his papers and being ordered to explain why he was visiting this concentration camp.

He nodded at Steadman who was sprawled in an armchair. Steadman did not acknowledge him but continued speaking to Sunderland. Quinn paid no heed to this discourtesy: Steadman taught Biology and considered human beings to be animals motivated solely by self-interest. Looking around the untidy room, he failed to spot his briefcase. Distracted by his search, he half heard Sunderland wish Steadman goodnight and the latter grunt a reply as the door closed under pressure of the over-powerful spring - something else he must remember to ask Robinson to see to.

'Have you seen my briefcase, Steadman, old chap?' he asked. Pleasantly enough, he thought.

In reply Steadman emitted a prolonged, howling yawn, stretched his arms till his elbows cracked and stood up decisively.

'Could have sworn I left it up against this table-leg,' muttered Quinn.

Steadman ran the tip of his little finger around the whorl of his right ear and stood under the fluorescent strip-light examining the flakes of skin and dried soap scooped out by his nail. After a few seconds' consideration he placed his nail under the ball of his thumb and carefully flicked his off-scourings straight into Quinn's face.

Quinn was too astonished to speak. He stood dabbing in fastidious repulsion at his shirt front. Steadman regarded him in contemptuous silence, picked up an expensive-looking briefcase with complicated brass locks and strode to the door. He paused only to switch off the light.

Quinn continued to stand in the centre of the room dumb with shock and bewilderment. Was there some sort of conspiracy to insult him? One involving even Robinson the Caretaker? He knew that most of the staff considered him of little account; were probably bored by his stories about Beryl and his advice on *cordon bleu* cookery; made sexual jokes about the fact that he lived alone.

Thought of home made him glance at his wristwatch. He stared numbly at his wrist. The watch was missing. He knew he had not taken it off. He never removed it, except to take a bath. One of those expanding links must have snapped. But surely he would have felt the sudden loss of its weightsnug?

Then he remembered. He *had* removed it while sitting at his desk in his classroom, just before going into the stock cupboard to check the fifth year literature titles. He had noticed that it was displaying the wrong date again and had tried to correct it. He recalled his irritation at having to move on the figures right through the month to come back again to the correct date. He was reminded of that strange sadness that had gripped him as he watched the dates changing in their tiny box. But he could have sworn he had put the watch back on.

He felt suddenly very tired and confused. Perhaps he was coming down with the flu that so many members of staff had caught these last few weeks. He held the knuckles of his right hand against his forehead. His skin felt neither hot not cold. He rubbed his face. It felt peculiarly numb and rough, as if he had forgotten to shave that morning. Had he, in fact, shaved? He remembered switching on the bathroom transistor radio for the Eight o'clock News and Beryl come running in and knocking it over. She often did when he forgot to feed her. She would be loudly complaining of hunger now.

The thought gave him sufficient energy to stride towards the door. He was going to find that Robinson fellow and demand that he unlock his classroom. He yanked the doorhandle venomously. It did not budge. He tried again. There was no doubt: this door too was locked. That damned caretaker must have waited for Steadman to leave but not checked if the room was empty. He leaned forward and rested his forehead against the woodwork. It felt neither smooth nor rough, cool nor warm. An ineffable weariness seeped over his body. He would have to sit down. But first he must try just once more to open the door and hurry home to Beryl.

The handle would not even move downwards. Almost weeping with frustration, he turned back helplessly towards the centre of the room and sat in the armchair that he tended to occupy at lunchtimes. What was he to do? Break a window? Phone the Head? The chair embraced him like a mother. He would sit and wait a while. Someone would come, eventually ....

He surfaced abruptly on hearing the Head's voice. It had that level of volume and authority normally reserved for addressing staff-meetings. He glanced around furtively to ascertain whether anyone had noticed that he had dropped off to sleep.

'I will tell you all I know, ladies and gentlemen,' the Head was saying. 'Apparently, shortly after opening the school this morning, Mr Robinson found Aubrey dead at his desk in his classroom. His head was resting on his open markbook and he had his watch clutched in his left hand.' He paused to clear his throat.

'Dr Bromfield, whom I called in at once, told me - off the record, I hasten to add - that it was probably a heart attack, early yesterday evening. The funeral is on Friday afternoon. I shall represent you all. There are no relatives. Mr Robinson did tell me, however, that Aubrey had a rather elderly Burmese cat. In fact, rather than see it have to be put down or allowed to run wild, he has very kindly offered to take care of it. Finding Aubrey like that was a nasty shock for him. He said he was very fond of him. They had both, in fact, been fourteen years on the staff here - in their different capacities.'

Horror in the Night

by

Wendy Martyn

Forty five years ago I was eighteen when we moved into an old vicarage. It was a gloomy austere looking Victorian building, very different from the gracious cheerful late Georgian house we had just left. Loving that one as I did, it was inevitable that I should dislike this one on sight. For one thing, the house was close to the main road; the other had been set among fields, reached by a winding lane and commanding a superb view of the Lincolnshire Wolds. The main rooms were dark and very high, they all led off from one side of the long dark hall; on the other side a mahogany staircase hugged the wall and gave onto a small half landing from which opened a large square north facing bedroom, built over the kitchen. On one side of the black cast iron fireplace was an ornate brass bell handle set into the wall. This bedroom was allocated to me and I *hated* it after the small sunny cosy little room which had been mine in our former house, and which had looked out over fields and hills instead of the dreary overgrown laurels which was all the view this room obtained. The rest of the bedrooms lay side by side along the main landing, looking out onto the main road.

Downstairs in the passage, above the kitchen door, a row of old fashioned bells hung, each labelled with the name of the room it served. We tried them all. The only bell which did not work was the bell for my bedroom.

Being over the kitchen, where the old Cook & Heat stove burned night and day, meant that my bedroom was always warm. Warm that is until eleven o'clock at night.

We had been living about a month in the house when I discovered this phenomenon. I was one who always went to bed at nine o'clock and was therefore fast asleep at the hour of eleven, but one night something woke me a few minutes before the hour. The room felt full of distress and a deathly coldness seemed to emanate from the far corner beside the fire grate. Terrified, I leapt out of bed and rushed out of the door and down the stairs. My incoherent claim that there was something horrible and horrifying in my room caused my father to go and investigate. There was nothing there and the experience was put down to my having awakened after a nightmare. But it was half an hour before

I dared return to bed. That to me was the beginning of a horror that occurred every night at eleven o'clock; usually I was asleep at that time but now *wanting* to be asleep I often awoke and every time that feeling of deep distress and fear would fill the room and that deathly coldness reach out from the far corner beside the fire place.

We made enquiries in the village but no one knew of any explanation for the horror. But one night in late December something else happened. My mother and sisters were sitting in the kitchen one night after I had gone to bed, when suddenly one of the room bells outside the passage began to ring violently. At first they thought it was my father pulling the bell in his study but going into the passage they saw it was the broken bell for my room jangling. They made for the stairs and met me hurtling down.

The atmosphere in my bedroom was terrifying; icily cold, fearful and full of unbearable anxiety and distress. The bell continued to ring violently for about fifteen minutes before it stopped its clangour and swung slowly to a standstill. The time was eleven o'clock. My father suggested mice, but the whole time we never saw a trace of any mice. It remained a mystery.

Several years later, after we had left the house and moved elsewhere, I was travelling on a local bus. The bus was full and an old man sat down beside me. After a few moments silence he commented on the weather and then began to chat. He informed me he had lived in and around this area as man and boy.

'I could tell you many a tale of folk that lived round here,' he said with a grin, 'Some happy, some funny and some downright sad.'

We were passing through the village where the Old Vicarage stood and I looked out at the house with loathing.

The old man caught my look, 'Do you know that house?'

'I did once,' I said briefly.

'Ah,' he said, 'It was real tragic what happened there.'

'Why?' I asked, 'What did happen?'

Glad to have caught my interest, he leaned back in the seat and sucked on his pipe. 'Well' he began. 'It was just before the turn of the century when I was a young man. The vicar at that time was a nice chap, very well liked. He married in middle age, a real lovely woman, just a bit younger than himself. They never reckoned they'd ever have children, but they did; one child, a boy. He was the apple of their eye. They fair doted on him. Loveable little chap and he grew into a real grand lad, always had a cheerful word for everybody. Popular he was. When he was eighteen he went to university. The world was his oyster.' The old man sighed. 'When he was nineteen he came home for Christmas as usual, suffering from toothache. Well it got worse and worse until by the day after Boxing Day his dad took him into town to the dentist.' The old man grimaced, 'Dentists in them days fairly pulled your head off! The poor lad had several teeth took out and came home feeling very poorly. His mother put him straight to bed. The doctor came and gave him something for the pain and told him to stay in bed for a few days, then he'd be as right as rain.'

The old man fell silent shaking his head.

'Well?' I prompted 'What happened? Did he get better?'

The old man shook his head again. 'He began to improve,' he said slowly, 'Then on the 29th December the Vicar and his wife had promised to attend a dinner party given by a Patron of his living three miles away. The Bishop was going to be there so they couldn't very well get out of it. The lad was improving, so though the Vicar's wife didn't really want to leave her son, they went, leaving him in the care of the old housekeeper. They set off early evening, promising to be back by midnight. It was a frosty night. Perfect carriage ride. Now the old housekeeper was very deaf and couldn't hear the room bells and the housemaid was out for the evening. The old lady checked on the lad, found him sleeping peacefully and went back to the kitchen where she dozed by the fire.

The Vicar and his wife got back at midnight as promised and the lady went straight upstairs to see her son. She opened the door and let out a scream. When the Vicar rushed upstairs he saw his son sprawled in the corner of the bedroom near the bell pull, covered in blood. It was obvious he'd been pulling the bell for assistance because there was blood on the handle and on the mantelpiece, where he must have tried to steady himself. The clock had been knocked on the floor and smashed. Its hands had stopped at eleven o'clock. The poor lad was quite dead. The doctor said he mush have had a sudden haemorrhage from his teeth and bled to death. It was a terrible tragedy, it broke his parents; they never got over it. The following year they moved right away; couldn't bear the house no more.'

The bus began to slow down at the end of a lonely lane and the old man blinked.

'Ah well, it were a long time ago. Here's my stop missus, it were nice chatting to you. Good Day.'

He began to move away but I put my hand on his arm for there was something I must know before he went, even though in my heart of hearts I knew the answer.

'Can you tell me which bedroom he slept in?'

'He looked at me shrewdly before beginning to move down the gangway.
'Yes, m'dear, it were the one over the kitchen.'
It was a hot day but I felt chilled to the bone as the bus moved on.

If You Can't Stand The Heat

by

Linda Crust

Last week was Margaret's ruby wedding party. There was a happy family gathering full of cousins and grandchildren. I kissed Margaret fondly. She was still a pretty woman with the same slight, attractive twist to her lips when she was listening to someone.

'It seems like yesterday,' I said fatuously.

It was exciting to have a grown-up cousin who wore lipstick and high heels. I loved Margaret's visits, her high, twinkly voice and her glamorous way of tossing her hair back and looking over her shoulder to check the straightness of her stocking seams. To a ten year old, Margaret had the allure of Garbo, Ingrid Bergman and Betty Grable rolled into one, with a bit added.

Naturally any man would be honoured to marry Margaret and I listened agog as Margaret recited one conquest after another. It was no surprise that the winner in the contest for Margaret's hand was Charles who was as dashing as his fiancée.

Charles drove a sports car and played rugger. It was apposite to say that Charles sported a moustache - everything he did was orientated to games and the pursuit of success. Margaret simpered and giggled and wrapped his long scarf round her neck and his like a figure of eight and called him darling even in front of Auntie Eva, which made me blush.

Auntie Eva was not so much straight-laced as a woman of her time. Some years ago she proudly told me that she had become a modern woman and would defiantly hang out her washing on a Sunday. To be accurate, she was as modern as was possible for her nature.

'I wouldn't hang out knickers on Sunday of course,' she admitted. This was the woman who suffered almost the cruellest blow to a daughter that could befall a mother.

I was to be a pink bridesmaid with Joan, my cousin, and Audrey, my sister, in blue and cream - like a bunch of sweet peas Dad said. My happiness was so huge that I tried to hide my smiles to keep it secret. It was the most enormous thing that had ever happened to me.

Then I blue it. Margaret and Joan and Auntie Eva were coming over on a visit to us to choose the dresses in our town because the shops were better than theirs. Clothes had just come off coupons and we were going to go mad. Although I wasn't the most helpful child in the world I wanted to do everything I could to make the visit a success so I decided to wash up the breakfast things for my mother. Our hot water system varied greatly according to the reaction of the old boiler to the prevailing wind so, to hurry things up, I put a pan of water on the stove.

My mother was busy preparing a bedroom for the visitors. Audrey was tidying the living room and Dad was keeping out of the way. I stood on tiptoe to get above the pan of boiling water and with shoulders clenched, I lifted it carefully from the stove. They asked me silly questions afterwards like, 'Why did you drop it?'

'It just dropped,' I said through my tears. The pain was excruciating. It felt as if my legs and feet were in a fiery furnace. My plaid kilt was drenched and I hoped that no-one would think I'd wet myself.

Audrey reacted quickly to my screams. She rushed in and pulled off my socks and sandals. The skin came off with it like a sock lining and I screamed more at the sight of the bloody stumps. My mother's face appeared white and startled. I expected her to scold me but she didn't. My feet were wrapped in clean towels and Audrey was sent round the corner to fetch the doctor as fast as she could.

'I can't go to hospital,' I tried to tell the ambulance man. 'I'm going to choose a bridesmaid's dress. Margaret's coming.' The pain inside was as big as the pain outside. How could I spoil this happy day!

'Hush' said my mother. There was nothing more useful she could say to me. I expect it eased her to say something. The men carried me out on a stretcher. To my astonishment there was a little crowd outside on the pavement.

My mother had always taught me to greet people politely but I had no training for this sort of occasion. Did I wave regally from the stretcher or did I bellow out in pain while they beat their chests for me? Not knowing what to do in this unexpected flurry of attention, I closed my eyes until I was safely inside the dark, frightening ambulance.

I didn't know it at the time but my friend Janice had been in the crowd and, seeing me carried into an ambulance with my eyes closed, she had rushed home and told her mother that I was dead. I might just as well have been dead for the use I was now. Things like this just couldn't intrude into Margaret's glamorous, fun life.

As I lay in the hospital cubicle I thought of the visitors arriving, of their amazement at my clumsiness, of Margaret telling Auntie Eva, 'Of course she can't be a bridesmaid now.'

'No,' I groaned, 'Please no.' But the picture in my mind wouldn't go away. People would laugh at a bridesmaid in bandages hobbling down the aisle. The wedding was only ten weeks away. I would never be better in time. I groaned and prayed for death.

'Can you give her something for the pain?' My mother asked the sister.

I was still in hospital when they came to visit me a month later. It was a kind thought. They brought their dresses to show me. Margaret was sweet and held my hand and looked soulfully at me through her mascaraed lashes.

'Charles was devastated when I told him,' she said. I felt a little thrill hoping it was true. 'He would have come to see you today but he's playing rugger.' I pictured Charles, strong and debonair playing rugger with a wistful smile on his face for my pain.

Margaret gave me a bottle of real grown-up scent called 'Evening in Paris' and Auntie Eva gave me a canvas tray cloth with a transfer of poppies on it which she said I could embroider. This later proved impossible as no needle would go in and out of the canvas but my mother said the thought was there.

What I remember most about the visit was the extraordinary thing that happened to Joan. As the grown-ups stood at the end of the bed discussing the wedding, my cousin Joan was leaning against a chimney breast near me. I could see her but the others couldn't. Before my eyes Joan slid down the wall and ended up in a heap on the floor. I concluded that the sight of me was too much for her and I kept quiet.

Auntie Eva, who was a champion talker, sometimes flung a remark over her shoulder without looking or taking a breath.

'Didn't we Joan?' 'Joan?' 'Joan! The girls fainted.' Everyone was galvanised into action. I lay and watched the incident from start to finish like an observer at a surrealist pantomime.

'Oh no! Not another bridesmaid hitting the dust!' Wailed Margaret. 'This wedding is fated.'

I couldn't help it. I giggled. I giggled ferociously. I didn't want to but I couldn't stop it.

'Try to have a little feeling,' my mother hissed at me. That was ironic. I'd done nothing else but agonise mentally and physically for four whole weeks.

When I came home there were more presents and a real basket of fruit with a ribbon round it. I rode in a wheel chair which was fun and made people sorry for me and the pain was at last a little better. The best present of all came from Charles. It was a doll in a pink net dress. I was a bit old for dolls but I lavished love, sentiment and endless care on Caroline.

Stretching the truth a little, 'It came in a box covered in red hearts and it said, 'Love from Charles'. ' I told my envious friend Janice who was in a difficult position as I wasn't actually dead now and she had to be nice to me because of the wheelchair and crutches.

Years later when I was grown-up Auntie Eva told me that Charles hadn't bought the doll himself but had asked her to get one for him and he would pay her the money.

'Another promise unfulfilled.' Auntie Eva pursed her lips and I felt hot with shame for the dastardly Charles and my feelings of misplaced gratitude.

As it happened I was asked to be a bridesmaid twice more in my life but those occasions just missed the thrill of anticipation that I'd felt for Margaret and Charles' wedding-that-never-was.

Auntie Eva was nearly ninety now but not nearly senile.

'Thank you Bob,' she smirked ingratiatingly at her son-in-law as he offered a plate of sausage rolls. 'You're the best thing that ever happened to me.'

Now I was older I could appreciate the mother's outrage that Auntie Eva had experienced forty one years ago when Charles had jilted her daughter.

Safety Zone

by

Shelley Thomas

I closed my eyes and once again I am transported to my own special place. All around as far as I can see there are green fields, with grass as I remember it from my youth. The sky is deep blue, so deep it seems as if it was copied from a child's colouring book. Here I am always alone. I do not have to think, just feel. I run across the fields towards a river as blue as the sky, but I get no closer to it.

Here I stay until the time comes for that alarm bell to ring. When I wake I feel great sorrow, because I am not facing another longed for day - just the end of my wonderful night.

My days are becoming increasingly unbearable. The only time I leave the house is when I need to be treated at the hospital. They know there that I am not just accident prone, they know it is him. But as long as I don't betray him there is nothing they can do. They have pleaded with me to tell them the truth, but as usual I remain silent. I do not speak at all now, I have lost the sense of speech entirely. The only outlet for my emotions is to write, every day I write and then hide my diary from him and the world.

No-one visits us now. He has told them all I am mentally and emotionally unstable. He is respected in the community and no-one would ever believe the things he does to me. Sometimes he can be so nice, bringing me presents helping me with the housework. But these times are so few and far between that I am beginning to forget them.

Now that I can no longer speak, I do not cry out when he inflicts pain on me. Was my life always like this? I can not remember. The pains in my head are affecting my memory. I can not even remember my childhood. If I was in a boxing ring they would stop the fight, because I would not know what day it was.

Last week he raped me again. He is my husband but I still call it rape. He rapes my body and mind, leaving me totally dejected and demoralised. Then he beat me for my lack of emotion. It seems so straight forward to write it all

29

down. He broke my arm and I let him. I can not stop him from doing anything now. Could I ever? I don't know. Pain for me now is something I accept, a way of life. There are only two things that now bring me pleasure - my secret dream place and the knowledge that sooner or later it will all end. I do not know how much longer my body will stand this punishment. Maybe I ask for this life. I must deserve it or it would end. But one thing I believe is that I have to suffer, I can not take the easy way out, suicide is a sin.

Have you ever had a broken arm? Then someone twist it to try and make you scream? I didn't, no I couldn't, scream. I just passed out. That was wonderful because I immediately went to my own dream world. I think he must have kicked me to try and wake me, but it was too late. I was here to stay for a while.

Now I have no pain, no broken limbs or mind. I am free to skip and dance over the grass. Or I just lie and look up at the blue, blue sky. I feel euphoric. To be so totally alone in a magical place such as this, must be as near as I will ever get to Heaven.

I can feel a presence here. Not anything evil, the same feeling you might have when someone caresses your hair. Soothing but not sexual. This feeling is all around me. So am I totally alone? I still feel as though I need to reach the blue river. Sometimes it seems close other times far away. But it always eludes me. I will not reach it this time because I am being pulled back to that other world. But I feel that soon something will happen for me, so far now I can only wait.

Today I wrote a poem to try and explain how I really feel. I wonder if it only applies to me - or are there others? If there are, I will cry inside for them because they might not have anywhere to go, as I do when I close my eyes. If there are more women like me they will understand my poem.

I couldn't think what to call it but the title seemed appropriate. No-one will ever see it anyway. I have no children or family. Something else that seems to have passed me by.

The Pain

The pain comes like a lightening flash
Eventually dissolves like ash,
Then the pleasure slows the pace,
Knowing smile, trusting face.

Then it's time again for pain -
I don't know what he has to gain.
In him only, I place my trust,
Now nothing left but self-disgust.

The pain that comes from his hand
I try my best to understand -
And then from the world I hide,
Lick my wounds, look for my pride.

He says it's in the name of love.
I'm so weak and he's so tough -
I think I hate myself more
As once again I crawl the floor.

I hide my wounds with expert ease,
Waiting for the pain to cease.
He begs forgiveness from me, then,
The pleasure. Then I forgive again.

He has left me alone for a couple of days. He has been staying out late sometimes all night recently. Obviously he has another woman. I pray for her if he
has because I feel as though my body has been completely worn out. Soon I
hope it will happen. I feel deep in my heart it will be soon. I am not frightened
by the prospect of dying and no-one will miss me.

Tonight I am alone in my bed. Once again I close my eyes. I am there.

I look toward the river. I am not alone. There is someone sitting. From the
way he sits I can tell it is a man. But I don't feel threatened, so perhaps he is
the presence I have been feeling for a while. He is so far away but I can see
into his eyes. He is waiting. What for? For me. But I am not yet ready to meet
this man. So for now I continue to enjoy my near solitude. I lay down but I will
not close my eyes, there is no need. Here I never tire, never need to sleep.
When I look towards the river again, he seems a little closer.

Once again I wake up. Another day. How many more to endure? I move
very slowly, because that is the only way I can move these days. Automatically
I do the housework and prepare a meal for him. He might not come home but

31

his meal will be ready for him if he does. When I have cleaned the house from top to bottom, I start again. I clean until 3pm, when I allow myself an hour's sleep.

I lie on the bed and close my eyes. Then I start to panic because nothing is happening. Dear God please don't take away my only pleasure. Let me go there, I need my sanctuary. The tears fall from my eyes like a stream down the side of a mountain. The one thing in life that I could bear anything for was gone. I do not know how it feels to be deprived of someone you love dearly through death, but I must be feeling pretty close to that now.

Once again I am devoid of emotion. He has come home and eaten his dinner, now he turns his whole attention to me. Nothing is right. Obviously he does not want to be here. Thankfully he does not feel the need to assault me sexually, just physically. He didn't stay long, just a few bruises and a black eye. I lay where he left me not daring to move until he was gone. I was frightened to close my eyes in case I was refused my safety zone. But my swollen eye would not stay open, the other followed suit.

I was ecstatic. Not only was I here again but the man was closer, definitely much closer. I sit and watch him for a while. I know he is waiting for me and it seems the stronger the need for my safety zone, the closer he appears. But I need my solitude more at the moment. I will need him soon, I feel.

I wake up because my body is cold. I crawl up the stairs and get into bed. The cold sheets burn my body but straight away I am here again.

I feel a strange need that I have never felt while I have been here before. Everything seems the same, but I feel a yearning to be held, to be desired. I need something or someone else to be here, close to me. I run towards the river, I run and run and slowly so slowly the man gets closer. I can feel him but cannot touch him. Compassion and tenderness radiate from him. I could not reach him then because I was wakened. He had returned home and he was drunk.

I lay in bed waiting for what ever was to come. He ranted and raved - it seems he had been stood up. There was only me to pay the price. He pulled me from the bed and threw me across the room. My head hit the wall and I knew this was it. I must have smiled as I fell because his rage knew no bounds. I looked down on my crumpled body, watching until I felt the grass beneath my feet and a warm hand in my own.

Not an ending - a beginning.

A Holbein Portrait

by

Damon Hager

Déjà vu: *illusory feeling of having already experienced a present situation; something tediously familiar.*
                    - Oxford Dictionary of Current English.

Having hitherto viewed intimations of previous bodily existences with *more* than a modicum of scepticism, it was indeed with my accustomed air of banausic bounce and pragmatism that I ascended, one damp and minatory autumn morning, the steps of the Fitzwilliam Museum, in Cambridge.

I had completed, the day before, a rather stimulating dissertation on the theme of textile manufacture in early seventeenth century East Anglia - a recondite and perplexing topic, it transpired, which had left me feeling rather drained. Ergo, having several hours to kill until that afternoon's supervision, and being possessed (in good measure!) with the antiquarian's habitual affinity for the legacies and relics of the past, I donned fedora, voluminous overcoat, and trusty black brogues, and set off, with contented and leisurely gait, for the Fitz.

Turning from friendly Trinity Street into imposing King's Parade, a light drizzle began to fall, which I adventurously tasted with the tip of my outstretched tongue. The bracing fenland air gave a cold embrace to the welcoming contours of my lungs, as I amused myself (boyishly!) by molding suggestive shapes in the ether, with my hot and cloudy breath. The shop-fronts of the street, as if sharing the joke, glittered cheekily beneath their thin veneer of rain.

Moments later, I found myself at the threshold of the Museum, greeting, a regular patron, the personable porter with the flamboyant salute of one gloved and incarnadined hand. (This greeting was promptly and gracefully returned in kind.) The lobby, having only just opened, was as enticingly empty as the oesophagus of some large and hungry beast; and thus the question promptly presented itself of which *particular* exhibits I should deign to favour with my inimitable attention.

At last, ever the prey of my artistic soul, I opted for yet another tour of the Museum's extensive galleries, and found myself - with five majestic strides of my long and sprightly legs - amid the familiar and sensual presence of the impressionists. As ever, I was not to be disappointed. Here, once again (for example), was Edgar Degas's colourful and touching depiction of the *Laundress Seen Against the Light* (1882), side by side with an equally engaging portrait, by the same artist and from the same year, of two young women *At the Milliner's*. Nearby, in an exquisite mirage of sensual blue and green, was Paul Cézanne's panoramic vision of *The Sea at L'Estaque*, while just below, an alluring and fiery portrayal exuding an aura of seductive grandiloquence, was August Renoir's delightful *Gabrielle with Jewelry* (1910). (A self-portrait by Vincent van Gogh, meanwhile, stood, silent and formidable, a few feet beyond). It was not, in fact, until after some forty minutes' savouring of these exquisitely crafted legacies of a more innocent and civilised age, that I made my way, humbled and, in a very real sense, enriched, into the cavernous expanse of the Museum's adjoining hall.

This chamber, in resolute contrast to its unicameral predecessor, was eclectic and disparate in character, and was divided, thematically and by modest partitions, into four or five generous enclaves - each of which appeared to be preoccupied with the work of a particular century. Hence, over the region allotted to the seventeenth, some lesser-known works of Rubens and Schalken cast a mannered and curious gaze, while in the cloister of the eighteenth century, amid baronets and earls, a large and cheery portrait of one of Joseph Highmore's ladies presided coyly, with a feminine grin. The area assigned to the Victorian age was just beyond my field of vision, but, in the far distance, I could barely make out a lonely group of socialist realists, clustered, with an indignant but resolute air, by the side of the door marked *Gents*.

It was for the sake of curiosity, however, as well as proximity, that I first turned my attentive and expectant gaze to the area on my immediate right, which was predominantly taken up with a cluster of works from the early fifteen hundreds. One one side, emblazoned in fiery colours, was Hans Eworth's portrait of Mary FitzAlan, Duchess of Norfolk, while on the other, a depiction of the Third Earl of Cumberland (in the typical style of Nicholas Hilliard) could be found. My attention was more readily caught, however, by a tenebrous portrait in dark-hued oils, standing squarely on the wall directly before me.

Stomach heaving, heart pounding, pupils dilating and forehead sweating, I nonetheless managed to creep forward, on jelly-like legs, to examine the article in more detail. 'Hans Holbein the Younger (1497-1543):', announced the plaque beneath, with anodyne simplicity; 'Portrait of ...., Seventh Earl of................ .' (I have resolved to omit particular names, for reasons that will become clear). With masochistic rigour, I forced myself once more to examine the visage which, with self-assured demeanour, gazed down at me from the glossy surface of the painting. With a visceral shudder, I once again perused the generous eyebrows, the dark-brown hair, the pale complexion, the narrow mouth, the broad, red lips, and (last, but not least) the large, dark eyes which, altogether, formed an impression - No, wrong. Which *all in all formed a flawless representation of my own face*.

To clarify the point: *in itself*, it was not this bizarre - one might even say, photographic - resemblance which produced the overwhelming sense of shock which now paralysed my mind. A rational and practical chap, after all, I was, and am, quite capable of accepting that some inhabitant of a previous age (perhaps by some genetic coincidence, or perhaps by some lineal connection) might have been the bearer of the same outward physical characteristics that I have since - with the arrogance accompanying *de facto* possession - come to regard as my own. Such a phenomenon, indeed, though admittedly disquieting to the beholder, might in fact be more properly the subject for detached curiosity than for incomprehending dread. The matter, unfortunately, was not quite so simple as this.

In essence - and to strive to put in simple terms a phenomenon both nebulous and complex - the painting had acted on my mind and spirit like a super-potent catalyst, causing to return (with a crashing, *shocking* force) the memories of a former life long buried. In a terrible instant, as I gazed in disbelief at my own features on the wall, I immediately recalled every detail, every facet, of an earlier material existence - an existence, notwithstanding its venerable vintage, every bit as concrete and as real as the present. Thus, with Technicolour clarity, I saw my estates at --- and ---, my comely wife Anne (an excellent hostess!) and my jovial daughter, Katherine. I recalled my participation, as a young and sprightly nobleman, in a succession of tedious campaigns against the Scots, in the course of one of which, while engaged in a skirmish, I managed painfully to lose a finger. I recalled, even more clearly, my subsequent years at court, where I was a close chum of both the King and the Duke of Suffolk, was associated loosely with the party of the Duke of Norfolk, and during which I attended (in a senior official capacity) the executions of Sir Thomas More and Ann Boleyn. And I remembered vividly, last of all, my own brush with the block during the minority of Edward VI, my rehabilitation with the accession of Mary I, and (with a shudder of cold recognition) my eventual death, from peaceful old age, in a bedchamber of Hampton Court palace, during the early reign of Elizabeth. (At the same time as these recollections came crashing upon my mind, I also found myself unexpectedly fluent in Latin, Greek and Hebrew - a legacy of an excellent boyhood tutor, appointed by my father around 1496.)

I *do not* recall, precisely, how long I continued to contemplate the picture, before I managed, with phenomenal effort, to stagger out of the Museum, and make my way home. When I had regained sufficient composure, I telephoned tutors and friends, and cancelled my appointments for the following week. Indeed, it was undoubtedly a good three days before I ventured out of my small apartment again.

When I did emerge, timorously, into the open air once more, it was with all sense of a world both more mysterious and more opaque than I had previously imagined it to be. Above all, perhaps, I was possessed of a newly-found awareness of the dangers of prying, too insistently, into the legacies and artefacts of a bygone age.

A Boy's Eye View of Christmas

by

Jane Welsh

Christmas was a family affair at our house. Aunt Florence would come with Uncle Bert. Gran would stay for Christmas until we could get rid of her. I would do my best to keep out of the way as the house was transformed from orderly calm to Christmas chaos. Mum polished everything in sight and vacuumed areas never seen before.

Our Christmas tree would stand glittering to attention at the window. Holly decorated the house throughout catching you unawares as it clawed at your hair and scratched at your skin. Banisters were entwined with the stuff.

'Gives a lovely atmosphere to the hall,' said mum as she entered the bathroom with her bag of holly. Go to the loo with care in this house.

On this Christmas morning I sat reading by the fire being careful not to upset the recently vacuumed rug or unplump the recently plumped cushions. The reason for all this madness was gran.

'She won't catch me out on anything this year,' said mum as she vacuumed the cat.

'She's getting old she doesn't mean anything,' said dad.

I felt sorry for dad after all gran was his mum.

'They're here,' I shout as I watch Aunt Florence and Uncle Bert manoeuvre gran out of their car. I brace myself and prepare to be the perfect son. Aunt Florence spots me first.

'Well haven't you grown. What have you done to your hair? Come here and give us a kiss.' She reaches over and grabs me. Wham, the great pink lips suck onto my cheek as she squeezes me to her.

'Leave the boy alone Flo your embarrassing the boy,' said Bert struggling past laden with parcels.

'I'm not embarrassing you am I love. He loves his Aunt Flo, Father Christmas bring you some nice presents then.'

'Yes thank you.' I say politely. And I do truly mean it I just wish for once she would buy me something else, a boy only needs so many pairs of pants. I sometimes wonder what she thinks I do with them.

Florence gets out her knitting and clicks away humming White Christmas to herself happy and content. She sips her sherry oblivious to the chaos in the kitchen. Dad and Uncle Bert get into the Christmas spirit by tasting all the spirits.

I wander into the kitchen in search of food.

'I hope you've got proper gravy,' says gran lifting lids off pans and poking her head in cupboards. 'That instant gravy gives me wind. Don't leave the sprouts boiling too long I like a nice crisp sprout.'

I can see mum starting to simmer and if gran keeps on she will boil over. Mum glares over to me signalling, get her out, get her out. But gran is in her stride.

'Did you defrost that bird properly. I'm to old for food poisoning. Is there anything I can do to help, you know me I'm not one to sit back and watch while you slave away.'

'No. Really you go and relax, I can manage.' Mum says hopefully.

'I must say you look nice in that dress.' Gran said sweetly eyeing mum up and down.

'Thank you,' said mum somewhat surprised.

'That extra weight suits you dear I don't believe in diets, if you're meant to be fat there's nothing you can do about it, that's what I say.'

Mum was carving the turkey and I saw her hand tighten around the handle and for a moment I thought gran had seen her last Christmas. But Uncle Bert came in just in time slapped mum on her bum and started fooling around in his Uncle Bert way.

'Fool,' said gran. 'What my Florence ever saw in you I don't know.' 'Spreading Christmas cheer mother-in-law dear,' said Bert winking at me across the room.

'Got yourself a job yet Bert, or are you still on social.'

It was at times like this I realised gran was indeed the godmother.

Bert laughed. 'That's right I'm one of the millions unemployed. Thank goodness I married your daughter, landed on my feet there.'

Gran pursed her lips. The heat in the kitchen was getting too hot. I decided to make my escape before things boiled over.

'Everybody at the table,' shouted mum.

So here we are mum, dad, uncle Bert, Aunt Florence, the godmother and me.

'Happy Christmas,' said dad raising his glass. 'And may we have many more.'

Somebody groaned but it wasn't me honest.

The Chauvinistic Pig

by

Joanna E Hopkins

Charlie jumped out of bed and immediately regretted her haste as a piece of toast jabbed evilly between her toes. Christ she thought, this place is like a pig sty... and instantly tears of laughter and despair rolled down her cheeks, dripping onto a carpet of broken china and mouldy mayonnaise.

She supposed it was her dads fault in the first place. Of all the names in all the world why had he called a blue eyed blonde haired girl Charlie? But he had.

He had brought her a train set once but she had stamped and screamed until it had been replaced with a wee-wee doll. This she sat on his chair and fed with bottles full of coloured water made from smarties. Eventually his cushion became a soggy pulp of petrol puddled colours. She was very pleased, but secretly, she would much rather have had the train set.

She remembered vividly the episode over the jeans. Her best friend Elizabeth had a red pair with zipped pockets and flaps and buttons that went up the legs. She would have died for a pair just like it. She'd be able to do bigger handstands and wider cart-wheels, climb taller trees and swing round and round on the rotary drier. Oh yes. A pair of jeans would make everything possible.

It was Friday night. She came home from school and saw the 'Dixons' bag lying on the table.

'Go on,' urged her dad, 'Open it!' She undid the twisted ends and cautiously peeped inside. They were there. The longed-for jeans lay cool and crisp like a new bank note waiting to experience the surprises of life. With a shriek of delight she yanked off her plimsoll's, oblivious to their flight path as they zoomed across the kitchen. Her skirt fell to her ankles, and with one vicious kick, went sailing after the shoes. And then, at last, she stepped tentatively into the jeans. She could smell the newness as she raised them to her hips and felt the sexual cling as she wriggled to their shape.

'Look look,' she laughed as she pivoted and preened, jutting out her hip and slapping her pert back-side. Her dad laughed with her, elated by her joy.

'Oh Charlie you look great. A proper tom boy you are now.'

Slowly she turned and looked at him. Her face was as blank as a black board wiped extra clean at the end of term. She removed the jeans and flung them carelessly over a chair. She got dressed. Slowly, silently. And at last faced her father.

'Bugger you,' she screamed and violently shoved her skirt inside her knickers. She ran out of the door. Jumped on her bike and peddled like hell down the deserted street. Who needs jeans anyway, she thought. I'll conquer the world in my pants.

She was about fourteen when it first started. Elizabeth collected owls, Julia elephants and Charlie decided to collect pigs.

'Well why not?' she'd asked defensively of two pairs of raised eye-brows.

She'd gone home and swept the Welsh dolls off her bedroom shelf and gone out and bought her first pig. He was a money box, sat on his haunches wearing a school cap and tie. She looked at him every morning when she got up and rushed home from school every evening to stare at the pig. Something puzzled her about him. Something elusive that probed at the edges of her mind. It was, she thought, rather like dice being rolled and scooped up before you had time to add up the dots.

It was Tuesday. She hated Tuesday because that meant arithmetic. A drone of numbers chanted into the air like lost mantras. But today was different......

She saw him picking his nose and wiping his sticky fingers under the desk. His podgy face was mottled and marble-like as if his tie was restricting his circulation. She noticed, and smiled, as he opened and closed his mouth one beat behind the answers to the times tables. His cap was perched on the back of his head, uneasy on his ginger spiked hair. The teacher glared in his direction. He furtively pulled the peak forwards, and hunched his shoulders into his obese frame.

'Sidney. Are you paying attention?' asked an accusing voice. A low grunt came from under the cap. She suddenly knew. Her pig was called Sidney.

Her friends could not understand her infatuation at all. Every play time she was to be found dogging the footsteps of the revolting boy.

'Why?' her friends beseeched her. But she just smiled serenely and chased after Sidney to give him the pick of her lunch-box.

Many pigs followed. A brass pig in a rocking chair who was really Edward, her first flirtation with an older man. A spotted pig called Claude who had taken her to the pictures. And Ralph, a rolly-polly pig in a butchers apron who had won her heart when he'd given her a free Cornish pasty.

Soon the bedroom shelf was full of pigs of every shape and size. Sometimes she'd buy a pig and spend months searching for it's human likeness. She'd haunt bus shelters and supermarkets, concert halls and picture queues. Once she had bought a pig wearing a sailors hat and had travelled miles to Southampton docks in search of her very own Waterloo.

Men came. And men went. Pigs spread from the shelf to the window-sill, and from the window-sill to the floor. Posters of pigs covered the walls and a mobile of flying bacon fluttered in the breeze. Fat pigs and lean pigs lay hunched in the pattern of her counterpane until the fatal day arrived. There was no more room for any more pigs............

She was very sad at first. Her days of pig castration had come to an end. No more the hedonistic pleasure of dumping each and every one. No more would she hear the pleading squeal of why why why, all the way home.

She spent her days huddled in the sanctuary of her piggy counterpane, refusing to leave her room and eating only food that was left at her door. Gradually the sty began to form. Stale crusts and mouldy biscuits littered the floor. Meat turned green and cheese spawned a creeping growth. She was oblivious to the cries and pleas that came from the other side of the locked door. Until, one day, she heard the magic words.

'Charlie listen to me,' came her fathers voice. 'I've bought you the biggest pig you have ever seen. She could feel his excitement creeping under the door, like fog finding its way down the chimney. She did not answer. She lay, listening until the sound of rustling paper ceased and foot steps panted down the stairs. Only then did she drag the parcel in.

It was big. At least three feet tall. She ripped at the twine eagerly, her fingers twitching like an unsure harpist over the strings. Its head appeared first. It had glasses perched on the end of its snout and curly whiskers sprouted from its ears. She felt perplexed. The old feelings of known intimacy, but uncertainty crowded into her brain. She tore at the paper revealing a brown floppy cardigan that poked with familiarity into her fuddled mind. Frantic now she gouged at the paper, sending showers of confetti round the room. Suddenly she felt the waxing of bile rise in her throat and the waning of despair seep into her soul. She saw before her 'Daddy Pig.' Smiling, he tenderly looked down at the little boy piglet, dressed in red jeans that he was cradling in his arms...........

She hurled the pig at the shelf. Ralph and Claude and Robert and Paul, fell, in smithereens to the floor. But 'Daddy Pig' smiled on. She attacked again. She flung the pig at the mobile which flew across the room like witches on broomsticks. The sleeping pigs on the counterpane were hauled from their rest and ripped into bacon in one fell swoop. But 'Daddy Pig' smiled on. Exhausted she fell across the bed and drifted into sleep on the wings of a lullaby for the insane.

Charlie jumped out of bed and immediately regretted her haste as a piece of toast jabbed evilly between her toes. Christ, she thought, this place is like a pig sty......... and instantly tears of laughter and despair rolled down her cheeks.

The Bag Lady

by

Angela Morgan

In its way the park was as beautiful today as it was in mid summer. In fact even more beautiful, with snow covering the grass, and the frost hanging delicately from the trees and shrubs. The sun shining powerfully through gave the park a totally magical look.

The frail and rather scruffy woman created a flash of colour against the white background as she sat, huddled among the brightly coloured bags, on the old park bench. She was cold, bitterly cold. She looked first in one bag and then another, she knew that in one of the garishly coloured plastic supermarket bags was a box with some chicken in it. She had found the box outside the take-away in the darkness of the night before. Now she needed it, she was so hungry, and terribly cold. At last she found it, and joy! There were even a few chips left. She hungrily ate the remains of the chicken, carefully picking every scrap of meat off the carelessly discarded bones, and relishing in the few cold hard chips. As she went meticulously through every scrap of paper in the box, she made the best discovery of all. One of those little sachets with a wet-wipe, it was a real luxury, she would keep it for another day. She would be able to wash her face and feel really clean, and the smell of freshness, oh yes she could remember the lovely fresh scent, it would be heaven. She would definitely keep it for another day, so it was carefully stowed in the bottom of the bag that held all her treasures. She made one final close examination of the bones, she could not afford to miss a single morsel, she needed it all.

She did not even notice the passers by anymore, or the concern and pity on their faces. Just a few short months ago those looks had filled her with anger and horror, she wondered how they dare look at her in that way, had she not been as good as they were, in fact she suspected better. She was sure they had not lived in the grand style she had, the house was a real mansion with stables and orchards. She had loved the gardens, with the rustic seats not unlike the bench she was now sat on. But you can not blame people, if she was not to know what destiny held for her, how could they.

Carefully she pulled the bags together distributing the weight, it would make it a little easier to manage. After the cold night her limbs were aching and stiff

44

so she pulled herself painfully to her feet. Stretching gently she knew she had to tread warily along the icy path. The big old iron gates seized at her fingers with their frosty bars. Threading her way across the busy early morning traffic, she headed towards the station. Pushing open the doors of the waiting room, she felt the warm air from the overhead heaters surge through her body. A cold shudder came over her as the inner cold of her body surfaced. Shuffling to a seat on the far side of the room, where a newspaper had been left, she sat down. The newspaper gave a little dignity, and was a reason to sit for a while. Reading the paper gave her time, time to warm up and release the cold from her body, ready for another day. People were bustling around, no one taking any notice of her. The news was as usual all doom and gloom. Somebody gently tapped her knee, looking down she saw a dog, a handsome Kings Charles Spaniel, happily wagging his tail, his owner smiled, hurriedly apologised and pulled him away.

He was just like Bracken, her Bracken, a lovely Copper coloured Kings Charles Spaniel, Ben had bought him for her for their first wedding anniversary. He had been in a large box with a huge bow on the top.

'Happy anniversary Claire, something to keep you company,' and indeed Bracken had been a great friend, for Ben was busy with his career. It was to be many years before they had the baby they longed for, but although Bracken was getting old, he loved Jenny from the moment she was born, never jealous of the attention that was showered on this much wanted new arrival. Bracken faithfully followed Jenny everywhere when she was a toddler, never even whimpering when Jenny pulled his long ears. He was to be her protector, no one could be cross with Jenny, growling when anybody raised their voice to her. The day he died was a nightmare, Claire was so sad, and Jenny at four years was inconsolable. Jenny was Ben's girl when he was home, he played with her, and made sure she had anything a small girl could want. They were sad, but it seemed that as there was to be no brother or sister for Jenny, she often asked where Bracken was. The only answer, it seemed, was a new puppy. Claire could not imagine a new dog, but there was little choice. Claire went to fetch the new dog, it was so pretty, black, tan and white, with a constantly wagging tail. Jenny named him Waggy, which was soon shortened to Wag.

Time came for Jenny to go to school, Claire was heart-broken, Ben had decided it would be a Boarding School, it would be more suited. Ben and Claire argued constantly, Claire was usually happy to go along with Ben, but this was too much. A suitable school was found nearby and Jenny would be home every weekend. Claire was lonely, weekends were cherished. Jenny had settled into

45

school, and the days hung with emptiness for Claire. Depression really came on when Jenny was seven, and started as a term boarder at her new school.

Hosting the Dinners, that went with Bens work, were not her idea of pleasure. One evening on one such occasion, she found Ben manoeuvering her towards a lady she had not seen before. Louise was her name, Ben seemed to know a lot about her.

'Helping the needy,' Ben was saying, 'Very interesting work, yes Claire would find it interesting.'

Hold on a minute, Claire realised she was being put in a position she was not sure of. Feeling uncomfortable, no way of getting out, smiling politely, she excused herself, went to her bedroom and shook with confusion and anger. Tomorrow she was expected to help Louise!

Shyly standing behind the counter, Claire could not imagine how she was going to cope, what should she say to people, waiting behind the counter, it was like a safe area. Oh now what happens. A group of people came in chattering, happily they began rummaging among the clothes and bric-a-brac, each finding their own treasures. They came to the counter, Claire found to her surprise it was easy to chat. After all they, the customers, started the conversations. Time soon passed and life was so different, it had a purpose, customers were now friends. Caring people who helped one another when needed.

Ben was proud of Jenny, she was doing so well at school. Claire had finally adjusted to Jenny's education, now she was fully occupied, if anything it was Ben who felt neglected, he was so used to Claire always at home to wait on his every need.

Watching the customers, as she sorted through the clothes, looking towards Mike, she remembered the first time he had called in. He had looked painfully embarrassed, as he browsed through the clothes. Mike was a good friend now, they had many conversations, he was so interesting, she looked forward to his visits. Mike was carrying a bag and looking pleased with himself. He asked 'How would you like lunch by the river, I've managed to get strawberries, the first of the season.'

How could she refuse, it was only a few days since she had spoken of her longing for the strawberries to be ready. The river bank was peaceful and beautiful, they settled beneath a weeping willow tree, they were sharing much more than the sandwiches and strawberries, so much more, it was thrilling and exciting, no restaurant with Ben had compared to this feast. Laying in the shade of the tree wrapped in each others arms, eyes closed, neither able to believe, as neither had ever felt such strength of contentment. It seemed to melt through them, invisibly welding them together.

Telling Ben she was leaving, was harder than the decision to leave, that was the easy part. Ben was furious, what would people say, his firm would not like it, yes she had remembered when he had proposed, he had actually said it would be a good career move. But she was probably as much to blame, perhaps she had been in love with the house and all the luxuries that marriage promised. Ben told her to leave, not to contact them and never come back. Joy and sadness washed over her as she went into the tiny flat she and Mike were to share. Jenny was never far from her thoughts. Mike was very caring, it made her feel so special. Wonderful romantic meals ready when she got in.

Louise called by and said it would be better if she did not go to the shop any more, Ben had been talking to her. Claire could not believe Louise would do this, her work at the shop had often been praised, but no, it was not to be, the keys were all they wanted of her now.

Through Mike's love, chinks of unhappiness soon showed, it tore at Mike, he had nothing to give, he felt she would be better off without him. In despair he left, just a note, telling her he loved her so much, she would be better off without him. Soon the flat was gone, she would not go to Ben, that would be no good. For Jenny's sake she must not go, Jenny must never know.

Oh Mike, if only you knew, all that's left is a few possessions in bags, to carry around!

Jason Isn't Like That

by

K P Tipler

It started when Jason and Tracey decided to get married. Jason asked me to be his best man, we'd been mates since school, worked in the same electronics factory, played in the same darts team for our local, the Red Lion, although Jason had recently quit the team so as to spend more time with Tracey.

Unlike Angie and I, they didn't live together, they were a bit old-fashioned that way but the arrangement suited me. I had plenty of girlfriends before but Angie had been the first one I'd been serious about. I thought it suited Angie as well but as soon as Jason and Tracey became engaged she started hinting about us doing the same as them.

We'd be walking down the High Street and she'd stop to look in the jewellers' windows, remarking on the fact that they were offering an engagement and a wedding ring together at a discount. If I was watching the football on the television, she'd be sitting next to me, reading a magazine article on bridal fashions or how to plan the perfect reception. She'd make comments, thrusting the magazine underneath my nose usually at a crucial moment of the game much to my annoyance.

She resented the fact that I enjoyed a night out with the lads, a drink and a game of darts. Tracey had persuaded Jason to give it up, she hoped to do the same.

We argued about it. Her favourite line was 'Jason wouldn't treat Tracey this way. Jason's a real man, he doesn't go out boozing with his mates, he spends all his spare time with Tracey, not like you, go out till all hours and leave me here on my own.' I suggested she find an interest, join an evening class or something, but she wouldn't.

Things came to a head the night of the final. The Red Lion were playing the Rose and Crown, who'd held the trophy for the past two years. We won and in our usual style we celebrated with a pub crawl, finally ending up at a night club.

I must have got really drunk because the next thing I remember I was in the Team Captain, Jim's house, stretched out on the sofa. My head felt like it weighed a ton. I couldn't recall ever feeling so bad as I felt that morning.

I had a cup of tea at Jim's and despite repeated offers of breakfast from his wife, politely declined as the smell of her cooking bacon and eggs was turning my stomach. Finishing my tea, I headed for home as quickly as I could, my head throbbing all the way there.

When I arrived back at the flat Angie was drinking coffee and smoking a cigarette. Radio One boomed from the twin speakers, which didn't help my hangover. Silently I switched the radio off.

'I was listening to that,' she moaned, violently stubbing her cigarette out in the already full ashtray.

'Well, I wasn't,' I rejoined, noticing the redness around her eyes, an indication that she'd been crying.

Quietly, she downed the remains of her coffee and moved to the kitchen. I followed her and gently placing my hands on her shoulders, apologised for all the worry I'd caused.

'Jason wouldn't behave like this,' she murmured, sniffing a little as she rinsed her mug underneath the tap. 'You wouldn't see Jason get drunk and stop out all night.'

'I don't bloody care what Jason does!' I yelled, exasperatingly, the loudness of my voice severely aggravating my hangover. The way she always used Jason's name when we argued irritated me, as if he'd always been some kind of saint. She hadn't known him before he met Tracey, he'd been one for a good time as much as I was. It was only since Tracey had got her hooks into him that he'd changed. They were like an old married couple already and he hadn't even placed that ring on her finger.

But the last thing I wanted that morning was trouble so rubbing my forehead, I apologised for my sudden outburst.

'You're sorry!' snapped Angie, moving back into the living room. 'You're always sorry, aren't you. Well, I've had enough sorry's, Darren.'

'What do you mean?' I asked, following her. I watched Angie take the vacuum cleaner from out of it's cupboard and unrolling the flex, plugged it in the socket. 'What do you mean?' I repeated.

She bent up from unplugging the vacuum in and considered me for a second before replying.

'I want you to leave,' she said, her voice calm and level, emotionless. 'Today,' she added, with finality, as she switched the vacuum on, moving up and down the room with it.

'Look, Angie, I'll change,' I pleaded, my words drowned by the vacuum, my head throbbing as I shouted above the noise. Reaching the socket, I pulled the plug out and the vacuum whirred to a stop. 'I'll quit the team, we can spend more time together,' I promised. 'Just give me one more chance.'

'You've had all your chances, Darren,' she replied, bitterly, brushing past me to plug the vacuum in again.

I knew it was useless trying to reason with her so I went into the bedroom and packed a suitcase, deciding to stay with my parents. At that stage I had hopes that after a while she'd take me back. Despite everything I still loved Angie and if it meant changing my ways to keep her I'd do it.

But it was too late. We talked a couple of days later and she'd come to a decision that it was best to separate for good. Our relationship wasn't working, we both wanted different things out of life so it was best to end things now before we both got badly hurt.

I was genuinely sorry it had come to this. I'd had plenty of women before but none of them meant as much to me as she did. Despite all my pleas to give me another chance and promises that I'd change she was adamant it was over. She'd even placed an advert for a flat-mate in the local paper, which in a way seemed to finalise things. She'd never have me back.

Soon afterwards, Tracey got a part-time job in the Red Lion, working evening behind the bar which made things awkward whenever I went in there. She and Angie had always been good friends so I was quite prepared for the bitchy remarks as she'd never liked me. I don't think I quite fitted in with her view of what was a polite society. She'd always been a bit of a snob which was why it surprised me to see her working behind the bar. I expected with the wedding on the way she needed the money.

'Angie was very upset about you splitting up,' she told me in her usual fashion, like a teacher reprimanding a naughty child.

'It was her who chucked me out,' I reminded her, irritated at being lectured at while trying to enjoy a quiet drink. 'I was willing to give things another go but she wouldn't have it.'

'I'm not surprised!' she exclaimed. 'She was at the end of her tether. You were hardly ever at home in the evenings, always in the pub playing darts. And when you were at home all you did was sit at home and watch the television. She felt neglected.'

What the hell would she know, I thought.

'Jason never behaves like that,' she added, proudly. 'I know he used to when he was under your influence but he's a changed man now.'

I'd noticed. All the spark had gone out of him, all the sense of fun. He looked like a downtrodden husband already.

50

'We no longer want you as best man, by the way,' she announced, suddenly.

'What!' I exclaimed, nearly choking on my lager.

'Jason hasn't told you?'

I shook my head, dumfounded.

'We decided it wouldn't be right,' she explained. 'Especially as I'm having Angie as chief bridesmaid. It might cause a bit of embarrassment. I'm sorry,' she added, haughtily, as she moved to the other side of the bar to serve another customer.

I had to laugh at her 'We decided'. What she really meant was 'I decided'. Jason never had a say in anything. But at the same time I resented not being his best man anymore. We'd been friends for years, long before Tracey came on the scene. It wasn't right that she should ruin our friendship.

I stopped going to the Red Lion after that. Tracey working there ruined the atmosphere for me. It saddened me to quit the darts team but it was either that or having to listen to what a wonderful husband-to-be Jason was every time I went for a drink.

The wedding was in August. Jason invited everybody from the factory apart from me. He apologised but as Angie would be there they didn't want any nasty scenes. They needn't have worried, any feelings I once had for her had died long ago to be replaced by a kind of regret, a desire to turn back time and erase past mistakes. But I expected Tracey didn't want me there either. I might get drunk and embarrass her in front of her relatives.

I didn't actually learn what happened until the Monday after. The entire factory was talking about it. Firstly, the night before the wedding Angie had excused herself from being chief bridesmaid on the pretext that she'd caught a stomach bug. Secondly, when Tracey and her father arrived at the church Jason was nowhere to be found.

It was my replacement as best man who gave her Jason's letter. He was sorry but he'd decided long ago he could never marry her but at least the money he'd spent paying for the honeymoon wasn't going to be wasted. He was spending a fortnight in Majorca with Angie. I couldn't help laughing all day.

The Meerschaum Pipe

by

Jeffrey Hurst

Sir Dermot Conolly and his three dinner guests settled themselves into armchairs arranged in a semicircle in front of the fire. He produced a battered meerschaum pipe from his pocket and began to fill it. Paul Ballantyne, seated next to him, could see that the bowl, carved into the head of a Viking, was stained with age and the stem had been repaired with adhesive tape. He expressed surprise that a man of wealth should use a pipe in such condition.

Sir Dermot smiled, 'It's a link with the past and is of strange origin. Would you like to hear its story?'

'Certainly,' said Ballantyne.

Sir Dermot spent a moment getting his pipe going, then began.

'You are aware that I wasn't born sucking a silver spoon. I came from a poor family and didn't have much of an education. I drifted from job to job, trying to find something I liked. Many years ago I got the sack for day-dreaming. It was just before Christmas and I had to take the first job that came along. That is how I came to be a night watchman, looking after a building site in Wisbech.

On Christmas Eve it was below freezing with a brisk wind making things worse. I had just made a cup of tea and was stoking the brazier when I heard the church clock chime the three-quarters.

'Fifteen minutes to Christmas,' I thought, and I was pretty fed up I can tell you. Sitting in a watchman's hut is no way to welcome Christmas.

Suddenly I felt that I was being watched. I looked up and there, on the edge of the firelight, stood a man. I hadn't heard him walk up so it gave me a bit of a start. He was a real sight, dressed all in grey. He wore a threadbare raincoat, which looked as if it hadn't been cleaned in years, a scarf, and a pair of frayed check trousers. The only thing about him which wasn't grey was a pair of ancient plimsolls through which his toes were poking.

There were plenty of tramps around at that time and part of my job was to see that they didn't steal from the site. He was different though. There was still some pride left in his eyes. The firelight made his unshaven face seem thinner than it really was. He stood in the shadows, gazing at the brazier and looking even more lonely than I felt.

'Come in and take the weight off your feet mate,' I said. 'The tea's brewed and you look like you could use some.' He sat down on the bench in a kind of dazed way. I put it down to the lack of food and possibly drinking meths. I gave him a cup of tea, nice and hot with plenty of sugar, and a slice of bread pudding. He drank the tea quickly and wolfed down the pudding, staring into the fire as if he was trying to soak up every ounce of warmth he could. Finally he spoke, in a voice that belonged more to a stately home than a watchman's hut in Wisbech.

'It was most kind of you to take me in and give me food. I was rather cold out there in the wind.'

He looked so sad as he said it that I just mumbled that it was what anyone would do in the circumstances.

'Ah there, sir, you are in error. Most men would take one look and spurn me. Even on the eve of the birth of Our Saviour, there would be no compassion for a tramp. They may realise their error too late, as I did, thinking themselves secure and awakening one day to ruin. I was not always as you see me. Once I could have bought a hundred cups of tea and not noticed the difference in my pocket. Now they are empty. I have only one remaining possession.'

He showed me. It was a small thing, of no great value. I poured him another cup of tea. He moved closer to the brazier, the flames flickering in his eyes.

'It's surprising what you see in the depths of a fire when you look carefully: bits of the past, bits of the future.'

'I've heard people say that,' I replied, 'but when I look, I see only bits of coke.'

'That's because you don't allow your mind to roam.'

'The last time I did that, I got the sack!'

'Yes I can see that,' he said in an odd way, 'but, mark my works, it will not always be so. One day you will see something in the coals which will turn your life around. When it happens, do not turn your back on those less fortunate than you. I know what it feels like and would wish it on no man.'

I confess, I laughed at the poor man. It was ludicrous to hear him playing the prophet.

'Oh yes, just like a crystal ball. Perhaps I should cross your palm with silver?'

He stood up and looked at me in a kindly way.

'I know you have little enough for yourself. Just remember my words. Accept that which is given, for it comes from a grateful heart.' With that, he waved farewell and stepped into the night.

53

The clock began chiming midnight as I got up and walked to the door of the hut, thinking to watch him go. I looked up and down the road but he was nowhere to be seen. I thought he might have fallen down the trench so I took my torch and looked all along it, but there was nothing except frosted earth and a rat. As I turned away I walked straight into a policeman. We both jumped, then we recognised each other and laughed.

'Merry Christmas Dermot,' he said.

'Merry Christmas George,' I replied. 'Fancy a cuppa?'

'Yes, but I could do with a drop of something a bit stronger than milk in it.'

'Oh really?' I said as we turned and started back towards the hut. 'The cold getting to you is it?'

'Oh I don't mind that,' he replied. 'Fact is, we had a bit of a do tonight and it upset me a bit. About an hour ago I checked the derelict houses around the corner and I found an old tramp, frozen to death. Couldn't scrounge enough money for warmth or food I suppose. No room at the inn and all that.'

A chill ran through me. I just had to ask.

'What did he look like?'

'Oh, the usual thing you know; thin, unshaven, old clothes. All grey they were, good clothes too, once upon a time. Someone must have stolen his boots in a doss house because he was wearing a pair of old plimsolls.'

I felt the blood leave my face and my head swam. George caught me as I fell and helped me into the hut. He laid me on one of the benches, my mind was spinning. Had I dreamt it all? Was I ill? Nothing seemed to make sense.

George kept his eye on me while he was pouring the tea. He gave me mine, sat down on the bench opposite, and looked concerned.

'Been celebrating early Dermot? You should lay off it a bit.' He looked down and picked up something from the bench beside him. 'Bought yourself a present then have you? I didn't know you smoked.'

'I'm not with you,' I said, feeling that I was still in a dream.

'This of course,' he said, holding out a small object for me to see.

I almost passed out completely when I saw it. Not valuable, but the last possession of a broken man.

'Accept what is given,' he had said and he had meant it. In George's hand was a brand new meerschaum pipe with the bowl carved into the head of a Viking. The thing that the tramp had shown me. The one he left for me.'

Sir Dermot sat back drawing reflectively on the pipe and gazing at the crackling logs in the fireplace. After a few moments, Ballantyne asked in a tone that he tried very hard to make casual.

'And the prophecy, Sir Dermot? Did it really happen in the way he foretold?'
Sir Dermot smiled archly.
'That, my dear fellow, is my ticket to dinner at your house.'

A Little Relaxation

by

Kevin Ball

Eric drew the last little morsel of smoke from the end of his cigarette, almost burning his lips. He stubbed the smouldering filter into the small ashtray and slid it back into it's compartment under the dashboard. After winding down the electric window, he slipped on his seat belt and started the engine. He'd had an awfully hard day at the office; tension tightened round him like a vice. This tension needed to be relieved and he knew the very thing.

Eric pulled out of his parking space and headed across town towards the station where the street girls hung out. He flicked on the radio; soon be time for the ten o'clock news. Some thumping pop ditty filled the car.

'Loada shit,' he muttered to himself.

Yes, Eric knew exactly how to relieve his tension. He'd soon be happily relaxed. He was going to pick up a whore, with just one thing on his mind......Murder!

How he hated them, the cheap little sluts! They disgusted him: flaunting their wares for all and sundry to see, selling themselves to men they didn't even know. How could they do that?

But Eric didn't kill them because of 'messages from God' or 'voices in his head.' And the devil didn't make him do it. It was a conscious decision. He hated them and he wanted them dead.

But, no, it was more than that; it was like a hobby, a recreational pastime.

He'd done four now; all within six weeks. But he'd laid off for about a fortnight. Too much attention. Headlines splashed all over, nationals as well as the local press. And of course the police were every-bloody-where. Well they would be, wouldn't they?

The first one he'd stabbed. He's lost count how many times. A rage sort of welled-up inside him and he sort of went blank. But anyway, that was much too messy. Even though the sight and smell of it excited him, it also made him sick. Then there was all the bother of getting rid of the blood-stained clothes and car-seat covers. No not very pleasant at all, stabbing.

So after that he'd decided on strangling. Much more civilised. He loved the feel of their soft necks in his strong hands. The feeling of power and control that it gave. He loved the rasping as they tried to scream, the way they struggled and thrashed.

The ten o'clock news was just about finishing as he turned the corner by the station and caught sight of the mini-dressed-peroxides standing under the orange-glow of the streetlamps; pouting and posing at him as the car cruised by.

'And now the weather.' No mention of him tonight. Wouldn't have mattered if there had been, he'd had a hard day and he needed a little relaxation.

'It's no good,' he thought. 'They're all in pairs. Gotta find one on her own.' He drove a little further, rounded another corner.

'There. The one with the long blonde hair. Pretty too.' Like all punters he preferred the pretty ones. He drew up carefully beside her and glided the electric window down. 'Working, love?' He smiled.

'For the right price.' She said; voice all lipstick and chewing gum.

'How much?'

'Fifty.'

'Well, okay. Hop in.'

She scuttled round to the passenger side door with tiny stilettoed steps and squeezed into the passenger seat.

They drove in silence to the end of the road; he eyeing her shapely legs instead of the road, her gazing nonchalantly out of the window.

'You gotta place, love?'

She turned and shook her head. 'Wouldn't you rather do it in the car?'

'Yeah, I know a place.'

Eric sped through the neon streets of the town centre. He knew exactly where he was going to take her. His heart stepped up a gear, sweaty palms gripped the wheel. 'Soon be gripping something else,' he told himself.

The car stopped behind some old warehouses on the town's industrial estate; the buildings casting black shadows over the car and it's occupants. Eric was screwed tight: head buzzing, heart thumping, blood rushing through his veins like a freight train.

'Want to get down to it, then?' She had no idea what she was saying. He grinned, leaning towards her, his hands flexing open and shut.

She was reaching into her bag. 'Must be getting the thingys out.' His hands were barely six inches from that slim, porcelain neck.

But what was this? Her hand flicked from her bag. A glint of steel. She's got a fucking kitchen knife. This wasn't right. This wasn't supposed to happen.

Sonya wiped the blood-stained kitchen knife on her long blonde wig, put the knife back into her bag and dumped the wig on the wasteground by the old warehouses. She had a long walk back to town but it was worth it.

Sonya hated kerb-crawlers. They disgusted her. Fat old business-men; stale and sweaty. Forcing their filthy perversions onto young girls with little choice. Getting their cheap thrills in the back of a car whilst their wives sat at home worrying where they were. How could they do that?

The Sofa Bed

by

Alison Hutchins

From the advertisement in the local paper, the second-hand sofa bed appeared to be just what I wanted. Ever since buying my first, darling little flat I had known that the purchase of a sofa bed was inevitable. I was far too well placed - only four stops on the tube from Oxford Street - to expect not to be inundated with visitors. To my surprise, the woman who answered my telephone call told me that it was still for sale, and that six o'clock would be a convenient time to view it. As I noted down the address, I felt guiltily pleased that I recognised it as a 'nice' neighbourhood. Well, as my mother always says, you can't be too careful these days.

At precisely three minutes to six that evening I was standing on the steps of a large, beautifully kept Victorian town house. Hoping that the sofa bed was in a similar condition, I knocked on the door. The door was opened by a man whom I could only describe as stunning. I suppose he wasn't strictly speaking hand-some, but I was so bowled over that for a moment I just stared greedily. He was quite tall and very slim - his tightly-belted jeans suggesting that the latter was a fairly recent development. His hair was dark brown and straight and worn neglectfully long, as though a barber had been the last thing on his mind for a number of months. The lock that fell over one eye looked as though it was so used to being pushed back that it could have jumped there all on its own. The dark stubble on his chin should have contributed to give the impression of a thoroughly disreputable character, but somehow the expensive-looking jersey and the small child clutching at his left leg managed to suggest instead a very weary respectability. He looked about thirty five, but I was sure that he was the sort of man who was older than he looked. There were lines around his eyes, but when he smiled he could suddenly have been eighteen. It was a kindly smile, totally lacking in any sexual overtones, but for a moment I was rendered speechless by it. It was almost as if there was something about him that I re-cognised, although I knew for certain that we had never met before. I had never before believed in love at first sight, but I felt drawn to this man by a magnet-ism so strong that I could put no other name to it. He appeared not to have been

59

the victim of a corresponding thunderbolt. Still smiling, he ushered me into the hallway, warning the child gently to keep out of the way.

'Hello there, my name's Mark. I take it you've come about the sofa bed. It's in the sitting room, if you'd like to follow me.'

Hastily I pulled myself together and followed him along the hall and into a large 'Homes and Gardens' sitting room. Sprawled elegantly on what I presumed was the sofa in question was a beautiful and immaculately groomed woman of about thirty and a girl of about eight, who showed every sign of taking after her mother in later years. My heart sank at these oh-so-obvious signs that my dream man was well and truly married.

'This young lady's come to look at the sofa bed,' Mark said almost apologetically. 'Could you both sit elsewhere for a moment, please?'

Giving me a pair of identical, frosty glares, mother and daughter relocated silently to the other side of the room. The toddler who had entered the room with us showed none of their reserve. He rushed up to the sofa and jumped on, proceeding to bounce up and down on it gleefully. The corners of Mark's mouth twitched.

'As you can see,' he said gravely, 'it's very good for bouncing on.'

'Just the sort of sofa I was looking for, then,' I answered with matching gravity.

At this he allowed his hidden smile to emerge, and I felt my throat dry up once again. I hoped I wouldn't be called upon to speak for a few moments. Luckily, at this point the woman glanced across at us, and noticed the bouncing.

'Joseph! Stop that at once! Mark, what are you thinking of? Really, I don't think you know what the word discipline means.' Having delivered this pretty speech in a well-educated yet shrill voice, she returned her attention to the magazine on her lap.

'I'll take it,' I said quickly, finding my voice all of a sudden, 'and I don't mind at all if your little boy bounces on it.'

'That's very good of you,' Mark said evenly, and I couldn't be sure if he was referring to the purchase or the bouncing. 'Don't you want to see it opened out into a bed?' He prompted politely.

'Oh, yes, I suppose so,' I said feeling very foolish.

Mark smiled again.

'That's just the sort of thing I would forget about. It drives Delia mad.' He looked across at his wife and the smiled faded.

He opened the sofa bed out for my inspection and I assured him that I still wanted to buy it.

'Will a cheque be ok?' I said anxiously. 'I'm afraid my card only covers cheques up to fifty pounds.'

'That's fine,' Mark said. 'Just put your address on the back.'

Delia looked across at us again and seemed about to say something, but then obviously decided not to bother.

'Will you be able to get it home ok?' Mark asked when the financial business was sorted out.

'Could you help me get it into the car? The back seat drops down, so it's quite roomy. Once I get to the flat my neighbour will help me to unload it.' I wished that my conscience had allowed me to pretend a greater helplessness than really existed. My remaining time in the company of this lovely man was becoming horribly short.

We struggled together with the sofa, watched by a grinning Joseph, and managed at last to get it into my car.

'Promise me you'll enlist the help of more than one neighbour to unload,' Mark said seriously. 'It's really far too heavy for a woman to lift.'

I agreed that I would.

'Thank you very much,' I said, then kicked myself mentally for sounding like a well-drilled schoolgirl.

'Happy bouncing,' Mark said with another heart-stopping grin, and waved goodbye as I pulled gingerly out of my parking space.

The following evening when I got home from work I took something brown and ice-encrusted out of the freezer and threw it into the microwave, then slumped down on my new-to-me sofa in front of the television. I knew that it was stupid but I had the horrible feeling that every time I sat on it I was going to think longingly of the man who had sold it to me. It was very depressing. I changed channels several times but nothing was showing that was the slightest bit likely to pull me out of my gloom. Then the doorbell rang.

I hastily ran my fingers through my hair and went to open the door. On the step stood Mark, looking even more tired and dishevelled than yesterday, if that were possible. Maybe they'd had a row last night, and he'd had to sleep on the floor now that I had their spare bed. I didn't dare imagine why he had come.

'Can I come in?' he asked.

'Of course.' I led him through into the sitting room. 'Did you suddenly remember you'd stuffed your savings down the back of the sofa?'

61

'Nothing so prosaic.' He looked very nervous. 'Look I don't even know your name.'

'Jane. Jane Reynolds.'

'This is probably going to sound dreadful, Jane. You can kick me out at any time, ok?'

'Ok.' I was starting to have a glimmer of an idea as to why he had come.

'I know I'm probably at least ten years older than you...'

'I like older men.'

'...and I know my divorce won't be finalised for several weeks yet...'

'I don't mind.'

'...and I know it'll be difficult, having Joseph come to live with me...'

'I like children.'

'...but can I see you again?'

'Yes, please.'

Mark looked me properly in the face for the first time. 'I didn't dare show any interest in you last night. Delia would have caused a scene. We don't live together any more, you know. She and the children were only there last night to discuss the division of the spoils.'

'And you got the sofa.'

'Yes.' He glanced at it. 'Lucky for me you like second-hand goods,' he said wryly.

I looked at it too. Suddenly I realised why it had seemed like a reassuring old friend. The fabric was identical to that of my sitting room curtains. It must have been fate.

Swallows

by

Sarah-Jane Evans

Steven was just five when I first knew him. I was fifteen. For a while, I was his protector and guide, but if anyone had noticed our childishness, I would never have been left in charge of him.

Steven had eyes too big for his elfin face, it seemed. Everything was a wonder. His heart was a rage, even then. All was a quest to be conquered. He had a toothy smile that was almost constant and a mind that simply ached for knowledge.

'Look! See! There!' He would shout, already in mid-flight scattering the bleating animals around us. I would laugh with him, chasing rabbits or crows, catching leaves in the early days of Autumn.

We flew my kite here too, on this same hill, squinting in the glare of the same sun.

'Hang on, hold it!' I would shout as he struggled with the kite.

'I'm holding...'

But every time, every single time, it would hit the ground and my father would have to mend the broken wing. It was a wonder it ever left the ground with all that tape holding it together.

But we all feel like that sometimes. It just hit me, lying here with the sun on my face, wondering if I'll every fly again. I mean really fly, face the world with a determination to enjoy and to treat happiness as an ongoing project.

'I'm going to be a fireman,' he said once.

'Why?' Was my question, getting my own back for a change.

'Because I want to travel fast and get wet,' he replied, throwing stones into a stagnant pond.

'Don't you want to do what your dad does?'

'No. He comes home smelling of inside, and ladies' perfume, mummy says.'

Then, I remember, we giggled like we were both five, hearing or seeing something childishly funny for the first time. We giggled until the tears coursed down our angelic faces, until lack of oxygen made us hurt and we heard his mother opening the outside gate.

I remember that he cried when I went away.

'I'll be back soon,' I promised, holding his watery eyes with my fickle gaze. It was the first time I had seen him cry. He clung to my cuff as I loaded my car, sucking his baby thumb, watching me with those big blue eyes that knew so much. Four summers we had spent together, but now there were new children in the village. He had to grow up without me: I had my own life to move into.

School had been fairly drab, now University loomed like an unavoidable diseased giant. The insanity of the place beckoned to me with handsome fingers and jewelled promises.

'Oh, you'll be alright,' I said. 'I know you will. I'll come home soon, I promise.'

Like a lover, 'I promise.' Like a God, 'I promise.'

He had gone back to his mother then, chewing his sleeve.

'I want to be a farmer,' he had decided once.

'Why?'

'Because I want to chase the sheep and watch the grass grow.'

'They do more than that.'

'And live in a big house and have lots of dogs.'

My heart grasped his innocence tighter to protect it and keep some for myself.

'Will we ever fly again?' I asked myself as I drove away from him. The answer saddened me more than a little, for the question was wrong. Not 'we', but 'I'. Will I ever fly again?

We have sloughed off the years, every shedding getting thinner, and thinner, and weaker, and weaker. Some were laughing, some were pained, but they all slipped from us so full, yet empty. A tinge of regret for all the things I never did, taints the edges of the paint-by-numbers life I have so far had.

I'm thirty now. I have a child and a divorce behind me. And I never flew again, until now.

I came home. Here, the sky always seems bluer, the clouds softer and whiter. I came to the hill where I spent my time with a little man I never really knew, until now.

Steven is twenty now. He lays beside me in the grass. The scent of youth is in our nostrils. Adult feelings linger at the places tingled by our games when my own youth was a fresh garment on my face.

Our pulses are lazy in the heat of the sun and the spent passion. I did fly again, with him today, but the feeling is lost now like his fruitful seed.

'A boy-toy, I suppose!' my mother said, disgust sharpening her features into a huge pair of puckered lips.

'The phrase is Toy-Boy, mother.' I replied, wearing her acidity in my own voice. 'It's not that bad, men have been doing it for years.'

But, of course, it is that bad, for her anyway. I feel like a teenager again, with the argument over the discoloured love-bite on the neck, being batted too and fro by the racquets of parents' opinions and blames. I feel like a naughty girl with a souvenir of her sins hiding in her pocket.

But at thirty, I no longer welcome the sense of rebellion that once would have exhilarated me.

'And what about your son?'

Why must mothers always be nothing more than mothers?

My son? Thomas, yes. Of course. Sweet Thomas is with his father today. Sweet Thomas is just five years old with eyes too big for his elfin face it seems.

'What about him?'

'Where does he fit in? Would your Toy-Boy fit him into his young life?'

Yes, probably mother. I don't know, mother. No, probably not, mother.

I shudder thinking.

But it is just for today, this flight. Tomorrow, I should go home. I have to land sometime. But will I still have the roar of freedom in my ears, the carefree spirit and wish for escape pumping in my body?

'I had a dream,' I say. Our eyes watch the swallows high up in space, our warm fingers mingling with the grass.

He stays silent, waiting for me to continue.

'We danced, you and I, for a contest. The jive. We both wore blue and the judges were our family, all sat with stern faces and cross mouths.'

'Did we win?'

I watch the swallows. I can hear their chatter and it thrills me. I think of my son, and my heart weeps.

'No. We were told we had, so we went up on stage to collect our prize. But when we got there, it was just a joke. Everybody laughed. Our parents walked off, and all the other contestants went home.'

He laughs a little, finding my hand with his fingers. Tears sting my face and I wish he could see them. I wish he could see me cry as I saw him cry once, when his eyes were rimmed with red and he was chewing his sleeve.

'What about all the shame you've caused me and your father?' My mother said. 'How are we going to cope with their rejections?'

I thought of my son and my hands went to my shamed face, as if I would find his eyes and ears to cover with my guilty palms.

'I don't know! Maybe if you reject me, they might accept you.'

She never spoke. Her swift hands cleared away the cups. With her back to me, I let the tear fall that had blurred the eye that bore it, and wiped it away with the back of my hand. I was tempted to chew my sleeve.

'How are we going to cope with the shame?' I ask him. I hear his laughter. It thrills me.

'You're just too serious. It's just another game. It's supposed to be fun. Life is. Sex. Fun!'

I am silent now. We are worlds apart. Acres of mundanity separate us and I realise that I have flown for the last.

'It's a migration. Life,' he says. 'You see, swallows go with the weather, they don't sit in the cold, starving hungry and hapless. They sun themselves constantly, have rich diets and warm climates.'

'You don't know how thirsty you are until you drink, or how hungry you are until you sweep up the prize you've been chasing.' I say, turning to him. But he is lost, I think. Our sex, my leaving, I was stretching my wings. Yet I would not have been without it, this escape from earth. I'm glad I was free on this hill once more. Free where the wind has blown my skirts and hair like my ambition, fanning my life into a rage. A wind that gathered everything up into a neat package and scattered the fragments into the air. They flew. I flew. Everything flew about me for some days in a lifetime of days.

I watch the swallows as they swoop above our heads. Steven pushes himself onto one elbow and smiles his toothy smile at me.

'Everything is wonderful,' I say and his smile broadens.

I can hear the flapping of the kite canvas we used to torture and I smile back. Everything feels wonderful.

Overhead, the swallows smile too, their beaks clicking as they catch another juicy meal and reach out for the next.

The Tea Garden

by

Elspeth Veness

It was late last Summer when I meandered along the lanes of the Suffolk countryside and took the turning which led to one of the many little coastal hamlets. The heat of August had barely diminished and the rush of air through the open windows of the car was still too warm to bring relief to my moist hands and flushed face. The excitement that had been surging through me was tinged with a shade of apprehension as I drove past the familiar thatched houses towards the neat triangle of the village green. Pink and blue lupins fused into lilac before my blurred eyes and a cluster of golden nasturtiums spreading over a low stone dyke evoked a sudden rush of nostalgia.

Incredibly there seemed little change as I slowly acknowledged the flourishing clematis and honeysuckle protectively shading the old brick walls from the heat of the sun. Glossy green ivy still crept over the outhouses and vied for room with the creamy-flowered vines. Such a luxuriant profusion blending with the gentle lines of the weathered cottages so that it seemed impossible they had been built and had not grown there naturally amid the tangle.

Enticed by the cloying scent of the meadow-sweet along the verge, my mind was drawn back some twenty years to the time when I had reluctantly accompanied my parents on their annual holiday to this part of the coast. Awkward and shy, I had longed for romance, imagining my lover to be an impossible mixture of the wild and brooding Heathcliff and Jane Austen's perfect gentleman, Mr Knightley. Irritated by my long-suffering family and yet acutely aware of my own inability to achieve my desires, I spent long hours wandering the cliff tops and the beach, day-dreaming in a world of my own.

One of my haunts was the little tea garden where white-painted rickety tables balanced on the uneven grass amid overgrown lilac and unpruned roses. Their heady perfume wafted back into my mind as I recalled sitting on one of the odd assortment of chairs with a glass of lemonade in one hand and the other preventing the pages of my book from fluttering in the breeze. An overpowering longing to step back into those days of fantasy and unrecognised happiness drove me in the direction of that garden.

My romantic notions had dimmed when I left school and began working as a library assistant. Unwilling to respond to the few ordinary boys who ever made the effort to approach me, I filled my life with humdrum occupations and secretly waited for the handsome, debonair man who would sweep me into his world of excitement and glamour. Having neither the appearance nor personality to make this a possibility, I had finally given in to the future of spinsterhood that seemed inevitable.

Increasingly aware of my hot and swollen feet and the need to sit down, I was dismayed to find that the sign advertising teas had vanished and although one or two tables were still scattered about, there was nothing to indicate any activity. Having clung desperately to the improbable hope that I would find things unchanged, the realisation that my dreams had been shattered yet again brought such a feeling of frustration that I stood with my hand on the gate in shocked disbelief.

Daisies flourished among the overgrown grass where once the tea-drinkers had kept the ground flattened. The bench bear the kitchen window where the trays of cups, saucers and plates used to be stacked for collection was now scattered with old stone pots holding artists' brushes and the paraphernalia attached to painting.

Where were the village girls carrying their trays laden with still-warm scones, the little curls of butter and the tiny pots of home-made jam? The laughing, energetic woman bustling in and out with big brown earthenware pots of steaming, fragrant tea?

A voice startled me from my reverie and I was suddenly aware of the presence of a woman who had obviously spoken already and was smiling at my confusion. Stammering my apologies for being half-way through her gate and encouraged by her friendliness and a faint feeling of recognition, I voiced my disappointment. Her smile widened and assuring me that I was not the first to be dismayed by the change, she invited me to share the pot of tea she was about to make for herself. Normally reluctant to impose on anyone at all, I was surprised to find how easily I accepted her kind offer. Reassuring myself that such a departure from my usual behaviour was due to my heat and discomfort I was forced to admit that I was partly attracted by the easy manner of the woman herself.

Ducking my head as I followed her into the cool stone-flagged kitchen, I sank, at her invitation, into a cushioned bamboo chair and became accustomed to the sudden change from the bright sun-light to the shadowy interior of the house. Completely unaffected by the presence of a stranger she made unhurried preparations with tea-pot and cups while I took in my surroundings, aware still of that nagging vague remembrance.

I gazed in silent envy at the artistic style of the rural kitchen: the white rough-plastered walls and the mellow pine furniture; the brown gingham curtains and the mass of greenery tumbling from terra-cotta pots suspended by natural coloured macrame ropes from hooks on the beams. Drawn back to my companion I secretly admired her gleaming dark hair which was secured at the nape of her neck and then released in thick strands on her tanned skin. A rather matronly thirty five myself, I judged her to be about ten years older though quite youthful in appearance. At first glance she had seemed attractive but closer inspection revealed a face which was quite plain, almost ugly. Then she caught my stare and the warmth in her eyes brought back the attraction I had immediately seen.

Inwardly ashamed of my perpetual reassurance in finding flaws in others I smiled back, feeling a sense of affinity that I could not have achieved in the presence of a more beautiful woman.

Following her indication I bowed my head to pass through a low archway into the living area of the cottage. Sunshine flooded through open windows bringing golden rays to the stained-wood floor. A couple of settees covered in a soft blue William Morris design formed an L-shape round a low oak table nestling on a shaggy cream rug. The litter of books scattered across the table and strewn against the tiny wall appalled my methodical librarian mind and then recognition dawned.

I had been in my mid-twenties and senior assistant at the small library in our Midland town. Too withdrawn to indulge in carefree chatter with the customers I concentrated on giving them efficient service and confined myself to observing them unobtrusively and allowing myself silent speculations.

I first noticed the dark woman when she regularly asked for specialist books on the history of Art and I wondered about her profession. Several years older than myself and not particularly pretty, she managed to convey quite a pleasing appearance by some considerable effort. I became aware that her visits seemed to coincide with those of a local schoolmaster whose requests were mainly for scientific volumes. He was hardly the type to feature in my romantic dreams with his mousy, uncontrolled hair and his bony, bespectacled face. Sometimes appearing with holes in the sleeves of his nondescript pullovers he seemed to me to be typical of a lonely batchelor and aroused a vague feeling of pity.

They would acknowledge each other with a formal greeting at the counter and then head towards their different shelves. Engrossed one dreary November

Saturday in pruning the dead leaves from the base of one of my cherished plants in the Travel section and obscured by a stand of paperbacks, I thought I heard their voices. Turning my head I saw them standing side by side and I was surprised by the rapt expression on her face as she looked up at him. Suddenly realising that their hands were surreptitiously entwined I was conscious of being an intruder and moved quietly away.

The apparent secrecy of their meeting intrigued me momentarily but as neither of them were glamorous enough to excite my imagination the incident would have been forgotten. Its revival was brief.

On a cold wet day at the end of February I saw the glossy dark head over at the Travel section when the threadbare sweater appeared at the counter. Beside him stood a plump fair-haired woman whose neat slacks and blouse seemed offended by his presence. He fumbled with his books and dropped a ticket while his companion stood stiffly beside him.

As I stacked his volumes ready to be restored to the shelves I instinctively glanced in the direction of the other woman and was alarmed to see that she was coming eagerly towards him, oblivious until the last moment of his unexpected partner. Unable to conceal her confusion she stopped dead, her colour ebbing away as he moved on apparently unseeing.

After that he was always accompanied and the dark woman took to coming in the lunch hour. Several weeks later I was transferred and they were both forgotten in the bustle of my new appointment.

Coming back to the sun-filled room with a sense of unreality I realised that the woman had been speaking and gratefully accepting the proffered cup of tea I struggled to adjust my thoughts. The clinking of the china had attracted an unsuspecting third presence as the door of an adjoining room opened. Ten years older but instantly recognisable in the unkempt, baggy jersey his still thin face seemed to have acquired a boyishness at odds with the passing of the years.

He smiled without any trace of recognition when we were introduced and as we sat down I reflected that the newly acquired knowledge of their names laced them apart from the unknown couple I remembered. Somehow I was not surprised to learn that his name was George, associated as it was in my mind with someone rather dull and staid.

Curling beside him on the sofa, her brown legs tucked beneath her, Hannah, as I now knew her, leaned her head back against his outstretched arm and rubbed her face affectionately against the rough wool of his sleeve. Unconsciously responding, his fingers twined the silky strands of her hair into ringlets and then loosened them again on her shoulders.

The sudden beauty of their intimacy surprised me and I realised for the first time that the romance for which I yearned might have been discovered outside the pages of my books if I had given it a chance. Their obvious mutual understanding evoked a feeling of envy of which I would not have believed myself capable and belatedly I saw them as they must have seemed to each other. Into my head came the irrelevant thought that Emma's Mr Knightley had also borne the name of George.

All of a sudden I felt awkward and out of place outside the confines of my ordered but dull routine and was sharply conscious of the contrast between their shared affection and my inhibited and lonely life. Despite their warmth and friendliness I resisted all attempts to prolong my stay. Outside in the lane again the feathery branches of the overhanging tamarisk brushed my face like the soft touch of a hand and I was overcome by a flood of self pity at the emptiness of my own existence. An aching longing to be back again in the past, cocooned in the undemanding safety of parental protection brought a tightness to my throat. Viewed in retrospect, those long ago summer days acquired an idyllic charm, bathed as they seemed to be in endless sunshine.

Shivering, despite the late afternoon warmth, I retraced the steps of the monks in the shade of the interlocking trees leading from the ruins of the priory to the sea. Flies buzzed over my head in the leafy tunnel until I came out onto the open cliff top. On an impulse I clambered down, half slipping and falling in the soft sand until I stood breathless on the shingled beach and gazed once more at the scene I had mentally revisited so many times. The cries of the gulls wheeling above my head seemed to mock as the figures in my dream refused to materialise. Sky and sea merged into a misty haze as long suppressed tears blurred my view.

The Job Club

by

Arthur Richards

I pushed open the door of the charity stained church hall, to be instantly greeted by a slightly built round faced man, beaming a smile right at me, as though the door was transparent and he had seen me coming.

'Good morning, I'm sorry.....' I said, about to apologise for being late, but he interrupted with a cheery,

'Hello, are you for the Job Club?' and without waiting for a reply 'Have a seat and I'll fetch you a coffee. How do you like your coffee?' This time he waited for an answer.

As I parked myself on the nearest available seat, I looked up to see an Asian man who, I only then realised, had been about to sit where I had. I think he scowled, so I leapt to my feet with a loud 'Sorry', but he merely looked blankly at me for a second or so then turned and shuffled off muttering like Peter Sellers.

'My name is John Williams, call me John,' said the first man returning with my coffee in a half empty cup and a full saucer, 'I'm the Job Club leader.' He apologised. I apologised for being Arthur Richards while shaking the out-stretched hand and taking the coffee from the other.

On the next seat a lady with artificial looking hair apologetically introduced herself, and on the other side of her, a small balding man, too nervous to apologise, merely grinned through teeth that would have looked happier in the mouth of a rabbit.

Our leader, John Williams, asked us all to fill in two forms, one giving name, address, age, number of years unemployed, etc., while the other, very cunning I thought, was an expenses claim form. They had my attention! Only later did I learn that travelling expenses were paid one day in arrears. *Very* cunning. I would have to turn up tomorrow if I were to get todays expenses. And so on.

We sat in a partly partitioned section of the hall. Chairs were arranged in a tight arc around a display board on which hung large white sheets of paper. John wrote on these sheets with a thick pen and in large, but nevertheless mostly unreadable, letters, while he explained the aims of the club and the facilities it had to offer. We were issued with a folder each, and the first sheets of what was to become, over the next few weeks, a thick wad of information.

All this was intended to help anyone, even us, find happy and gainful employment.

The next step on the stairway to an employed heaven, was to introduce ourselves to each other. We were told to pair with the person next to us and exchange relevant personal details. I paired with the lady with the tea-cosy haircut, who proved to be very nice and called Betty.

John only allowed five minutes for this procedure, so I only had time to hear about her three husbands, her unfortunate medical history, her service in the WAAFs, her Mother's unfortunate medical history, the reason she lost her last job, her cat's medical history and her career as a Jazz Pianist. However, luckily for me, there were eleven more days to go yet.

'We have plenty of time to chat,' she assured me sweetly.

Then, one by one, John had us tell everyone else what we had learnt about our respective partners. The following are the details as best I can remember.

The first to be described was a young person named Kim, occasionally referred to by her partner as 'she'. I mention this because 'she' was more like a 'he' than most road diggers. She had long but lank hair, broad shoulders and narrow hips, was ugly and wore men's clothing. She was well over six feet tall and walked flat footed and stooping. Her gruff voice was rarely used, her main means of communication being a grunt for yes, a groan for no, a grin for don't know and a shrug for maybe.

Then came George. George seemed to have done every job one could think of except for brain surgery, although he had tried chiropody. He had laid bricks and laid out corpses, he had tried dentistry (on his wife) and peered into the mouths of London sewers in his youth. He had raised chickens and slaughtered pigs. He had demolished houses, some of them when *not* employed as a Gas Board fitter. He claimed to have taken watches apart, but did not claim to have repaired any.

George's problems arose from his need to try something different. As George put it, 'When I get used to a job, I get bored and lose concentration. Then things go wrong.' When asked to name his favourite job, he grinned and said 'Breeding.' It was the Greek gentleman who asked George what he liked breeding most.

Next round the arc came Rabbit-teeth. But for his teeth he would have been forgettable. I do remember he had been a Merchant Seaman, as Betty asked to see his tattoo's. The reply came sharply, 'No.'

John had great difficulty with the Greek's name, but eventually mastered it, I never did. The Greek had also been at sea, as an accountant - I'm sure he had. He had difficulty in obtaining an accounting position because of his lack of formal qualifications. He had been on the catering staff of a large cruise liner, with responsibility for the book keeping, and seemed to know his subject thoroughly. I suspect his difficulties really stemmed from his speaking. Not that he couldn't understand or that he couldn't be understood, with a little effort, but that he could not stop himself talking. No one could say more than a few words before the Greek would interrupt, offering opinions or reminiscences, or merely repeating the speakers words like an echo. One merely had to look in his direction to start him talking, and he would continue to talk for as long as he felt he had a listener. If, while he talked, one were to look away, he would tend to fade out, even in mid sentence, unless he could catch another eye, whereupon his voice would pick up and continue as if uninterrupted. Consequently, we all learnt to studiously avoid exchanging glances with the Greek. Better to stare at the wall or ceiling.

Shah came to this country from Uganda some twelve years previous but had yet to find the right job. He had many children and was always eager to talk about them. When not actually giving birth his wife suffered intermittent health problems and needed Shah at home to help her with the children. Now, his wife could bear no more children and nor could he. A job for him was the only answer.

Then there was Kate. Kate suffered from a scarcity of confidence and an abundance of misery. She inspired us all to gloom and despondency. She could kill any happy occasion stone dead. One look at her drooping bloodhound eyes could wipe the smile from the face of even an extreme optimist. She was a nice person, but very depressing. She didn't so much want a job, as somewhere to hang a pall over, to cast a shadow on, an opportunity to bring a little gloom to somebody's life. A friend had suggested she might like to become a Hospital Visitor!

Next was Betty, who related in glowing terms, the information I had given regarding myself, and then I, the last on the arc, tried to tell a very much condensed version of the Betty chronicles. Even so, John rather pointedly glanced at his wrist, twice.

I began to feel like the only fit person in a class of chronic invalids, and ashamed of not having a job because, of those present, I was the only one who had no excuse for being unemployed. That feeling did not last long, as it occurred to me that they may all have been thinking the same about themselves.

74

Perhaps Kim thought herself beautiful; maybe Betty thought herself interesting, Rabbit-teeth the life and soul of the party, Shah overworked, George an entrepreneur, and Kate cheerful? No, I couldn't believe it. Even John seemed a little odd to me. He had often pulled back his cuff, stared at his wrist and referred to the time, but he did not wear a watch.

John looked at his wrist again and suggested we have a coffee break. He explained that coffee was free but we had to help ourselves, and would we mind washing up the cups occasionally.

First to reach the kitchen, and eager to demonstrate managerial ability, I attempted to organise coffee making, but fell at the first hurdle.

'George,' I demanded 'Would you ask the others how they like their coffee?' George's eyes met mine but his mind was elsewhere. His blank face suggested he was concentrating on some bodily function, he seemed tense as though straining.

Not completely deterred, I tried the same words of command on Kim, who made a noise somewhere between a grunt and a groan, looked over my head and stayed still.

Kate said 'Can I help?' but made the question sound like an apology.

All during this time the Greek talked continuously in low confidential tones into my left ear. He must have known I wasn't really listening, but still he droned on, boosted occasionally by my unwitting glances in his direction. I now turned to look at him full face, using a pretend conversation as an excuse to forget the coffee making. Five minutes later, my brain aching with the effort of listening to the tedious droning voice, I made coffee for myself - and the Greek. And still he droned on and on and on..............

My eyes searched the room for a diversion, I tried to attract John's attention, willing him to re-start the session, but failed.

I then attempted to involve Rabbit-teeth in the one sided conversation, but he just grinned and looked away. Rabbit-teeth was definitely not as stupid as he looked.

'Excuse me, I must use the lavatory.' I told the Greek gentleman as I turned away.

'Yes me too,' I heard him say behind me. My heart sank to my pelvis as he began to follow me, still droning on about.......... about..........I really can't remember what.

On the way to the lavatory I spotted Betty leaning on a battered old piano, and remembered her claim to have been a Jazz Pianist.

'Betty,' I exclaimed loudly, hoping for a diversion, 'Why don't you play something for us?'

'Me? oh no. It's been too long..........' she muttered, lowering her ample hips to the piano stool. She lifted the lid and waved goodbye to the keys - presumably to flex her fingers.

Perhaps the piano needed fixing? Or maybe she played a way-out type of Jazz? Anyway, it was awful. If it wasn't actually the Death March it was very close. Nevertheless, my ruse had worked as the Greek was now talking at Shah about Jazz. I carefully backed away, and headed for the lavatory.

When I returned, the 'Jazz' had ceased and John was in the process of calling order, while beside him, waiting with not very well concealed impatience, stood a fat man wearing a dark suit and a back to front white collar.

John said, 'I'd like you to meet the Reverend Dave Pullman,' As he paused, we heard a loud donggg........... George had sat on the uncovered piano. John continued nervously, 'Dave is my Boss. It was his idea to start this Job Club, and he very kindly allows us to use this splendid hall.' He paused expectantly. No-one spoke. 'I'm sure we're all very grateful,' he pleaded.

The Greek saved him. 'Tha's good,' he said ' Iss always ze church. Than' goodnez, eh?'

Everyone avoided looking at the Greek, except the now smiling Reverend Dave Pullman. The eager little man from Athens, attracted by this show of interest in what he had to say, crossed the floor to the fat Vicar, and proceeded to enlighten him on the intricacies of catering and accounting. At least, thats what I gleefully presumed. As my smile grew, so the Vicar's faded.

After a few minutes the Reverend Dave began trying to edge away from, and even turned his back on, the little man, but could not deter him. His patience soon exhausted, the Vicar suddenly declared out loud, that he had a sermon to write and turned sharply to leave, shrugging off the Greek in what I thought was a very rude and unfeeling way.

'How dare he treat our little Greek friend like that?' I thought.

I was surprised to note that I was not alone in my thinking. As fat Dave said his goodbye to John, the rest of us were drawn to where the Greek stood. One moment he was alone, the next surrounded by colleagues, eager to talk with him.

The remainder of the morning was interesting but uneventful. On my way home, I felt excited about the prospect of another morning at the Job Club. I wouldn't be late tomorrow morning.

Ben Is Coming Home

by

David Wicking

John Taylor took down the dog lead that was hanging in the hallway, then turned and walked slowly to the kitchen.

'Come on old chap, its time to go now' he said very quietly as he bent over and clipped the lead to the collar. The old labrador had been going down fast over the recent weeks, off his food and listless, nothing like his usual self, he seemed to have lost interest in everything. He gave out little yelps every now and again, John noticed they were becoming more frequent of late.

It did not seem fifteen years since he had brought him home. John had been walking down by the river one evening when he first saw the tiny pup, covered in mud and whimpering. He had stopped to stroke him, then, after picking him up, the crying had stopped, as he cuddled him the pup had put up his head and licked John's face.

'Right' mused John 'I'll take you home little fellow, feed you up, then it's round to the dog pound.' He had never had any intention of ever keeping a dog, or any other pet for that matter, but just could not bring himself to walk away and leave the pup all alone and frightened. Later that evening, when John had brushed out all the mud from his coat, and his tummy looked as though it would burst, the pup had climbed on to John's lap, he gave a great sigh and promptly fell fast asleep. By the morning that tiny little bundle was following John all over the house and garden, almost as if he was John's shadow, his little tail wagging non-stop. John knew then that he could never part with him. He called him Ben.

'I'm sure you've made the right decision' said the vet. 'He's had a long life, until recently he's never had much wrong with him, but you can see there's no more enjoyment left for him, and with all the pain he's getting now he just doesn't want to go on any longer I'm sure.'

Looking back over the years, John recalled the day when Ben had thoroughly disgraced himself by going into the grocers shop, and had helped himself to a large amount of sweets from one of the shelves. Most of the locals had a good laugh that day, but to John, who had to compensate the grocer it was far from amusing. Not long after that episode Ben had raced across the street to grab a ball from a neighbour's boy. It had taken an hour to retrieve that ball, by then of course it was punctured and quite useless. The ball had been a birthday present, which did not make the situation any easier. The parents of the boy were very angry, they were never friendly after that.

'Oh Ben, why on earth did you have to pick on the snootiest family in the street anyway?' Later still, there was the occasion when Ben had ripped the postman's trousers. Luckily for John, the postman was a dog owner himself, and whilst he was not actually bitten, he could see the funny side, especially as John paid up for the invisible menders bill of twelve pounds.

'You'd better not do that too often you old devil' mused John.

Speaking softly now the vet said, 'There's a good boy, you are a brave old chap, I won't hurt you I promise.' He gently shaved the right front paw below the joint, then, talking quietly, stroked his head, 'Now that didn't hurt did it?' The old dog looked up at John not quite sure what was happening.

John now wished that he had never beaten him, Ben was still quite young when he had chased after a lad on a bicycle. The lad had fallen off, not injured at all, but very shaken.

'He has to be taught a lesson' said John at the time, 'he might have caused a more serious accident.' He had never forgotten the look Ben had given him, or the way he had slunk off with his tail between his legs, staying away for several hours, only to return later, bounding up the path, his tail now wagging furiously, knowing that all would be forgiven.

The vet took a syringe from the cabinet, then, gently taking the old dog's paw, inserted the needle.

'Soon be over Ben, no more pain old son!' Ben lifted his head and stared straight at John for several seconds, his eyes flickered then closed, his legs twitched, now he was quite still. The vet placed his stethoscope on Ben and listened for a few moments, then, turning to John enquired, 'I expect you'd like me to dispose of him for you?'

'Thank you, but no,' answered John. 'Ben is coming home with me.' He wrapped a blanket round the old dog and carried him out to the car, laying him on the back seat; then he drove home slowly, back through the streets where he and Ben had walked so many times before. Going past the vicarage John thought of the ginger tom cat that always used to sit on the wall, Ben would bark frantically for about five minutes, then when the novelty had worn off, would race back to John, just his bit of fun. On arriving home, John went into the garden and began clearing a space by the apple tree, Ben had always loved this part of the garden, he would sleep away the hours on long summer days. When John had finished digging he laid Ben in the grave and covered him with earth. The task completed, he returned to the house.

Everything seemed so misty now, and he felt quite shattered. He tried to do some small jobs around the house, to help take his mind off some of the sadness he felt, but the reminders of Ben were everywhere it seemed, the empty food and water bowls, the collar and lead, the many scratch-marks by the back door. John sat on the settee with his head in his hands.

'Ben, what am I going to do without you. No more dogs, I couldn't go through all this again.'

Several weeks later the telephone rang, it was the vet.

'Hallo John, how are you? I know it's early days yet, but I've a problem, and it's crossed my mind that you may be able to help. You see, I've a lovely young pup here in the surgery. He's only four months old and very healthy. His owners are moving to a flat where a strict 'no pets rule' operates, I'm afraid, so he has to go. I may have to put him down if we can't manage to home him. I'm sure he'll turn into a fine dog, what do you say John are you interested?' John thought hard for several minutes before answering, then,

'I really don't think so at this stage. I miss the old fellow so much, I know I'll never get another quite liked him. It's strange, but do you know, sometimes I imagine he's running up the path. I suppose I'll get over it eventually. It might be different later on. Yes I'll keep in touch of course, thanks anyway for thinking of me, goodbye.' As John turned away from the telephone he glanced at the photograph of Ben which was on the bureau, it had been taken on holiday a few years back. There was Ben, standing on the beach with the surf swirling round him, he was holding an old piece of driftwood in his mouth. Still holding the photograph John moved to the window and stared out to the bottom of the garden, to the mound of earth at the foot of the tree. He remembered that evening many years ago, when that tiny pup first came into his life. He remembered too, all the happy times, with all the fun he and Ben had shared together. As he stood staring down at Ben's grave the memories came flooding back. Turning once more to the telephone, he quickly dialled the vet's number.

'Hello John Taylor here. I've been thinking. If that offer still stands I'll take that pup after all. I can't bear to think of him being put down because of a stupid regulation in a block of flats. Will it be alright if I pick him up in the morning. That's fine then, goodbye for now.'

Crossing over to the bureau once more, he stared at Ben's photo and mused.

'Ah well, at least the grocer now has all his sweets under glass counters, and that snooty family from over the road have long since left the district. Now let me see, that just leaves the problem of the postman; I wonder how much invisible mending costs these days?'

The Carer's Prayer

by

Pamela Willison

She pulled the door to, not quite closing it as she knew he like the comfort of the landing light.

'Please God let me have some rest for a while.' She descended the stairs and caught sight of her reflection in the hall-stand glass, and for a moment was aghast at her untidy appearance. Where was the once smart secretary, before she'd given up her job to care for her father? She entered the kitchen and made a cup of tea. She stoked the fire and settled down thankfully, quite exhausted from the day's never ending chores. She closed her eyes, and in spite of herself, tears of self pity trickled through her closed eye-lids. She slept, and her tea grew cold.

Upstairs, the old man also lay exhausted after the nightly ritual of undressing, catheter changing, teeth cleaning etc. His wispy white hair became tousled as he turned on his pillows to settle for the night. His face was surprisingly un-lined, his mouth sucked in as his teeth were out.

'Good,' he said to himself, 'She's left my teeth in the glass.' He like to nibble a biscuit sometimes in the night. 'She's a good girl,' he thought, 'but I wish she weren't so short tempered.' His wife, long dead, had been even tempered all the years they'd been together - except for a few occasions which he recalled with guilt, when he'd asked for it! He looked round at the familiar room he and his wife had shared for............... how long was it? 49 or was it 50 years? His pale blue eyes rested on the wardrobe, still full of his wife's clothes, he hadn't let them take them away. He often opened the doors just to smell the old familiar fragrance of violets. She always like a bottle for her birthdays, saved him the trouble of thinking of something to buy. He felt a sudden stab of pain in his chest.

'Oh God, how long was it since he'd lost her?' His mind wandered in the ef-fort of struggling to remember............

He'd be late for school again! Old Williams would knock his block off! He'd caned him in front of the class; and what was worse, he'd wet himself! His body stung with humiliation at the memory; urine dripped slowly down the

81

pipe into the bag. Then he cheered up, remembering his 'finest hour' - a chuckle escaped from his lips. He'd proved himself handy with his fists in spite of being so small built. He and his brother, no bigger than himself, joined the Boys Club when they left school at the age of 13, having first earned a certificate to allow them to leave early. So when he saw his little sister in tears from a caning, he'd marched her back to school and confronted old Williams, threatening him with a 'bunch of fives' if he ever laid hands on her again - and he didn't, he thought with satisfaction! Then he saw his father standing slowly removing his belt in preparation of dishing out another beating, for some petty misdemeanour. He'd stood up to him too, and found it worked again!

However, it was the beginning of the end for him, he'd had to leave home. Even his mother had said she thought it would be for the best, fearing further confrontation. So he left his job with a firm in the city making chandeliers - they'd made them for the ill-fated 'Titanic' before he'd joined the firm as a tea-boy, and general factotem, at the princely sum of 2/6d a week (as he was learning the trade & lucky to be there). He left home and joined the R.A.F. as a Tool-Maker apprentice, surprising himself by passing the entrance examination. He was stationed at Halton, Bucks, miles from Brum and home. He got two guineas a week in 1922, and his bed and board, he'd never been so well off! He sent his mum 10/- every week, saved 10bob and spent the rest. He was never one for drinking or smoking as he represented the Service as a Fly-weight. Did quite well too, had plenty of medals and cups to prove it. One particularly big one was won at Dreamland Hall, Margate when he was later stationed at Manston, Kent, prior to being sent to India. The RAF were more niggardly with their prizes, some were quite small, though the bouts had been important.

'I wonder where my cups are now?' he thought. When his wife was alive they'd been cleaned regularly, and stood proudly on the shelf opposite the living-room door, so visitors couldn't help but notice them as they entered the room. It often created a topic of conversation to strangers, and he could bask in remembered glories as he re-told the fights he'd had to win them. His wife's face would beam with pleasure. and she never tired of his tales, indeed often added something he'd forgotten. Though she'd never attended any of his fights, they were all before he'd met her, but she knew the stories by heart.

'Wouldn't have watched anyway,' she'd say, not wanting to see him hurt he guessed. His daughter must have put them away, he remembered she'd grumbled at having to clean them - he'd ask her about them tomorrow.

Many of the cups had been won in Karachi, he was there for five years. He'd met and made friends with Colonel Lawrence, (of Arabia), only now he was called Shaw. He'd widened his knowledge beyond belief with the books he'd lent him, and unlike some of the others, he always made sure he returned them in good order. He'd still got one he'd been given to keep, a small battered book of the 'Wisdom of Bernard Shaw', the binding had become torn over the years. Pity neither had signed it, would have been worth a bob or two by now he mused. Might still be worth something, it must be out of print now. Shame none of the children read much, brought up on too much TV. His wife read, they'd stayed up till all hours discussing religion and politics. He remembered how they'd argued over the riddle of the Sphinx, got quite heated about it. God, how he'd love to have the old girl lying beside him now, and they could talk till one or the other fell asleep. Great one for poetry she'd been, could recite for hours, and one night, when he couldn't sleep she'd amazed him by reciting the whole of the Sermon on the Mount without faltering. Smiling at the memory his eyes clouded over, he looked round the room in bewilderment, closed his eyes and mercifully slept.

Downstairs Molly was woken by a knock at the door. Sleepily she rose, wondering who it could be calling at this hour. She looked at the clock it was only 8 o'clock. She fingered the cross at her neck, 'Oh God, I'm so tired. Please, please lighten my burden.' It was a prayer she asked more and more often these days. She opened the door, it was Bill, one of the ambulancemen who called twice a week to take her father to the Day Centre. Her only opportunity to shop and catch up on neglected household chores. Bill had a sprinkle of grey in his thick untidy hair, and a kind face that reminded her of Syd James - 'lived in' was the idium of the day.

'The old boy left his cap behind Molly,' he said. 'I was passing, and thought I'd kill two birds with one stone, so to speak. Can I come in a minute?'

'Of course,' replied Molly, only too glad to have an unexpected visitor.

'I was wondering if you'd consider letting your spare room to me Molly, my sister is having another baby, and I know they need the room, but won't say so; they've both been good to me since I lost my wife, as you know, and I don't want to out-stay my welcome. No rush to answer,' as he noticed a rising flush on her face; and added, 'I know it needs a bit of thinking about.'

Upstairs the old man's voice rose querulously, 'Where's my cup of tea Molly?'

They looked at each other understandingly, and she made to go up.

'No, let me,' said Bill. 'That's another thing I was going to say, I'd be able to help you when I'm off duty, and I'd be glad to. The old boy likes me I know.'

He bounded up the stairs, and she heard her dad say, 'Oh Bill, it isn't Centre Day is it?'

She smiled, and whispered to herself in wonderment. 'Thank you, oh Thank you God, you heard my prayers.'

The reminiscences of the old man (my husband) are *all* true, he was in India the same time as Lawrence, and I still have the book mentioned. I have been relieved as a carer, for he is now in Holbeach and E. Elloe Hospital in the latter stages of Parkinson's disease. I nursed him for 19 years.

The Fly

by

Keith Hazelton

Spring had come early this year. The temperatures were well above the seasonal norm. Phil Bates made the most of the lovely weather by leaving the patio doors open as he relaxed on the sofa reading his newspaper.

The first time he became aware of the fly was when it made a low altitude pass above the sports pages. Phil made a desultory swipe at the insect almost by reflex. The fly alighted on top of the wall unit. It waited a few seconds and then again took off and buzzed around Phil's head.

This time Phil made a more virorous attempt to swat the flying beast but he was far too slow to make contact. He watched as the fly made its way back to its favourite perch. It landed and seemed to stare straight back at him, challenging. Its eyes were black and fathomless but they radiated evil and hatred. Phil felt a shiver run down the length of his back.

Christ, its only a fly for God's sake, he thought, what's the big deal. And yet he couldn't return back to his paper. Ah, the paper. He rolled it up and decided that very soon the fly would be an ex-insect.

To reach the fly he had to gain extra height. He stepped onto the foot stool. The fly hadn't moved: it just continued staring straight at him. He raised the paper to strike. It swished through the air. At the last second the fly took off, not to escape, but to return the attack. It flew directly at Phil's eyes. Phil ducked and lost his balance. His arm went out to avoid the fall. That was his biggest mistake.

He grabbed at a shelf of the wall unit. It was not fixed to the wall and as he fell the unit came crashing down knocking the wind from his lungs. Everything went as black as the fly's eyes.

Consciousness returned. He had no idea how long he had been out. The first item on the agenda was the terrific pain that seemed to flood the lower half of his body. He tried to move: that was a bad idea. He was laying on the floor with the heavy wall unit pinning his body from the chest down. Judging from the pain at least one of his legs were broken.

He looked up at the wall clock; it was three o'clock. Mary and the kids were due back from the pool at five. Two hours of agony. The thought didn't fill him with glee. Moving, though, was out of the question.

For the second time in his life. Phil Bates became aware of the fly. It was still perched on the wall unit but this time somewhere near his ankle. If flies could laugh Phil was sure this one would be having a good chuckle. What a state to be in over a stupid fly.

'Why don't you buzz off,' he said aloud and burst into waves of hysterical laughter at this, to him, extremely funny remark.

The laughing didn't last for long. It soon gave way to tears of pain, and yes, a little bit of fear. Phil Bates would not have been able to explain that fear but the presence of the fly filled him with a strange sense of foreboding.

The fly took off and flew around Phil's face, studying him. Phil's strength seemed to have gone and he couldn't raise his arms to attack. He tried blowing the fly away but this futile gesture had no effect.

At last the fly seemed to have had its fill of gloating. It flew out of the patio doors into the bright sunlight. Phil relaxed and dropped into a light slumber, confident that soon this nightmare would be over.

Phil opened his eyes. The clock told him he had dozed for an hour. The pain, if anything, was worse. The top of his body had turned numb and he felt delirious. He heard a sawing sound from outside. I didn't know Jack had brought a chain-saw, still some of his bushes do need a good trim, Phil thought to himself.

But the sound did not come from next door. A shadow blocked out the sun coming into the room. Phil turned to look towards the patio. What he saw defied belief. An almost solid black mass was flying into the room. It was an impenetrable cloud of flies; millions and millions of them.

The mass stopped halfway across the room. Phil couldn't believe the noise that millions of tiny wings could make. His attention switched to the end of the wall unit. Sure enough a fly with penetrating black eyes was motionless near his feet. It can't be, Phil thought, no fly is that intelligent. It was almost as if the fly was acting as air-traffic controller for his companions.

The fly turned its attention to its colleagues. As if of one mind they flew down and landed on Phil's body. It was like being covered in flowing treacle. Phil tried to close every orifice but the need to breath became overwhelming as flies started crawling up his nose. He found the strength to move his arms and tried brushing the mass away from his face. But he was heavily outnumbered.

He had to open his mouth to breathe. But that was fatal. He was now eating flies. He could feel thousands entering his windpipe. No air was reaching his lungs, only flies.

Phil Bates knew he was going to die. He just hoped it would be sooner rather than later. His last wish was granted. He could feel life leaving his body, and with it went his last thought. Why didn't I leave that bloody fly alone?

The fly allowed its followers to feed for a while. But now it was time to leave. It cast one final look at the pathetic bundle on the floor, took off, and flew out of the doors into the afternoon sunshine.

Silent Night

by

D J Hedges

Four men in the Gynaecology Ward.

Such a thing had never happened before. But it did at Christmas 1988 and I was one of the men.

It had all started several weeks before. I was laying on the couch of the Eye Consultant at Peterborough District Hospital when his Secretary asked, 'Are you going away for Christmas?'

'Oh no, I shall be at home with the family,' I replied, thinking how nice it was of her to make small talk, probably trying to calm my nerves, as I lay waiting for him to start whatever he had to do.

It was late November and I had been waiting for an operation to correct a cataract, on my left eye since the previous January. That day exact measurements were to be taken for the implant lens I was to receive, which I was assured would correct my sight.

Three days later a letter advised me a bed was reserved for me on December 22nd and I would be in four or five days. It hadn't been small talk at all but an information seeking question. I was to be in hospital over Christmas.

I went in during the morning of the 22nd and was prepared for the operation the following morning. During the late afternoon an Indian doctor came to explain to me what was to happen. An incision was to be made around the top of the iris and the lens removed. A plastic lens would be inserted and the iris stitched up. It sounded quite gruesome.

Later I was visited by the anaesthetist who started to reassure me and explain his part in the operation. I had in the past had operations for two hernias and one to remove a stone in my kidney so that I was fairly familiar with the procedure.

'Just make sure I wake up,' I told him jokingly, yet dead serious, 'I'm not really interested in anything else.'

'That's no problem,' he assured me, ' I shall be very worried if you don't.'

'So will my wife,' I informed him. We had a nervous laugh together and he parted with a cheerful, 'See you tomorrow.' His confident attitude was very reassuring.

The operation was successful and I duly woke up with a patch covering my left eye. During the afternoon the nurses told us that those not going home for Christmas were to be moved into another ward to reduce the staffing requirement over the Christmas period. A highly sensible move, no point in having several half empty wards. It then emerged that the men, four of us were to go downstairs to the gynaecology ward, something never heard of before.

The transfer took place on Christmas Eve, the four of us in a curtained off section. I was in the left hand corner near the window. Opposite me was Fred, a man in his late sixties, a pleasant, quiet man, quite lucid if a little scared of his first stay in hospital. Along side him was Tom. His daughter had told me he had been a very intelligent headmaster but recently his mind had started to fail and he had become very absent minded. His whole manner was that of a gentleman, the way he spoke and constantly folded his clothes. Opposite Tom, and next to me, was Reg. Poor Reg had big problems. He had an operation on one eye and had very poor sight in the other. Combined with this, without his hearing aid he was almost totally deaf. He was the only one of the four who enjoyed a smoke and seemed always out in the day room having a cigarette or asking to be taken there.

Behind me was a solid wall but only a curtain behind Fred and Tom divided us from four ladies who we could hear but could not see unless we chose to look when we went to the toilet which was past the entrance to their section then off to the right.

The day was relatively normal and passed off without it being apparent that it was Christmas Eve, and at around ten o'clock the nurses started to settle us down for the night. Tom and Reg had been sleeping for some time when the lights were eventually put out. As usual I was asleep very quickly, quite pleased that the worst was over and that all I had now to do was to recover. A couple of days and I'd be at home.

I woke with a start. Shouts and screams seemed to be everywhere. For a few moments I could not be sure where I was. Nurses came running, calling, waking the whole ward. In the dead of night every sound seemed amplified. Those of us awake, Reg hadn't heard a thing, gathered that Tom had got out of bed to go to the toilet and instead of turning right had turned left and sat on the bed of one of the ladies. Hence the screams. The nurse calmed everyone down and Tom was helped back into bed totally confused at what all the fuss had been about. Peace was restored and I was soon tucked back down into bed and asleep again.

I had no idea how long I slept before suddenly being awakened again. This time it was trolleys rattling in the corridor. Trolleys with loose wheels, they could have been square wheels for the noise they made, trolleys that clattered and squeaked over what must have been very uneven floors. Trolleys that turned out to be just one bringing clean clothes for Tom's bed. It had been thought he was returning from the toilet when actually he was going towards it when he took the wrong turning. He had never got there and now had wet the bed. He was quite distressed as one nurse changed him whilst another changed his bed. The rest of us were wide awake, at least Fred and I were, Reg wasn't aware of what was happening. Tom was finally settled down and the trolley rattled its way back along the corridor to its normal resting place while we curled down into our beds and yet again gave way to peaceful sleep.

It was broken again by Reg calling for the nurse. He had woken and wanted a cigarette. He couldn't or wouldn't understand that it was the middle of the night. He wanted a smoke and that was that. The nurses decided the quickest and quietest way was to take him to the day room and let him have his cigarette. One went off to get a wheel chair, which of course squeaked. He was helped from his bed, put into a dressing gown, moaning all the time, and taken off squeaking all the way up the corridor. I was still awake when he returned. At least he was satisfied.

Once again I succumbed to sleep only to be woken by a high pitched whistle. The nurses came running once more. No one could tell from where it came until one of the nurses identified it as coming from Reg. It was found his hearing aid had dropped out of his ear and he was laying on it creating an unusual oscillation. It was taken away from him because he wouldn't need it whilst asleep.

'That's it, off to sleep gents,' called one of the nurses. We did.

It seemed only minutes before she was shaking me, 'Wake up, Happy Christmas.'

Hark, the Herald Angels sing.

Was it they who disturbed our rest that night?

Silent night, Holy night. What a night!

Done!

by

David Gray

I found myself a job and saved up, I suppose I could have been doing something more interesting, but nothing springs to mind. Eventually I thought I would give myself a treat, I was beginning to get fed up with walking to and from work, and with my weekly budget set aside I had nearly two thousand five hundred pounds begging me to enjoy it. So one Saturday I set off to the showrooms to see if I could spot a bargain.

They were all there, all shapes, sizes and colours, the prices varied a great deal too and there was no shortage of salesmen trying to separate me from my hard earned cash. I tried to be sensible and not grab the first shiny object I came across. I looked at everything that was on offer and after almost too much hesitation I plumped for what I thought would be right for me.

Looking back, I did feel slightly pressured by the salesman, but I really did believe that this was the one I wanted, even though it would cost me all of my savings. I couldn't contain my excitement on the way home, it was everything I had dreamt of and more. I thought about taking it round to my friends house to let him have a look, but I didn't want to show off, I didn't want it to seem ostentatious of me, and anyway, I wanted to enjoy it on my own, while it was still new.

Later I went to bed with a feeling of satisfied exhaustion, and the smile still clung to my lips as I took one last look out of my bedroom window at my new toy, it stood there gleaming in the light of a street lamp, all brown and creamy, I couldn't wait for the morning.

Next day, before breakfast, I dashed outside for another look. There it stood, still new, still perfect, not quite as big as I had imagined it from the night before, but it wasn't such a novelty being a day later. I know it sounds silly now, but it wasn't until then, as I studied it, that suddenly the reality dawned on me that it was a Swiss roll.

I bent down and picked it up, numbed, a few bits of grit stuck to the bottom but basically it was still as good as new. Straight away the shock of realisation hit me, yes, I had been done! I didn't want a Swiss roll, I didn't need one, and anyway it was far too expensive. I thought about taking it back but it was

Sunday and the shops were closed. How could I have been so foolish? I ought to have known those salesmen were sharks, to be talked into a purchase like that was totally humiliating and I thought how much the man must have laughed. I would have to wait until Monday to take it back and with no guarantee even then of getting my money back.

I took it back anyway, Monday came and down I went, the same man was still there, I put it on the counter and he looked me up and down.

'I'm not happy with this' I said, 'it's not what I expected, in fact it's totally unsuitable and I'd like my money back please.' I thought the direct approach was best, try and brazen it out. He picked it up and straight away he hit me with a 'crippler'.

'Got the receipt?' He said.

I didn't panic, 'no of course not,' I blustered, 'how long do you keep receipts, I bought this in good faith and reserve the right to return it if I'm not satisfied with it.'

He picked it up and turned it round in his hands, 'seems alright to me,' he said, 'no damage, good as new, as I remember you had a good look underneath it and saw the list of previous owners.'

'Well,' I said, still trying to look stern, 'I think it was misrepresented, I didn't want a Swiss roll,' but then I dried suddenly and all I could do was stare at him.

'I won't give you your money back,' he said, 'but I'll buy it back off you if you like.'

Thank goodness, I thought, at last I can unload it.

Then, cool as a cucumber he said, 'I'll give you thirty pence for it.'

I couldn't believe it, my legs began to tingle and I gripped the counter. 'Thirty pence!' I said, with not a little surprise.

'Well what would you pay for a used Swiss roll,' he replied as he put it back down on the counter.

'The wrapper hasn't even been off,' I said, 'It's as good as new.'

'Pre-owned,' he retorted, 'and by more than one person.'

I had trouble speaking, 'I, I paid two thousand pounds for that,' I poked it, leaving a little dent in the packet.

He sighed again and remained silent. I knew I was losing the argument, and I wasn't ready for his offer when it came.

'I tell you what I'll do,' he said. 'I'll exchange it for you, I can't say fairer than that now can I?' He half turned and put his hand in the edge of a row of shelves behind him loaded with sweet comestibles, and smiling asked me to make my choice.

92

I knew I had to be canny, I won't get caught again I thought, and I scanned the shelves with total concentration. Eccles cakes, jam turnovers, cream and apple puffs, bakewell tarts, packets of biscuits by the score.

He thinks he's got me again I thought, expecting me to pick some rubbish off those shelves. I glanced through a wired glass window in a door leading from the right-hand side of the room we were in, into the garage area at the rear, and there I saw it. Royal blue with orange stripes gleaming in the sunshine that bounced through the garage skylight. Those smooth lines captured my mind and this time I wasn't going to be cheated. I pointed through the window and declared, 'I want that!'

The man looked at me and then through the window, a frown cut across his forehead and it was his turn to stutter.

'No, no, on here,' he said as he patted the shelves. 'That's not for sale.'

'You said make my choice, and I have,' I declared emphatically.

'But you've only got a Swiss roll,' he wailed. 'Do you realise how much that costs,' he pointed into the garage. 'That's brand new,' he said.

'And just what I want,' I replied triumphantly, adding, 'a deal is a deal, honour it!'

I got my bargain, and on the way home this time I felt different, a success, a man not to be trifled with. That night as I gazed through my bedroom window into the street below, I made my plans for the following day. I would take it round and show everyone I knew, I deserved a little praise and admiration now, God knows I had suffered enough the past few days.

Next morning I made myself wait and had breakfast before doing anything, I felt like teasing myself, I felt like a little boy. I eventually left the house and went outside onto the pavement.

I reached out my hand and placed it gently on the shiny blue roof. The chrome trim sparkled in the morning sun and the windows gleamed spotless, the aerial quivered in the light breeze and I steadied it as I walked round to the front. The headlights glared pop-eyed ahead and the chrome grill grinned the widest grin imaginable across the broad front of this blue marvel. I walked along the other side and around the curved back end with its twin chrome tail-pipes sticking out like two shiny teeth. I came to the door and gripped the handle, impatient to smell the leathered interior.

'Hey, what's up, get away from there.'

I let go and swung round, the boy from next door stood scowling at me, a bunch of keys rattled as he shook them impatiently. I said nothing as he pushed passed me, unlocked the door and got in! The engine coughed once and caught first time, dying away to an even hum. I saw him clip on his seat-belt and then with a short squeal as the wheels spun in the dust, he shot away down the road.

I was dumbstruck, what was happening? I stared down at the vacant kerb and there, in the gutter close by my feet, I saw the crumpled remains of a full box of jaffa cakes, squashed into the road by the spinning tyres. Straight away I knew...

I had been done again!

The Gypsy's Word

by

Ann Warren

'Oh dear' Ruth exclaimed aloud. Putting a vase of flowers on the window-sill she had seen an old lady fall on the path near her gate. Opening her front door she ran down the path.

'Let me help you up,' she said, 'are you hurt?'

The old lady was a Gypsy pedlar and her basket of trinkets had spilled over the pavement. Moving the basket aside Ruth helped the old lady to her feet.

'Thank you my dear I'll be alright now,' the old lady said. Ruth collected the things and put them back in the basket, but as the old lady held out her hand to take it Ruth could see she was shaking.

'You must come inside and rest,' she said, 'I will make you a cup of tea.'

The old lady was obviously shocked and she allowed Ruth to take her arm and help her to the house.

Sitting in Ruth's kitchen with a cup of tea she began to look much better: and when Ruth asked where she was staying and if she had far to go the old lady said her son was meeting her by the last house in the street, and he would take her home.

'He has a blue truck, perhaps you can see it from your window,' she said.

Ruth could see no vehicle from the window but offered her visitor another cup of tea while she waited.

While they were having their second cup of tea the old lady said she could see Ruth had been unhappy and had recently lost someone dear to her. Ruth was amazed.

'How can you tell?' she asked.

'Just by looking at you my dear,' replied the Gypsy. Ruth then told how she had given up her job six months earlier to nurse her mother, 'now she has gone I feel very lonely,' Ruth said, 'I just haven't got round to getting myself another job yet.

'Give me your hands,' the old woman said reaching out. As she took her hands Ruth felt a tingling like a small electric shock go up her arms. 'Your sad time is over,' the Gypsy told her, 'you are about to start a new way of life and you will be leaving this house.'

95

Ruth smiled when she heard this, 'I was born in this house and I can't imagine living anywhere else,' she said.

'It must be time for me to go,' the old lady said getting to her feet. 'Thank you very much for your kindness, you know kindness never goes unrewarded.'

Ruth looked out of the window and saw the blue truck parked down the road, 'let me walk with you,' she said picking up the basket.

As they got near a young man jumped out of the truck: he had black curly hair and dark skin.

'What's the matter mam?' he asked the old lady as he took her arm.

'I had a bit of a fall and this kind lady looked after me,' she replied, 'but I'm alright now.'

The man helped his mother in the truck and then turned to Ruth to take the basket. 'Thank you very much for your help,' he said 'I am indebted to you.'

'That's alright,' Ruth replied, 'but she did have a nasty fall, perhaps she should see a Doctor.'

'Thank you again,' said the man getting in his truck, 'Goodbye.'

The truck pulled away and Ruth went back to her house: but she could not forget what the Gypsy had said about a new start. As she washed the cups she made up her mind to go out and get herself a job the very next day.

That evening answering a knock at her door Ruth was surprised to see the Gypsy man standing there.

'Hello,' he said taking off his hat, 'do you remember me, I'm Rob Buckley, you were kind enough to help my mother this morning.'

'Yes of course I remember you,' answered Ruth, 'is your mother alright?'

'She is none too well,' replied the man, 'she asked if you would come and see her.'

'Yes of course I will,' Ruth said, 'come inside while I get my coat.'

Rob put a blanket on the seat and helped Ruth in the truck. the Gypsies were camped in a little copse at the bottom of Kents Drove where they came every year to help with the fruit picking. As they pulled into the clearing Ruth could see six caravans, they all looked very smart with pretty lace curtains at the windows. There was a fire burning at the centre of the clearing with some men sitting round it: and as Ruth got out of the truck some children came over to stare at her. Rob took her arm and led her over to one of the vans.

Inside the caravan was spotless with shining brass ornaments, and at the far end the old lady lay in bed.

'Are you awake Mam?' Rob whispered.

'Yes,' came the reply, 'leave us now, sit down dear,' she said to Ruth pointing to a chair by the bed.

'I'm sorry that you are not so well,' Ruth said, 'is there something you want me to do?'

'No,' replied the old lady, 'I just want to talk to you. You see in our family one of us has always had the power, but I am the last. My two girls died very young and I only have my son left now.'

'What do you mean the power?' Ruth asked as the old lady paused for breath. For answer the lady reached out and took Ruth's hands: and once again Ruth felt that strange tingle run up her arms.

'The power is healing hands. You have that power in your hands I felt it when I touched you this morning. Now I am giving you my power as well, always use it for good and never for money. You must go now I am tired,' the Gypsy said.

Ruth stood up, 'Goodbye and thank you,' she said.

Rob was sitting on the steps outside waiting for her. 'Will you have a cup of tea with us before I take you home?' he asked.

Ruth thanked him and followed him to another caravan where a young woman was already setting out the cups and saucers.

'This is my cousin Roma,' Rob said.

'Hallo my name is Ruth Telford,' she introduced herself.

When the tea was ready Roma left the caravan and Ruth asked Rob if he knew why his mother had wanted to see her.

'No,' he replied, 'but it must have been something special as it's the first time anyone other than our own people has been inside my mothers home.'

Ruth did not tell him what his mother had wanted but said it was time she was going home.

When they reached her home Rob thanked her for going to see his mother and said perhaps they would meet again.

Watching him walk down the path Ruth was hoping they would.

The next morning Ruth decided to cycle to the Gypsy camp to see how the old lady was. When she reached the site all the vans had gone and there was nothing except a few ashes to show they had ever been there. As she turned to go Ruth met Mr Kent walking his dog.

'Morning Ruth you're out early,' he said.

'Yes I came to see the Gypsies but they've gone.' She replied.

'Yes, Rob came to see me last night to tell me they had to go, but they will be back in time to pick my apples,' Mr Kent told her.

Wheeling her cycle Ruth walked with Mr Kent back to the road.

Suddenly the little dog sat down and whined.

'It's his leg,' Mr Kent told Ruth as they walked back to the little dog, 'sometimes he just can't move it.'

Ruth felt again that strange tingling in her hands and arms as she put down her cycle and picked the dog up. As she gently rubbed his leg the little dog licked her face and wagged his tail. When she put him down he ran to Mr Kent.

'Well I'm blessed,' he said, 'all you have to do is rub his leg for him, I'll remember that next time it happens.'

Ruth smiled, she knew there would not be a next time, the little dog was cured.

For the rest of the day Ruth felt quite miserable, she knew she had gone to the Gypsy camp with the hopes of seeing Rob again: and her mind was still on the Gypsies that evening when she sat down to watch the television.

Suddenly her attention was caught by the word Gypsy, and looking up she saw the television cameras were in a field with dozens of caravans, and the presenter was saying traffic had been held up all day in this area with so many vans on the road. Then to her surprise there on the screen beside the presenter was Rob, telling him they had all come here to bury his mother.

'The funeral is tomorrow and we shall all be gone the next day,' he said.

'Where will you go?' asked the newsman.

'I shall go back to the place I left last night,' replied Rob. Then, looking straight at the cameras he added, 'there is someone there I want to see.'

Sitting in her chair beside the TV Ruth knew he meant her. The Gypsies word had come true: her life was about to change.

Do You Take This Man?

by

Nick Plumb

Dominic opened his eyes and glanced at his watch. He'd been asleep for over an hour. Fay was asleep in the seat opposite, her long blonde hair partially covering her face gently caressing her pale cheek as the train vibrated along its track. Dominic turned his head and gazed out of the large oblong window. The miles flashed by; greens and browns merging into a one long wall, the colour of sludge.

Each field like a memory, filled with detail for the briefest moment then smudged into time, fading around the edges, details lost in the confusion of the past. Details such as how Dominic had come to be on a train heading for a tiny holiday village on the East coast, on a cold February morning.

He shifted his gaze to Fay, who was still asleep, her chest rose and fell regularly in a deep comforting rhythm. She seemed so at peace with the world, so calm; indifferent to the towns and country flashing by, ignorant to the complications of life, unaware of the unpredictability of time.

Dominic sighed, closed his eyes and returned to his land of dreams.

He awoke to the rattling of door handles and the sound of heavy footsteps on concrete. They had arrived.

Still dazed with sleep, they wandered out of the station and toward the village. The cold crisp air reflecting the warmth of their breath in white streams. The crunch of frozen grass underfoot thrust memories of their recent wedding into his consciousness. That small ceremony, that even smaller church and her beauty, her overwhelming brightness that filled every corner of that cold ancient building. He remembered her smile, her vitality, her eyes so filled with life.

He spotted it, a small public house and suggested that a glass of something would help warm them up. What he really meant was that he felt awful and needed a drink.

God how he needed a drink.

The pub was empty with the exception of a dark figure, huddled over half a pint of brown liquid, backed into a corner, melting into the shadows.

99

Dominic shivered more with fear than cold, the figure was that which he feared, the very thing he was running from, the very thing Fay was saving him from.

The landlord was leaning over the bar reading the Sunday paper, he looked up and smiled, a worn smile, thought Dominic, on a worn face, a face that had seen lives change, people grow, people die, a face that had gazed upon a world within a world and had not liked what it had seen.

'Brandy please,' Dominic handed over a crumpled five pound note. A creased photo of Fay fell from his pocket and he hastily grabbed it, pushing it deep into his coat pocket, fearing its loss.

They sat by the log fire at a small dark wooded round table, flanked by two stuffed birds and a fox's head nailed to the wall behind them.

The empty glass eyes watched them, deaf ears listening.

The hours and the brandies slipped by, soon the numbing sensation had overcome the initial warming effect of the brandy.

Dominic waved goodbye and headed down towards the sea front, he stumbled passed the shuttered kiosks, the empty crazy golf and the silent fun fair; where only the ghost of the Summer now played.

He walked on toward the open green, near the cliffs, to the small wooden bench where he and Fay had met. To the spot where Cupid fired his fatal arrow.

It had begun to rain causing the sea and sky to join in a false horizon and as he squinted through the rain, she came back into view, standing just a few yards in front of him. Her blonde hair blowing in the cold salted wind, her eyes bright and her smile filled with love. She stood in the exact spot where the bench had been.

She held out her hand.

The band of gold caught the last rays of the Winter sun as they embraced.

The body of a young man was found at the bottom of Milton Cliffs in the early hours of Monday morning. There was no means of identification except a creased photograph of a young woman, with blonde hair and a cutting from an obituary column.

Police are appealing for witnesses.

All Part of the Game

by

Ron Marshall

Everything seemed so quiet and peaceful in the park; even the hum of the busy Belfast traffic, muted by distance and the persistent drizzle, only added emphasis to the feeling of tranquillity. However, the young British Soldier standing alone in the centre of the large open area, knew only too well that peace and tranquillity were aliens on the lands of Northern Ireland. To him they could only be regarded as dangerous figments of the imagination, ready to waylay the unprepared and lead him onto the rocks of death and disaster. So the young soldier stayed alert and as watchful as ever as he constantly studied all and sundry which stood or moved within his vision.

It was now nearly three years since he, and the Regiment had arrived in Ulster. Nearly thirty six long arduous months of patrols, road blocks, stake-outs, bomb alerts and the never ending stand-by duties. It was these, which above all else, that sapped the mind and destroyed the spirit. And all for what? He had long since given up trying to fathom his reason for being in the Province. Someone had once said, 'The British Army's task was to contain the situation until the politicians could find an answer.' After all these years he was beginning to wonder if those politicians had even understood the question. Or, more importantly, if they even cared.

As he stood there his head constantly turned slowly while his eyes took in every single detail. Every bush and tree was subjected to the closest of scrutiny. Any movement, however slight, drew his utmost attention; nothing, no matter how mundane, was accepted without careful study and thought. Only when he was totally assured that all was quiet, did he let his mind and body slowly relax.

Taking a series of deep breaths in an effort to relieve the tension within him, he let his mind dwell on why he should even have joined the Army in the first place. The answer to that question was simple enough; he had had nowhere else to go. Having been born the unwanted child of a fast failing marriage, he had been condemned to life in an institution, therefore it was only natural that when at the tender age of seventeen, he had been told it was time to go out into

101

the wide world and make his own way, he had simply found another institution in which to reside.

Which ever way you looked at it, it was always better than the dole queue. He smiled at the thought of what his ex friends in the Lincolnshire Fenlands had said when he informed them he was joining up. If only they could see him now; well fed, well paid, well clothed and bloody scared.

The sound of a vehicle intruded on his thoughts and he turned to watch an old mini-bus, badly dented and seemingly in an advanced state of decay, slowly make its ponderous way along the path.

He studied it closely as it turned and came to a halt in the small car park a few yards from where he was standing. Then, as he caught a glimpse of the occupants through the dirty windows he felt the first stirrings of disquiet. The vehicle contained about a dozen youths, although perhaps young men would have been a more apt description and it was the big lad sitting next to the driver which held his attention.

For some reason he felt he knew the lad and he started to search his memory in an endeavour to put a name to the face. Then it came to him. The youth's name was Patrick McHarry, and with the memory of the name came the memory of when they had met some six months earlier.

It had been on the day when the IRA had buried two of its members who had been killed by the security forces. As is normal on those occasions, the proceedings had drawn huge crowds of mourners and, as is normal, some of the crowd were there for the sole purpose of causing trouble. When the trouble started, the young soldier's platoon was one of the first into the fray. It was then that he had come face to face with the young Patrick.

At the memory of that encounter his pulse began to beat a little faster and he looked more closely at some of the other passengers on the bus. Other faces began to bring, not only other memories, but also the realisation that every passenger on the bus was a Catholic. And the disquiet within him grew even stronger.

A sound? A movement? Or maybe his sixth sense, honed to perfection by training and constant duty? Whatever it was, something made him cease his study of the bus and look away to his left. At first he could see nothing out of the ordinary but still he searched, then he saw them. There must have been at least twelve of them walking up the path leading from the park gates to where he was standing. As they came, he studied them intently, trying to identify them. It wasn't hard for as they came closer he began to recognise face after face. This time they were lads he saw nearly every day of the week for they all came from his estate which lay alongside the Barracks.

And that estate was staunchly Protestant.

He watched them as they steadfastly marched to within twenty yards of where he stood. There they stopped in a tight knit group, looking from him to the mini bus and back again. Now, as he stood there watching them, he realised things were not going as he expected; the last thing he wanted was to be involved in a confrontation between two warring groups. The earlier feelings of disquiet were now steadily growing into the early stages of panic and the wish to be anywhere else but in the park, was growing stronger by the minute. However, he made no effort to move away and the thought of running never even entered his head.

It wasn't bravado that held him rooted to the spot, or even a sense of duty, but something far deeper that even he himself could not explain. What he did know was that every member of the group knew exactly what and who he was. There was no hiding it for his uniform was there for all to see.

Just as suddenly as they had stopped, so the lads started to move forwards again. Soon they were no more than ten yards away from where the young soldier stood. here they paused, and then without any sound whatsoever, began to spread out into what appeared to be a pre-determined formation. The young Soldier watched them, almost as though mesmerized, and although seemingly calm, he could feel the blood rushing through his veins as his heart beat furiously.

A loud bang away to his left shattered the afternoon air and as the young soldier spun in its direction, he instinctively dropped into a crouching position. It had been the slamming of the bus's door which had caused the noise and he now saw that the Catholic lads had now de-bused and were standing in a tight group. Slowly he forced his body and mind to relax but as he did so they also started to spread out and walk towards him.

Soon he was completely surrounded by the two groups and the young soldier looked around as though trying to implant the picture of every face deep into his memory. They in turn just stood there, watching and waiting in a strange foreboding silence.

The young soldier took one final look around, but apart from himself and the two groups of youths, the park was totally deserted. Even so, he knew the time had come and the next move was his, all the training and knowledge acquired during the recent course was about to be put to the ultimate test.

It was almost with desperation that he raised his right hand and stared at the whistle he was holding, then, placing it to his lips, he blew hard. The result was almost instantaneous and as the two groups burst into action, a violent rush of adrenalin flooded into his bloodstream and heightened his senses to a pitch he had never experienced before.

His first ever match as a newly qualified referee was on and his spirit was raised with the excitement of it all.

The Warriors Return

by

Roger Smith

It was a long day's walking, and the sun burned. Bandren shifted the large sword slung over his shoulder to an easier position. He called the sword Soul-Searcher. It had tasted many souls recently.

The mercenary glanced around at his companions. Warriors all of them. Many bore rags tied proudly to wounds. Some carried the belongings of those who could not return. Bandren was a tall, dark haired man, with a full set of whiskers. Most of the other warriors had similar features, like they were all variations from the same mould. They could not afford full suits of armour, most of the men wore pieces scavenged from the fallen of the wars they had fought in. They all dragged their feet wearily, yet there was the sense of a job well done. The company had done its job, and had done it well.

As they walked along the dusty track that crossed the Hanengrab hills the warriors started to pass a wineskin around. They each swallowed thirstily. When the container was empty it was thrown carelessly away. With mock seriousness they then chose another wineskin. After a few hours the fog of inebriation clouded their thoughts. Soon one of the men began to sing, then the others joined in, especially with the vulgar choruses. As they sang their spirits soared, and the oppression of death left them. They slept soundly that night, and the wine was more than a little responsible for that.

In the morning they drew lots as usual, to see who would prepare the breakfast. Bandren lost, amid the usual jeers and catcalls from the others. It was then the usual routine to care for the armour pieces, and weapons, as lovingly as any craftsman looks after his tools of trade.

The bacon was six days old, it was that long since they had stormed the gates of Penri Dortho, and earned the Kings bonus. Bandren ignored the green mould, and dropped the meat into the hot fat of the frying pan. The warriors wolfed the food down.

There was an eager feeling among the warriors that morning. Before nightfall they expected to be back in the wooded slopes of the valley they called home, Hanrebb Dalven. The youngest of the company, a beardless youth, was sent to fetch water for the rest. As he bent over by the stream, filling the pail he was pushed into the water. His spluttering indignation was met with resounding laughter. However the men then used the stream to wash themselves, many for the first time since they had left Hanrebb Dalven some six weeks ago. The bank was littered with various items of apparel, all of them dirty and smelly. When they finished washing they started on the last few hours of their journey home.

As they strolled along they started to brag to each other. Each man told of his bravery at the gates of Penri Dortho, and of the ferocious street fighting to hold the gate open for the King's men to storm the rebellious city.

Indeed the taking of the gates was a courageous action, the street fighting was an entirely different matter. Most of those slain by the attackers were unarmed women, children, and the aged. Yet these men would deny that to their grave.

They didn't stop for their midday meal, they were now eager to see their homes. Soon the dizzy heights of the crags guarding the entrance to their valley came into sight. They could hear the horns placed on those eyries blare. Normally they would call to warn of the approach of strangers. This time there was a welcome note. Within minutes a stream of women and children swept towards the returning heroes. Cries of welcome intermingled with grief-stricken wailing as the two groups met.

For the first time in six weeks Bandren smiled joyously. he knelt arms outstretched, as his children ran to him. As he told the children of the places he had seen his wife compared his booty with the other wives.

History is Junk

by

Peter King

A huddle of history society members stared into a pool which had nearly sub-
merged the blackened stumps of ancient wood.

'You are looking at the remains of a fortified bronze age boundary fence,'
said the plump, woolly-bearded guide in a woolly jumper that had seen better
days.

'That's not what you said last year,' said the club secretary with a furrowed
brow and goatee beard. 'Last year you said it was a long house - and whenever
you found something you could not understand you tried to pretend that the site
was religious.

'I suppose next year you will decide it is the foundations of a complicated
Spaghetti Junction that fed horse-drawn traffic on to a suspension bridge that
stretched across the North Sea.'

The guide gazed down at his reflection in the murky waters beneath and reflected on his archaeological tour of duty in this bleak corner of the Fens. He
thought of the line of trees that marked the original coastline and the surrounding settlements that had been islands in the area's watery past.

He thought about how the theories concerning the site had changed as regularly as clockwork - and he looked at his watch and remembered that the next
party, the school group from Winterbech, would be arriving soon.

Winterbech, like the site being excavated at Bunting Fen, had at one time
been a coastal settlement, but as the Wash silted up it had moved inland. The
boys knew it was not a long journey they were making that morning, but as
they clambered with their clipboards on to the Pigg's Luxury Tours bus they
cast their minds back to some of their previous 'luxury' excursions.

They remembered one return journey where the speedometer needle had
never risen above 20 miles an hour and they remembered the fateful day when
the vehicle had encountered a hill.

To reach the site the coach had to leave the road and turn down a long, winding track - and it was just as the vehicle was starting to negotiate this that one
of the wheels nestled into a pot-hole and the engine, as if in sympathy, ex-
pired.

The teachers conferred and decided it would take too long to walk the rest of the way. They told the boys to stretch their legs for ten minutes while the fault was being repaired.

'The children are late,' thought the guide as he glanced at his watch once again. 'If I don't see them soon I'll have to ring the school.'

But the only phone was in the visitors' centre, on the far side of the site. That could wait for the time being, he thought.

'You have ten minutes only!' called the teacher in charge. 'Be back in your seat by 10.30.'

The boys clambered down the steps and jumped on to the dusty track. Stops were usually all right - especially if you could buy some vinegar-soaked chips - but there was not much they could do here. They listened to their Walkmans, ate sweets and told jokes, but really they were bored.

By 10.30 all but three of the children were back in their seats. The missing boys had walked further from the coach than the rest - and just out of sight of the others they had discovered a scrapyard. For once the Alsatians that patrolled it were silent and the gate had been left ajar.

When the three red-faced boys came running back to the coach five minutes late, they were reprimanded, but the bulges in their pockets went unremarked.

Everyone was back on board, but the engine would not respond. The driver tinkered with this and fiddled with that. The boys' sweets were finished and the minutes were ticking by.

'If they turn up, what theory shall I tell them today?' wondered the guide. 'I'll have to go and make that call.'

The windows steamed up and the teachers consulted. 'There isn't enough time left. We've got to be back by lunch.'

Then the driver chipped in: 'I need the 12 biggest boys you've got. It'll go with a push.'

With a heave the boys lurched the coach forwards and the engine spluttered back into life.

'Home, m'lady?' laughed the boys in their best Thunderbirds accents. And that is exactly where they went.

The boys' headmaster, a historian, was patrolling the grounds when he bumped into a group of three who had just returned from the trip. He did not notice the extra weight concealed beneath their blazers.

'Are you any the wiser for the outing or are you just as muddled as ever?' he asked.

'Just as muddled,' they all agreed.

'I sympathise,' said the headmaster. 'They keep changing their theories all the time. No wonder they say history is bunk.'

As the boys nodded, a car badge from a bulging pocket tinkled to the ground. The boy reddened, stooped casually for his trophy and quickly vanished.

'History is junk,' he thought quietly to himself.

The headmaster looked puzzled, but there was no time to ponder. His telephone was ringing. The riddle would have to wait.

Gazelle

by

J H Clarke

Today is a horrible day, and I am feeling all sixty one of my forty nine years. Two of my trainees haven't turned up for work, one of the others has a bad attack of hay fever and the remaining two have been bad tempered and quarrelsome since we started work. The van had to be towed before it would condescend to start, and is still running roughly; probably it will fail completely before we reach the depot.

Pedestrian crossing ahead! The two vehicles in front of me ignore the lady waiting to cross, and I am briefly tempted to follow their bad example. I stop.

She is tall, with long black hair; dressed in white shorts and a flowered blouse. Long slender legs and large dark eyes make such an impression that I am instantly thrown back in memory twelve years to a blistering day in an Arabian desert, when as though by magic a beautiful little gazelle doe appeared out of the mirage and stopped just a few yards away, watching me with great lustrous eyes, uncertain and poised for flight with one forefoot raised. Now, as then, I wait.

The lady also hesitates, takes one step, then looks at me with a question in those dark eyes. I check the road in both directions, no moving traffic from either way; I smile, nod my head and wave a hand to indicate that she may cross in safety; she passes confidently in front of me, and I am given a lovely smile before she is lost to sight in the crowd of shoppers across the street.

Briefly, I see again my little gazelle walking gracefully away, trusting me to do her no harm, and in a few seconds she has again become a part of the mirage which starts only twenty five yards away. The memory fades, it is time to move on.

Today is a beautiful day, and I am feeling all twenty one of my forty nine years.

2066 and all That

by

Irene Wilkins

Nicholas stepped out from his Family Unit in the tall tower block onto the Monorail, which stopped at every block. He inserted the card which gave his place of work and sat down. Several other people from his block got on also, but as other rails and carriages joined theirs or sections of theirs peeled off, these people were carried away to other parts of the city. It was summer and the upper part of the carriages rolled back.

There was a certain point every day where his rail came near, but didn't join another rail. It was here lately that he had seen the girl. She wore, of course, the identical blue boiler suit that he did with a number on the breast pocket, but the contrast of her curly chestnut hair and white skin with her large dark eyes was quite beautiful.

He longed to meet her and wondered if and when she went to the Leisure Parks. One went down by lift to ground level to get on the rails, or moving pavements, which led to the Leisure Parks, Walkways and Shopping Precincts. One day when he saw her rail approaching he called out ... 'Do you ever go to the Leisure Parks ...?' - but they were carried away from each other before he could hear if she answered.

An elderly man said sourly, 'No shouting is allowed on the commuter rails.' Nicholas noticed he had a low number on his pocket and so judged him to be over sixty. The young people had longer, higher numbers. His own grand-father who lived in the Family Unit with them, had a very low number, and was due to be Phased Out soon. Some of the old people still spoke of death or dying as if it was a natural thing. They remembered life before the New Order.

Next day as the rail carrying the girl came towards the young man, she called 'Park 5, Day 6.' Day 6 was what used to be called Saturday and was a leisure day.

When Day 6 came Nicholas went down to the ground and onto the rail for Park 5. He arrived at the park gates and hurried in, looking eagerly about him for the girl, After about half an hour she arrived.

'I'm Saskia,' she said smiling.

'I'm Nicholas,' he answered, and she was even more beautiful now he saw her close to. Her dark eyes were the colour of the stones called sapphires, which some of the old people still had in rings.

All day they wandered in the park, sat on the grass and ate the food they had brought. It only occupied a tiny packet, but when soaked in water from the drinking fountain, swelled up to appear like meat and vegetables ... substances no longer in existence.

'I have a Fitness for Matching Ticket,' he said tenderly. 'I'm twenty-five.'

'I too have a ticket. I'm twenty-four. I had four applications and refused them all. The man at the Ministry said I must not refuse again. I must be matched before I'm twenty-five.' her lip trembled. She'd been in trouble for being difficult. If she refused again her permit would be stamped 'Single. For work only.' and she would become a second class citizen.

'May I apply?' said the young man eagerly.

'Yes.' she said shyly. 'I would accept this time.'

'I'll go tomorrow to the Ministry to apply for you. As they want to get you matched there should be no difficulty.' They kissed quickly and guiltily. Kissing was illegal in public, but they left the park hand in hand.

Two days later as he saw her rail approaching he called joyfully,

'I've got my application.'

'I accept it,' she called back.

'All this shouting,' grumbled the man with the low number on his pocket.

'I don't know what the young are coming to. Time those two were matched, then we might have a bit of peace.' He remembered when people had had cars.

Nicholas, his application granted and in his pocket, stamped for the permitted two children, and now accepted by Saskia, felt there was no word to express the warm glow which suffused his being. The old people called it happiness.

Untitled

by

Barnie Ledger

All the scientists, politicians and major businessmen were gathered in the great hall in Brussels. Dignitaries from the Far east, Asia, the Arab countries and Israel were sat in tiered seats stretching into the vastness of the great hall. Lights hung like the blaze of a thousand suns, pouring brilliance on to the fifty metre wide stage.

Calvert, waiting in a patch of shadow at one end of the vast auditorium, watched the array of dials in front of him as the huge generators two miles away, steadily built up the voltages necessary.

As he half listened to the Director giving his opening speech, he thought back over the last three years. The hundreds of Scientists, technicians and electronics engineers who had worked so hard to complete the project in time for the political integration of the United States of Europe. So this was it, after the Common Market, food mountains and the like.

It was the start of a new era, he mused, and lit a cigarette as the director droned on. The United States of Europe. No more wars. No more famine, crime cut down to almost zero. Freedom for everyone, with no national borders, no need for passports and only one kind of personal identification.

Calvert looked at his hand but the number was quite invisible. They've really cracked it this time, he thought. A number, electronically printed and instantly available wherever you go. No need to carry cash, cheque book or bank card. All the information was stored in the great central computer. Strangely, as Calvert looked at the huge one hundred metre cube, filled with the accumulated knowledge of a thousand years, a slight shiver of apprehension ran through him. He would be glad to get away when his shift had ended.

The Director had almost finished now and Calvert knew they would have to switch on very soon. The instruments were now showing the huge amounts of power which would be needed and he moved towards the small lever which would set the massive computer in operation for the first time.

Calvert acknowledged the Directors signal and pushed the lever over. The instruments in front of him showed the surge of power flowing to the Beast, as the technicians had named the computer. Indicator lights flashed on and except for a gentle humming and the occasional chatter of relays, there was total silence in the great hall.

The director motioned to the head of sciences, who had been chosen to ask the Beast the first question. He stepped forward, cleared his throat and spoke. 'Is there a God?'. The Vast audience leaned forward eagerly, relays chattered wildly as power surged through the circuits. The lighting in the auditorium dimmed, came up again and dimmed again. Calvert knew something was wrong and leaped forward to disconnect the power. Too late. He was thrown off his feet as a brilliant flash of lightening welded the contacts closed. Slightly dazed, he heard a thunder of sound echo round the auditorium.

Yes, now there is a God'.

Horoscopes

by

Joyce Lawrence

It was a bright, cold, November day as the group entered the chapel. A day to lift the spirits. This was a funeral, marking the passing of a man to whom death was a release both for himself and for the women who looked after him in his last years.

Hardly a happy event, but certainly not a doleful one except that it was significant of the end of all men. But Jack welcomed it as his loneliness and isolation increased with his lack of mobility and the decline in his mental capacity, that cruel cerebral process, slow enough for him to recognise what was happening while being powerless to stop it.

The daughters watched in silence as the coffin was borne, shoulder high and placed before the alter.

Noise poured from the walls as he shouted for his dinner, his shoes thudded on the floor, a pint mug of tea slapped the table, knife and fork rattled. Dad was home from work.

Mam rushed around seeing to his every need, no-one else counted as this supreme being was served. This was the man of the house in the 1930's. Lord of all he surveyed; wife, daughters, fire irons and kettle.

He was the sun to their moons, they paled when his dawn broke, silver grey to his blood-orange, delicate cascades to his Niagara. Such energy filled the house that there was room for nothing else.

But this vitality could easily turn from happiness to rage if something went wrong. To displease him was to suffer extraordinary consequences for very minor offences. Mam placed the pretty flowered china jug on the table. It stood on a small foot which had become chipped, but the jug was well loved so Mam would not throw it away. It was not well balanced and Jack caught it slightly lop-sided and milk splashed out.

The atmosphere changed, darkened. He picked up the jug and flung it out of the back door and down the garden, as he withdraw his arm the milk dripped all over Mam who was standing behind him.

Once temper was allowed scope there was no turning back, so next the table was overturned, then the shouting of abuse started.

'Stupid old goat, I've told you to throw that jug away. You knew it wasn't stable. Do as you're told in future...,' and on and on it would go.

The women clustered together in fear of the physical violence which sometimes followed these outbursts. He was like English weather, high summer and bleak winter succeeding one another with a rapidity that dizzied the senses.

And he was the boss, the one who wore the trousers. Joan the elder daughter was due to leave school at fourteen that July, and one of Dad's workmates asked if she would work for his wife doing housework. Joan was indignant.

'A skivvy, no thanks.'

That comment was enough.

'You think you're too good for that do you? Right, you start next week.'

And nothing would move him from that decision. The daughter had to be humiliated to prove who was the boss. She was willing to tackle any other kind of job but housework, and Mam was against it too, but the tyrant prevailed.

'I earn the money so I say what goes.'

Joan was stuck with that miserable job for four months, then, when she had learned her lesson, she was allowed to leave.

Pat passed the eleven plus, but Dad would not fill in the forms for her to enter the grammar school.

'They only teach them to look down on their parents in them schools.'

The immovable object.

A hard core of bitterness grew in the sisters.

They married and left home and had their own families and, seeing less of Dad, also saw less of the irascibility which had ruled their lives.

As life became smoother for Mam and Dad, money becoming more plentiful, then retirement, there were fewer storms and more periods of full sun. But the leopard doesn't change his spots. He can't.

At ten o' clock Jack was ready for bed and usually Ada was ready too, but tonight there is something interesting on the box.

'Come on then, I'm ready.'

'I want to see the end of this programme.'

'Oh, come on.'

'I'm watching this.'

Jack unplugged the television and, with his pen-knife, cut off the plug and took it upstairs to bed with him. Once a tyrant always a tyrant.

Yet he loved his wife, and even more surprising, she loved him, not his moods, but the faithful husband who had provided for her and the family through the good and bad times.

And so sixty years passed. Joan and Pat organised a party, presents galore, and this was a successful marriage for working-class people of that era.

The following month Ada died. Jack was alone. Now the daughters trotted to and fro cleaning, washing, cooking. That hard core of bitterness remained. They felt immensely resentful of this man who demanded allegiance from them in his old age yet had refused them training for a career.

As his physical decline set in he became a gentler human being, though that centre of strong character with immovable convictions remained constant. he was still awkward and obstructive at times refusing any help other than that of his daughters, making life difficult for them, but remaining true to his own ideas formed long ago when life was harsher, and there were still flashes of the man who was interested in everything, charmed by life's patterns and struggling to affect fate however fleetingly, to make his mark, to matter in this world.

He had fought unemployment, industrial accidents, and any other of life's vagaries, as hard and as steadfastly as he could. He had been true to his beliefs. At the end, those last weeks when life drained from him, he attained that awful dignity of the nearness of death showing those qualities of courage and constancy that were his characteristics.

The daughters wondered what motivated this man, what forces acting on his personality caused him to do some of the apparently unreasonable things he did.

The ham and tongue tea was in full swing and the mulling over Jack's beginnings started.

His mother died in childbirth when he was eighteen months old, his father died of no-one remembered what when Jack was three.

The youngest of six, Jack had a rough upbringing as older brothers took their share, and more, of whatever was available, usually very little.

No-one was there to ensure Jack went to school every day, so he didn't. He fought for anything he wanted and fought against anything he didn't want - to do, to have - against assumptions. Life was a battle and Jack's response to it was predictable. He was set in a mould by life's treatment of him. Anyone knowing his origins could tell his fortune - and Joan's and Pat's.

Sheena

by

Diane Davis

The damp fog closed around Sheena's shoulders like a shroud as she hurried through the grey streets to her basement flat at the end of the block. As she neared the corner memories of the recent week flitted through her mind,

'Damn him!' she couldn't help the words escaping through gritted teeth.

'Damn him to hell!' the venomous sound came louder than she realised and as she pushed her key into the lock a startled passer-by quickly crossed the road and disappeared into the enveloping fog.

Thankfully entering her cosy room and closing the door behind her she kicked off her shoes and pulled off her coat then reached for the light which threw a warm, comforting glow around the flatteringly arranged room. Putting on the kettle and preparing her meal took her mind off her problems for a short while, but they were soon back, clouding her head like the clammy mists outside in the busy streets.

Peter, the ever trusted Peter had been leading her a dance for the past three months, how could she not have known, but he was so clever at hiding the fact that he was married, and now, now. . . when she was expecting his child he'd shrunk away with a sickened look and shifted uneasily from one foot to another.

'I'm. . . I'm. . . sorry' he'd stammered and slunk out of her life leaving nothing but distaste for his actions.

Sheena slipped into the bathroom and ran herself a relaxing bath, her honey blonde, shoulder length hair gleaming in the steamy confines of the bathroom and her strong gaze looked back at her in the cracked mirror, blue eyes stared at a pretty mouth with the faint flicker of a smile.

'Come on girl, we'll see this through,' she said to herself and valiantly made an effort to smile again, but her strength gave and she sank into the bath with sobs racking her tired body.

Later Sheena slid into bed and hoped sleep would come quickly. Eventually she fell into a restless sleep and Sheena began to dream deeply. . . The red sports car sped round the country lanes and the scenery flashed by at an incredible rate. Peter glanced nervously across from the passenger seat,

'Sheena. . . please. . . just slow down,'

'Oh don't be so jittery, it's alright I know what I'm doing' Sheena smiled reassuringly. Suddenly without warning Sheena whipped the wheel through her hands and the car slew across the road. The last thing she remembered was the look of sheer terror on Peter's face as the car shot off the edge of the cliff and hung for a milli-second in mid-air before crashing mercilessly hundreds of feet below.

'Noooooo!' with a startled scream Sheena sat up, sweat pouring off her.

'God what a dream,' she muttered and slowly settled back into a light sleep.

As the alarm woke Sheena the next morning she felt much better as though a great weight had been lifted from her she hummed to herself while she prepared coffee, orange juice and toast. The radio announced the news and Sheena's humming stopped abruptly as she listened with rising terror to the newscasters voice,'

The well known Mr Peter Salt was killed last night in a mysterious accident, his red Porsche was discovered at the bottom of Syke's Quarry early this morning. Police are investigating. Sergeant Foster said this morning that they believe Mr Salt was not the driver of the vehicle and would be pleased if the driver would come forward as he or she may need urgent medical attention!?

Just a Song at Twilight

by

M E Lavin

For sheer nostalgia this takes some beating. Memories are precious and you can picture the dewy-eyed sentiment these words evoke. The dim, distant past is crowded with family and friends exuding warmth and comfort. The upsurge of emotion is strong and difficult to control. I swallow the lump in my throat and blink away tears. How well I remember that sweet haunting melody!

I'm old enough to recall the Penny Rush and silent films at the local cinema. 'Ben Hur', 'The Red Shadow' and Rudolph Valentino, to name but a few, I sampled at the Saturday matinee. As the youngest in our family I may have had free entry. According to Nellie the Lanc, streetwise and local know-all, you don't pay for babbies - as long as they don't cry. I was a regular, even when talkies came in and we all had to pay tuppence.

Edgar Kennedy, Fred Emney, Buster Keaton, The Three Stooges and Charlie Chase were all part of our weekly diet. Slapstick was tops except for Buck Jones and Tom Mix in mortar, who rated higher. Sometimes we were really in luck and had cowboy films with slapstick as well.

One in particular, I remember well. The comic, doomed to failure, had made up his mind to shoot the singer in the saloon. She was a large, ample bosomed lady with a forceful personality. Erect, statuesque and formidable she distainfully ignored all attempts at annihilation and in high, piercing treble murdered her sole refrain - 'Just a song at twilight.'

Our comic hero shot himself in the foot, the first time, because his gun stuck in the holster. The second attempt he slipped, missed the singer and hit the bottles. The first effort failed miserably and he got a slap in the kisser from the swing doors. How we roared, every time the singer hit the top note our comic appeared for a pot shot.

Culture was not high on our list but occasionally there would be a Sunday concert. Nellie the Lanc read the notice - it says there's a tenor, a baritone, a pianna and a soaperanna. Most of us had heard tenors and baritones because of dads singing in choirs. The pianna was OK but the soaperanna had us foxed - we didn't like to admit it!

'Ee that'll be good' somebody said. So we all went the following night.

Normally we never noticed the hardness of the benches at the front of the cinema. At concerts kids, on their own, were confined to the first six rows. We fidgeted through 'Glorious Devon', 'Danny Boy' and a lot of piano music then we froze. The air was tense and heavy with dramatic suspense.

On she came, like a ship in full sail gracious, aloof and splendidly arrayed, We held out breath as she gave a curt nod to the pianist. We weren't as sharp as Nellie but, by gor, we knew a soaperanna when we saw one - she's that one that gets shot. With closed eyes and hands clasped firmly over her ample chest she breathed out those sweet familiar words. . . 'Just a song at twilight.'

As the words floated towards us we couldn't believe our luck. At the crucial moment - the high note - 'though the heart be weary' - all hell broke loose. Whistles, bangs, war cries, shouts - a lynch mob would have seemed soft, by comparison.

I'll say one thing in her favour. . . soaperannas are tough! She stood her ground. Like the trooper she was, she finished her song though her panic - stricken, wide eyes would have graced Landseer's 'Stag at bay'. Frosty-faced she stood throughout the stupendous final applause. We clapped ourselves daft!

I'm sure to disgrace myself some other time - perhaps at a musical soirée, when the upsurge of emotion is strong and difficult to control. 'I'll swallow the lump in my throat. With mounting hysteria, blink back the tears and mentally adjust my hip holster, wait for the high note and fire!

Ah memory! That sweet, haunting melody has a very special charm for me.

121

Petals on the Wind

by

Yani Birt

'Is that clock right?' she asked of the little ornamental, brass barometer that always sat on the fireplace. She always asked that as she sat with her back to the clock that lived on the sideboard. Grandad must have really missed Grandma when she died. I missed him so much when he died and I still miss him today.

I didn't miss Grandma. You see I was two when she died, so I didn't really know her like I did Grandad; I was too young to have known. It was so different after we lost him though, it was so sudden. Five days he was ill, then he died. I didn't even have the chance to say goodbye but, I have all the happy memories of him and the stories he told me about Grandma, no one can take that away. When he died it was as though my life had been tipped upside down. I was very close to Grandad.

'Tipped upside down' is a very good way of putting things, I think, as most of Grandma's belongings were usually tipped upside down or out of place in one way or another, when she was alive. This I know because I've been told so many, many times all the most marvellous stories about her by those lucky enough to have loved her.

Grandma was Florence Eva Maud or 'Loll' as she was affectionately known, although no one knew why.

Very rounded, five foot nothing with cheery blue eyes and curly white hair and gold rimmed spectacles, when she remembered to wear them, that is my very own treasured image of her.

'Look at her lovely, straight little legs,' she used to say about me as she held me with my straight, little legs hanging.

She hadn't got a lap hadn't Loll. She used to lodge me on her front with her folded arms about me, or so I've been told. Not that I remember being only six months old at the time.

Loll was a muddler, that I feel is the best way to describe her; for Loll everything had it's place in life and that was usually out of place.

The tall kitchen dresser, that should have housed the tea-service that Grandad won in a raffle at The Jockey Pub was empty expect for several boxes of tea. The crockery, with its vegetable pattern of carrots, peas in the pod, and tomatoes around the rim, was instead scattered about the kitchen. On tables and benches and in the narrow cream wall cupboard with red sliding doors and white handles that always hung on the left hand side of the wall, by the window over the sink.

That cupboard seemed so large and high when I was small, but as I grew in those years after Loll, it gradually shrunk, as I suppose did Grandad.

Grandad was without Loll for nineteen years in the house with the cupboard. A big, old house at the end of a long narrow path flanked by thick welcoming hedges. That was his home, and its surrounding gardens and orchards magic kingdoms for me.

My favourite, 'bestest' place of all when I was a child was underneath the huge, spreading walnut tree. As many children do, I loved to swing and the rusty, knotted chain that hung down between the gnarled branches of my sheltering haven was the best swing ever, in the best place that a swing could ever be in.

That place was my very own sanctuary, where I went to solve my problems; problems that all children sometimes get.

The garden at Sladefield, which was the houses name, was the prettiest, most exciting paradise a child could wish for and I remember Grandad telling me how Loll knew every flower in it by name.

She had a passion for all kinds of plants and once she even bought a tree home on the bus after one of her many shopping trips.

Shopping was one of Lolls favourite pastimes, and many times she went on daytrips out by bus. She would go anywhere and everywhere if it was to shop, either on her own or with friends.

One particular friend of Lolls was Cousin Annie Harlow. Each week they would set off together on yet another promising shopping destination and each week Loll vowed never to go with Cousin Annie again.

The reason being, Loll always ended up paying for their cup of tea and slice of cake as Cousin Annie never had any loose change, or so she said.

Very partial to a cup of tea was Loll. She would never waste any that was left in the teapot, finishing the last drop herself if no one else wanted it. She was so fond of tea that she insisted anyone she was out with at the time accompanied her to the nearest tea shop for elevenses, twelveses or oneses. In fact any time was a good time for a cup of tea; as far as Loll was concerned a cup of tea works wonders.

Apart from tea Grandma always bought things she didn't really need. At flea markets, fairs and jumble sales she bought bits and bobs, bits and pieces and more bits.

Hats for all occasions that were never worn. Perfume in bottles and sprays. Pieces of pretty fabric to cover the comfy chair that was never mended. Buttons in tins, jewellery in boxes. Ornaments to pack away in cupboards, souvenirs for family and friends.

Embroidery silks and threads in rainbow colours for the never completed table mats and chair backs. Balls of wool to never complete the unfinished jumper, its needles still attached and wound with unravelled strands of yarn and a painting by numbers to lie in its box uncompleted. Loll never finished anything she started. Once when she decorated she painted neatly around the radiogram and sideboard, she didn't move them. Her favourite saying was, 'I'll do it another day'. She never did.

She didn't even finish her sentences and while deep in conversation she wandered from one subject to another without a pause.

Going 'all 'round Wills Mothers' as is the saying of old. Now, please don't think that Loll was mad. She wasn't. She was just forgetful and disorganised.

I remember being told of the day she went shopping without her coat and after finding she was a bit chilly, she bought one; she never wore it again after that, but it added to the pile in the spare room. If it rained she bought an umbrella, if the sun shone she bought a sunhat, if it snowed she bought boots. I could never understand why she didn't take them with her in the first place.

Perhaps she forgot.

She bought the things she admired that took her fancy. She bought handbags that never matched anything and then used them for storing her pennies and ha'pennies in.

'They're too heavy to carry, those coins are', she used to grumble, and so they were hidden away in handbags, under half knitted blankets on half mended chairs, in the green front room with the piano to be found years later by me.

I've still got those coins today, hidden away in a dusty old handbag, under a half knitted blanket on the chair in my green room; such a strange coincidence that history repeats itself.

Grandad and Loll had a big, fat, faithful black labrador, whose name was Judy and who was a pedigree. She was fat because she used to help herself to the dog biscuits that were kept in a brown paper bag, on the stone floor, behind the door in the pantry.

When Loll swept the floor in the kitchen with the blue handled brush, she sometimes gave Judy a quick sweep at the same time. When Loll washed the floor in the kitchen with the greying floor cloth, she also sometimes gave Judy a quick wash.

Judy loved the garden at Sladefield, like we all loved it, and she lived very happily until she was fourteen.

Years later I too have a big, black labrador, but although he isn't a pedigree he is still loved.

In time I expect he too will be just one of my treasured memories as are Loll, Grandad and Sladefield.

Although our lives are constantly changing, our memories only get better as we remember the good parts, 'The Good Old Days', and try to forget the bad ones.

Our lives are like roses, beginning life as a bud, opening gently to bloom the best we can; then in the later stages of life, as strength begins to fade the rose begins to fall and its petals carried on the wind.

The memories of all the beautiful roses stay with us until the end, and so my Grandparents live on as roses not just as 'Petals on the Wind'.

Take These Chains

by

Roma O'Neil

Justin breathed in the crisp cold air. It left a vapour trail in front of him as he exhaled. The sky was clear and the rising sun was making a feeble attempt to warm the countryside.

Looking around him, Justin could see the other competitors preparing for the race. The top of the mountain was strewn with gaily coloured people, each busily getting everything in order for the 'big event'. Fathers, trainers, officials. each with a job to do. Nerves were beginning to get the better of him. With no one to offer friendly encouraging words the time was passing too slowly.

'How long before the first competitor?' Justin thought. He looked at his watch. Ten minutes. He jumped up and down, ran on the spot vigourously. 'Warm those muscles up!' The last thing Justin needed was a pulled or torn muscle. Not now. Not today. It had taken a long while to get to this point in his life. He had scrimped and saved for two years so he could spend a winter on the American Ski Circuit; so he could race and maybe make enough money to do it again next year.

Skiing had always been in his blood. When he was younger he had shown great promise in Junior European races. But just when things looked good, tragedy had struck. The vehicle had skidded on ice and gone out of control. Justin received serious leg injuries, but worse than that, his beloved father had been killed. His Mother had been a tower of strength, but with the death of his Father Justin felt that all stability in his life had gone. His best friend was no longer there for him.

Months in hospital did not help the long-term depression that set in. 'Would he be able to ski again?' 'Very doubtful,' came the medical experts replies. The weeks came and went and progress was slow. The weeks turned into months and the months to a year. He worked hard in the gym and against all the odds was given the 'all clear' to start skiing again.

And here he was. His first race about to start. His loving Mother was at the finish area. He knew she would be nervous - Probably more so than him - if that was possible!

'Number 35,' a voice bellowed out. 'Oh God, that's me,' he thought. He took his place behind racer number 34, who was in the gate. No time to be afraid now. This was it. He was in the gate. Three, two, one. . . Go!

He pushed out for all he was worth. Through the red and now the blue. The gates were coming up so fast. He was vaguely aware of cheering and cow bells in the distance. 'Aaaagh! He had nearly fallen on an icy section but it was Ok now. He felt good, his confidence growing. Just a few more gates. . . Yes! he had done it. Not the best time of the day, but a personal triumph. 'For you Dad, I did it for you.' He felt the warmth of his tears in his eyes.

'Justin, Justin,' said the gentle voice. 'Wake up now. Time for your injections. Come on now.' The Nurse lifted the book from the chest of the crushed and broken body before her. She mused at the title 'Astral Travel for Beginners'.

'Do you really believe in all that stuff Justin?' she asked.

'What do you think?' he replied.

Charles - English Gentleman

by

Sujen Ray

Charlie stood, posing in front of the mirror, a self satisfied grin on his face. Not bad for a man in his early forties he thought! Such was his conceit that he had convinced himself of this. The reality was he would reach his half century in just a few weeks. His grin widened as he remembered the remarks made by his colleague about his thickening waist and thighs. He had suggested that he join the 'Keep Fit Club' with him. Charlie grinned again, the man hadn't an inkling that the excess fat was his extremely well made money belt nestling round his lower regions. He caressed his hips and trembled with ecstasy, he had schemed and cheated for money for as long as he could remember. It gave him the biggest buzz he could ever have, far more exciting than any woman.

He checked his watch as he slipped into his jacket. Leanne would soon be arriving at their new luxury home. He had driven her to the airport earlier in the day, she would be there ready to welcome his arrival tomorrow with Jock and their belongings. He sighed a little sadly, after today his devious methods of obtaining money would belong in the past. He squared his shoulders and almost saluted, from tomorrow he would be known as 'Charles, English gentleman' respected and admired by the local residents. His enemies would never find him, those that had enquired his destination had been given a fictitious address in the South of France. He would, in fact be living in a select area of Portugal.

He checked the security system, satisfied all was in order he locked the outer door and left for his last evening at the 'Crown' with his so called friends. He knew he hadn't any 'real' friends, only acquaintances. His dubious business methods excluded friendships. He was still puzzled by their desire to give him a good send off, fools that they were. Had they forgotten how he had cheated most of them over the years. His craving for money had been satisfied through them. Perhaps they were celebrating his departure knowing he would not cheat them any more!

He patted his hips as he walked into the bar of the 'Crown', the feel of money always boosted his confidence. A group of men stood at the bar waiting for him. He greeted them saying, 'Hi lads, what are you having. The drinks are on me tonight.' He joined them.

Bill spoke cheerfully but forcefully, 'Oh no Charlie, tonight is on us and all the people you have known over the years. We wouldn't like you to leave the country without a 'good send off'. Who knows when we will all meet again?'

Charlie glowed with satisfaction, his money could stay in his wallet.

'As you like then lads, I musn't be too late though. Jock and his removal lorry will be at the house at an unearthly hour in the morning. I can't afford to miss the ferry, the move is costing me far too much as it is.' He felt miserable when he thought of the huge fee Jock demanded for transporting his possessions and the half payment, in cash, that he had demanded when the agreement had been made.

The friends grinned at each other.

'Cheer up Charlie,' they chorused, 'We'll make sure you are home at a reasonable hour.'

Bill called the Landlord giving him a discreet wink as he said, 'Drinks as ordered please Tom. Nothing alcoholic for Charlie though. He has a long journey tomorrow and must keep a clear head. We don't want him nicked for 'Drink Driving' before leaving the country!'

The drinks flowed as the Bar became more and more crowded. Business associates and people he had become acquainted with over the years wished him well in his new life. He was puzzled. Why were they behaving so generously? Had they forgotten the harm he had done most of them over the years? He watched them through bleary eyes. They seemed to be waiting. Waiting for what? He felt an ominous foreboding steal over him. Seconds later he slumped forward on to the bar. Out for the count!

The watching crowd breathed a sigh of relief. The joint plan of action had worked beautifully.

Bill called, 'Right lads, we all know what we have to do now.' He pointed to a group of people in the corner. 'Have you got your lorries in position in the orchard at the back of his yard?'

They nodded agreement.

'Right then, wait until you see Fred and me go through the side door with Charlie then follow us in. Move quickly and quietly and load everything. Leave nothing portable behind. We will meet later on, as planned.'

The crowd slipped away, each had their allocated tasks to perform.

Bill and Fred drew up at the door of Charlie's house. They took him upstairs and dropped him on the bed. Stripping off his clothes they found the money belt, filled to overflowing. They grinned delightedly at each other, an added bonus, there appeared to be thousands of pounds inside. They rifled through his pockets and found more money which they pushed into the belt. At last they were satisfied; with a final check on Charlie they left the room, disconnecting the telephone as they did so.

Charlie found himself on a long, long ladder, seemingly stretching to eternity. Terrified, he wondered what was happening, was he in a dreadful nightmare, or was it for real? He didn't know. There was no alternative though, he had to keep moving upwards, for as he climbed the rung beneath him disappeared. He looked up and saw a gleaming white door enhanced by a golden light. He breathed a sigh of relief. Life at last! The door opened, a tall gentleman clad in a long white robe with flowing hair and a long white beard stood before him.

He spoke in a gentle voice. 'Hello Charlie, what are you doing here? You can't come in, you belong below.'

Charlie stuttered: 'Wh, wh, what do you mean. I can't come in. Why not? And where am I?'

The gentleman spoke again. 'Don't you know where you are Charlie, or who I am?'

Charlie shook his head miserably. 'No, but please let me in. I feel so weak and ill.'

A crowd of people appeared as if from nowhere, eyes fixed sternly on him, their faces passive.

The white robed gentleman spoke. 'You are at the gates of heaven Charlie. I am St Peter and these men are your jury. They have just voted unanimously that you must not be allowed in. You caused them and theirs so much unhappiness on earth, they cannot allow the same to happen here!'

As the meaning of his words filtered into Charlie's brain he heard the crackling flames beneath him and smelled the sulphur fumes.

'Please, oh please let me in,' he begged. 'I am absolutely terrified, I'll be a reformed character from now on. I promise.' He glanced along the line of men and shook with fear knowing he was doomed before St Peter confirmed it.

'Sorry Charlie. It's not my decision,' and he closed the door.

The top rungs of the ladder disappeared. All that was left was a long line of rungs leading downwards. He felt the heat of the flames on his feet and heard the hideous laughter beneath him. What could he do?

Jock, with his mate drew into the yard of Charlie's house at six o'clock exactly with his huge container lorry. He jumped down from the cab and walked swiftly to the door. Strange, it stood open. He walked in peering through the open doors, every room was empty. Seething with anger he ran up the stairs and saw Charlie through the open bedroom door, lying on the bed. He gripped him by the shoulder and shook him like a rat.

'So you welshed on the deal again did you? My word you'll wish you hadn't by the time I have finished with you.'

Charlie came briefly out of his nightmare and whimpered: 'What are you talking about Jock. Everything is packed ready for loading. I supervised it all myself.'

Jock shook him furiously then threw him back on the bed.

'You haven't heard the last of this Charlie. I have your new address don't forget. There are many that would be glad to have it.' He slammed the door and ran down the stairs, smashing the bannister as he went.

Once more Charlie was back in his nightmare. The sulphur fumes made him gasp for breath. His foot slipped on the ladder, the hideous laughter rose up in a great crescendo of sound to meet him and deafened him as he fell backwards into the raging inferno below.

Charlie never did live the life of an 'English Gentleman'. The fear in his nightmare became the reality from which he could not escape!

The Bottle Hunters!

by

Roger A Metcalf

The Reverend John Tuddenham stepped out of his beloved church and made his way along the tarmac path to the vicarage.

Winter was coming and the nights were drawing in. Even though it was early in the evening it was already getting quite dark.

He unlocked the front door of the vicarage and hung his coat in the hallway. Walking into his study, he poured himself a small sherry from the sideboard and sat in an old worn leather armchair near the window. He sighed. This was how he liked to finish his workday. To ponder over church business. To all intents and purposes the archetypal village vicar. With one exception!

The bell rang. He put down his sherry and eagerly went along the hallway to the front door. He opened it and there stood two rather scruffy looking characters with grinning faces. Mick and Paula. They all ambled along into the study and made themselves comfortable.

Mick and Paula made rather an odd looking couple, sat in the old vicarage. Their appearance was more suited to the sixties than the nineties. Long untidy hair, under woolly hats. Multicoloured tops and flared trousers. They had made no concessions to current fashions at all! All this made such a contrast to the Reverend Tuddenham, not yet changed out of his cassock and surplice.

Mrs Clarke, who'd seen them arrive at the vicarage from her house across the road, remarked to her husband how she couldn't see what their dear vicar saw in them.

The Reverend Tuddenham could have told her straightaway. They were fanatical bottle collectors, as he was!

Now if you don't understand bottle collectors, please let me explain. As a rich art collector craves for masterpieces on his wall. Or a philatelist dreams of those elusive stamp rarities. A bottle collector asks for nothing more than to have his house full of ancient bottles, of every shape and colour. It becomes an all consuming passion.

The small group in the vicarage, sat and smiled cheerfully at one another.

'And tell me Mick, how has your research gone?' asked the Reverend.

'Aha! That'd be telling,' said Mick, winking at his wife Paula.

'Now don't tease,' said John, laughing.

'Well, as I said last week, I've been sorting out the position of an old dump I heard about. And all I can say John is you'd better hurry and get changed, or we're going without you!'

'You mean you've found it?' gasped the vicar.

'Yep,' said Mick, chuckling.

John jumped out of his chair and made for the staircase. 'I'll be with you in five minutes,' he shouted happily.

In no time at all they were on their way, in the vicars old Ford Cortina. The boot loaded up with spades and torches etc. They passed through a couple of villages, then pulled off the main road into a small wood.

'Here we are,' said Mick. 'I hope you're fit John, it hasn't been touched yet.'

They walked along by torchlight, until Mick stuck his spade theatrically into the earth.

'This is the spot, let's get stuck in,' he said gleefully.

They started first by clearing various bits of rubbish away, then the dig started in earnest. Secrecy was all important with a new dig, they worked by moonlight. Just a few feet down, they started finding broken glass and crocks. This indeed was a former rubbish dump.

Paula was the first one to strike lucky. She held an early Victorian lemonade bottle in the air triumphantly. This encouraged frenzied digging by the other two. And very shortly John smiled as he spotted something glistening. He picked up a glass object and began to clean it up. As he did so, it became clear it was no ordinary bottle. It was made of red glass and in the unmistakable shape of the Devil! He hastily put it into his bag and continued digging.

Three hours later, after carefully camouflaging the site from other bottle hunters, they prepared to go home. Mick and Paula were elated as they examined the mouth-watering finds of the night. John joined in, but felt oddly uncomfortable when he handled the red figure again.

After dropping Mick and Paula off at their ramshackle cottage, John arrived home at the vicarage. He went into the study and placed the contents of his bag on the desk.

'Quite a good haul,' he thought. Especially a poison bottle he'd found just before they'd packed up for the night. But the centre piece was undoubtedly the devil figure in red glass. He picked it up to examine it. There was something in it he thought, some sort of liquid. He took the cork out to discover what it was. He put it to his nose.

'Ugh,' he lurched forward. The stench was vile. As he did so, a small drop of the loathsome liquid spilt on the carpet. He put the stopper back in and placed the figure on the mantelpiece. What on earth was in it he couldn't imagine. He felt sick and found he was trembling from head to toe. He turned the light off and went to bed. Sleep did not come easy that night!

Old Tom the vicar's gardener, was busy digging the border the next morning. He happened to glance at the study window. His mouth dropped open in awe at what he saw! There in the window stood a young woman. Naked as the day she was born. As old Tom watched, she stepped back and disappeared into the shadows. His old gnarled hand shaking, he lit his pipe and puffed at it.

'I didn't even know the vicar had a lady friend,' he said to himself. 'Wait 'till I see the lads in the pub tonight!' He chuckled and carried on digging.

That evening the vicar returned from church. He was about to unlock the front door, when his attention was attracted to his study window. A red light shone out into the blackness.

'Odd,' he thought. 'I'm sure I didn't leave the light on this morning. Anyway it's not that colour!'

He quickly unlocked the door and ran through the hall, fearing burglars. He opened the study door and rushed in. Nothing! Just darkness. He turned the light on and looked round the room. Everything seemed normal. Wait a minute! His eyes were attracted to the devil figure on the mantelpiece. It was different somehow. As he watched with mounting terror, he realised it was beginning to glow. Dull at first, then brighter and brighter. The room quickly filling up with an unnatural red light. And yes there was no doubt. The foul liquid inside was bubbling. The cork being slowly but surely forced from the bottle.

Bang! The study door had slammed loudly. He spun round to face it. The naked figure of a woman stood there. Black hair flowing over her shoulders. He gasped as he looked into her face. It was not the face of a woman, but the unmistakable face of Lucifer himself!

Suddenly laughter filled the room. He turned round. Figures stood all round the room. Some male, some female. All naked. All with that same face of evil itself. The laughter rose to a crescendo, until he thought his eardrums would burst. He clasped his hands to his ears. Then he knew. He knew he had uncov-

134

ered some kind of ancient evil and his very soul depended on returning it to the earth from whence it came.

He rushed to the mantelpiece and grabbed the foul bottle, then made for the door. The laughing had stopped and turned into angry screams.

As he ran to his car he didn't look round, but heard screams behind him. He jumped in and started the ignition. Tyres squealing, he accelerated out of the drive and down the road.

At last he reached the small wood. He turned off the engine and listened. Nothing.

He ran blindly towards the hidden dump. Branches and brambles scratching him as he went. He reached it and desperately looked for something to dig with. A spade caught the moonlight. Forgotten when they left the night before. He grabbed it and frantically started digging.

Now he could hear angry voices, getting louder as they approached. He buried the evil vessel in the earth and fell onto his knees exhausted. Lucifer's children surrounded him, linking hands chanting. . .

The next day a man walking his dog found the battered body. The Police Pathologist remarked he'd never seen anything like it in his whole career.

The bottle lay in the earth waiting to be released again. There was no hurry!

Morning Encounter

by

D L Hall

It was a cold dreary late January morning with the dawn still about three hours away and rain had been threatened. Constable David awoke with the alarm after a restless night, his mind going over the sad events of the previous evening. He looked at his wife who had obviously not slept at all and kissed her tenderly on the forehead.

'He will be fine love. He is in the best place to tackle that fever. Doctors can perform miracles these days and with the nurses to watch over him I am certain that he will be home in a few days time, bursting with energy being his mischievous little self again, you'll see.'

She nodded as the tears rolled down her cheeks. 'I am being silly, come on let's get you off to work, it will soon be 5.30 and you will be hurrying down to your beat all of a sweat and a lather.'

With these thoughts he arrived on his beat. He left his case with his sandwiches in the police box, folded his cape and threw it across his left shoulder and walked to his 'On Duty' point which today was a short distance from the police box. The good people of this Welsh coastal town had already begun going about their business. It was just 6.00 am.

His beat stretched around the side of a hill which sloped to the main thoroughfare and the river which ran along the valley floor to the sea. He again glanced at his watch and reasoned that he had plenty of time to visit the bonded warehouse at the top of the hill and return well before he made his scheduled telephone call to the Central Police Station.

As he climbed the hill between the narrow street of terraced houses to the warehouse his thoughts were of his small son whom he loved dearly, wondering what had caused the raging fever which necessitated the little boy's emergency admission to the hospital. The hospital doctor said that they were very lucky as they had just caught the lad in time. The statement gave him hope - emphasising the possibility of successful treatment, yet the boy was so very ill.

Having examined the fastenings of the bonded warehouse which were secure, he made his way down the hill taking a short cut through the cemetery. He had been standing on the pavement of the main road for about ten minutes watching the early morning traffic build up when a young man in his late teens, early twenties came running towards him gesticulating frantically. He grabbed Constable David's sleeve mumbling, 'The cemetery, the cemetery.' He kept tugging the sleeve and pointing up the hill towards the graveyard. Such was his state of agitation it was difficult for the officer to understand what else the young man was trying to say.

They broke into a run up the hill towards the graveyard and the gap in the dilapidated boundary wall from where the well worn track began. The path wended its way upward around the graves and gravestones to the top of the hill and its opposite boundary wall. Constable David felt there was something seriously wrong and that the answers lay with the young man and the graveyard.

On reaching the gap in the boundary wall the young man stopped and would go no further. He looked at Constable David and shook his head.

'What's the matter, what is up there?' Constable David enquired.

The young man leaned against the boundary wall with the constable's torchlight on his face. Obviously the man was very frightened indeed.

'Come on now lad. Try and tell me why you are so worried. Is there anyone in danger up there?'

The constable's voice seemed to have soothed his anxiety a little. He blurted out: 'My girl's up there.' His face was ashen as he pointed up into the graveyard.

Constable David held him firmly by the elbow and said: 'I am going up.' There was nothing further he could get from the young man and there was no one else in the vicinity.

As he stepped on to the well worn earthen path inside the cemetery wall and began his assent he felt a strange sense of foreboding. There was something sinister about the old graveyard which he had never experienced before anywhere. He was acutely aware of an overwhelming feeling of dread. The chill damp January morning air suddenly became colder as he climbed the path between the gravestones. The perspiration which had been brought about by the exertion had now stopped and as he ploughed on upwards the colder and clammier he became. His legs felt like lead.

He had climbed about two thirds of the way to the top when he saw a young woman sitting on the wet earth looking dazed. He shone his torch.

'Are you alright?' He asked.

Whereupon on recognising the uniform she literally jumped up from the ground and grabbed Constable David around the waist tightly. Gradually he re-

137

leased himself in order to walk around the graves to the lower boundary wall. The young woman, however, still clung to his arm with surprising strength belying her rather slight stature. Gently he led her down the path, it was not an easy task as she buried her face in the top of his sleeve. He kept talking to her, encouraging her at the same time, praying that she would not pass out.

On stepping through the gap in the boundary wall she looked up and on seeing the young man she ran towards him and slapped him hard across the face screaming: 'You yellow bastard.'

Constable David moved in between them and managed to reduce the girl's anger.

'What happened, what caused all this?'

She was now able to tolerate the young man's presence and between them disjointedly they recalled what had frightened them so much. She still clung tightly to Constable David's arm.

The couple had been courting, lived near each other at the top of the hill and worked together at a local factory just off the main road. They started work each morning at 7.00 am and called for each other to walk to work together. This morning they were a little late for work and the young man had suggested that they take a short cut through the graveyard. They had gone about a third of the way down when both of them suddenly saw to the right of the path between the graves a human head slowly turning from side to side against the background of a pale shimmering glow.

Constable David smiled grimly and knowingly and said: 'Ah that will be old Bob the gravedigger, I'll have to have a word with that old so and so. He is deaf and partially sighted but he knows what he's about.'

Constable David explained that in all probability old Bob had a funeral early that morning and as was his wont and custom, started digging the grave about 4.30 am, by candlelight if the weather permitted.

As they neared the grave old Bob must have heard them and stuck his head up above ground level holding the candle at shoulder height. Neither seeing nor hearing anything further he probably got on with the preparation of the grave. As he finished rationalising the occurrence they saw old Bob walk through the cemetery gates further down the road and disappear into a side street as if in confirmation.

The young woman ignored the young man and requested Constable David to escort her back to her home. She was still very shocked. He took her home avoiding the graveyard. Once indoors she let go of the constable's arm and called to her younger brother who was about to go to his newspaper round. She thanked Constable David for his trouble as he left the house.

On the way down the hill Constable David decided to take the short cut through the graveyard to see if he could see the spot the incident happened. By torchlight he searched the entire path on both sides but he could find no trace of earth being disturbed. This experience had shaken him more than he cared to admit now.

As he passed old Bob's home further down the hill he saw a neighbour of old Bob whom he knew, leaving his home to go to work.

'Good morning Islwyn.'

'Good morning Les.'

'Tell me Islwyn have you seen old Bob the gravedigger this morning?'

Islwyn did not answer immediately but looked at Constable David strangely for a few seconds and said quietly: 'Old Bob died about a month ago Les. Are you alright?'

'Yes, I'm ok.'

Islwyn locked his front door, nodded and walked along the terraced street. Constable David released his cape and put it around his shoulders drawing it close. He was chilled to the marrow despite the heavy winter uniform. He thought how best he could classify the occurrence as he walked to the police box where he saw the sergeant waiting. He decided that 'Domestic quarrel' was appropriate and that is what he would enter in his notebook. He looked to the heavens and said quietly to himself: 'Still up to your old tricks Bob.'

A few hours later he telephoned the hospital and he was told by the ward sister that the crisis was over. His beloved son was on the mend.

139

Who's Sorry Now

by

Julie Barham-Brown

The autumn sun gleamed through the grubby windows of the bedsit, illuminating the dust motes spiralling round as Katie searched in the wardrobe.

'Damn,' she muttered, grimly shaking out yet another garment. The old baggy jumper lay there, on the saggy sofa. No, thought Katie, not today.

It would go with the skirt, though. As well as anything ever did on her at least. No risk of stretching and ruining that, certainly. Everything, after all, was stretched. The skirt waistband tightened as she turned.

But look what happened when I wore you last. Five months ago. Spring and the promise of a new start. She had met Michael at an evening class. He was the tutor of the group, studying the English novel. With pale blue eyes and jet black hair, he read *Wuthering Heights* and *North and South* as lovingly as if he had written them himself. She began to look forward to those evenings and even more so to the drink in the college bar afterwards. Gradually the other students drifted off, leaving Katie to nervously move the spare beer mat between the empty glasses.

'Look,' said Michael, 'why don't I meet you here tomorrow night. We could have a drink and I'll explain that essay. OK?'

She shot him a disbelieving look from under her flop of fringe.

'Yes, I mean, OK, I mean, what time?'

'Well, my class finishes at nine, so I'll meet you here at half past. Bye.' He got up and walked out of the bar, confident and assured, leaving a scene of pure disbelief at the table behind him. She wasn't worried or concerned. Just totally panic-stricken.

She was there the following evening. In an outfit she had chosen, changed her mind, taken off and then put back on. The clock on the wall had stopped - or it seemed that it had. Eventually he arrived, late. They sat and talked, or rather he had, about the essay and then, everything.

They met again. On the third occasion he mentioned his wife.

'Wife? Oh, I didn't know you were married.' She managed to keep her voice level, despite the crashing sound in her ears.

'Yes,' he said casually, 'but she. . . '

'Doesn't understand you?' She winced. It was corny. Around her, people were smiling, emptying glasses, carrying on as normal. She couldn't believe that the world had stopped for just her.

'No,' he laughed, a touch self-consciously. He put his hand up to his hair, pushing it back.

'She doesn't understand good writing. She's keener on balance sheets. She's an accountant.'

'Oh,' she replied, hoping her voice didn't shake too much. It's difficult to keep your voice level when you are internally combusting.

'Look, um, could we go somewhere, well, more private?'

She couldn't really believe he had said that.

'Mm, if you like.' She grabbed her bag. She felt about sixteen. The juke box played 'No Regrets'.

That was four months ago. Four months of furtive meetings. Four months of disappointment when he hadn't arrived. Four months of. . . well, it didn't matter now. She told him on Friday. She felt dizzy and sick as she anxiously scanned the pub doorway. He arrived, late as usual.

'Michael,' she began. The baggy jumper, knitted by her mother, hung there, over her handbag. 'Michael, there's something you must know.'

'What is it Katie?' He replied, not really listening, excavating in his document case for her essay, a meandering tale of nineteenth century wronged women.

'Michael, I'm. . . going to have your baby.' She was proud of the way she had put it, loading some of the responsibility on him for once. His face went blank, even drained.

'Oh. Are you sure?' He muttered. 'Really sure? I mean, women can be mistaken you know.'

'Yes, they can. But ultrasound scans aren't usually.' She sat up straight. He looked crumpled and stained, she noticed.

'I thought you were, well, you know. . . ' He forced the words out through clenched teeth.

'Well, I wasn't. And you never bothered to ask.' She had bought herself a drink. She sat back against the wall. His eyes moved swiftly around the room.

'Well, what are you going to do?' There was desperation in his last word. He rattled the legs of his stool on the ground.

'I am going to have your baby on December 28th. What else did you have in mind?'

'But, I, well. Couldn't you have done something about it? I've got my wife to think of and my job. . . ' his voice trailed away.

She picked up her jumper. It felt warm and comforting against her as she gathered up her bag.

'What are you going to do, Katie?' He looked up, pleadingly.

She stood, lifted her full glass. Slowly, deliberately, she poured its contents over his head.

'That,' she said, 'is what I am going to do.' She turned smartly and walked out. The juke box played 'Who's sorry now' as she slammed the door behind her.

A Mother's Loss

by

Danielle Wrate

Earth sighed as she looked down at the world she had created. From a distance the world looked beautiful, it was a perfect sphere, like a marble suspended in the dark depths of the universe. The sight no longer enchanted her it only filled her with a regretful sorrow for she knew like so many of its inhabitants the Earth's superficial truth; the earth was far from beautiful.

Only her eyes showed that she was old, for since creating the Earth she had physically barely aged but the weight of her great responsibility had left her mentally worn out. She tried searching within herself to find ideas hoping for some inspiration that would guide her into saving her creation but she had been exhausted of all inspirations long ago and she found only hopeless anguish which forced her to use every ounce of strength to fight back the tears which she knew would have to come. She did not want to cry for crying was a weakness and to her it showed that she had failed, given up the fight and that truth she could not yet face.

As she watched the years pass on her world, Earth thought back to the beginning. She knew almost as soon as she had placed them on her untainted world that the first creatures she had chosen to be the dominant life form would not last. So while they proceeded to lead themselves to extinction, with a confidence born through naivety she worked on creating what she thought was the ultimate creature. They were the most complex being she had created simply because they had more than instinct, she had given then the power of thought and reflection so that one day she hoped they would become a reflection of herself, she realised now on reflection that this was perhaps her biggest mistake.

At first she had tried guiding them with her words speaking down from what they called the heavens, but after a short while they failed to take notice of her wisdom and after a brief period when she left them on their own she decided she would have to visit the world herself. Placing herself inside a virgin woman's womb so that they would know she was special from the start it was not long before she was able to act. Using powers they had not seen before she gained the attention she needed and told her followers parables containing the values which she herself had once been taught. Her time on Earth could not last

143

though and as she had feared people became scared of her power and her difference and through their ignorance killed the body she had inhabited. Her only option was to return once to let the people know she had not been beaten. Her stories had surprisingly lasted but they were not enough and she understood that what she had created could not be controlled by such simplicity in a complex unfamiliar world.

It was true, the earth was a stranger to her now she no longer understood it. She could not dispute that the people on her Earth had come a long way and at first she had been impressed by their advancement, she had for a short time been proud but as she observed she realised that they were taking her world and creating a new one. The miracles of life she had given them no longer were enough and they were proceeding to destroy them (in every sense) to give way to an artificial world they had created. They had lost touch with nature and they were destroying the natural balance of the world she had worked so hard to create. At one time she had thought things would improve when people of her world realised that they were killing the very things that gave them their life but she was wrong, they were too used to their way of life to make sacrifices for a world and future that seemed so far away. They had no idea what she had meant them to be, they did not seek to look inwards, they only looked outwards towards the things they could possess. Materialism was not something she had imagined they would have for she had given inside each person the very essence of life, she hadn't realised that many would never find this. Materialism had bred greed and greed had made the world unethical, corrupt and in some respects evil.

Of course not everything was bad, things were never black or white and that was the hardest thing. Despite everything there were still aspects of her world which she was unashamedly proud of and that made it so hard to let go and face the truth. She had many regrets, many questions which haunted her conscience. She would be a fool to think that the nature of man had changed, the signs had always been there but she was either too blind to see them or she had chosen to ignore them, she did not know which, most probably both. Maybe if she had realised earlier that this was to be the Earth's destiny she could have done something about it. Oh what was the point of maybes and if onlys. The Earth (which she had, now regretfully, named after herself in a time when the world was going to be perfect) was the only way it was, she could do many things but she could not reverse time. She had been too young and naive to create something so significant yet that kind of knowledge could only come from experience for it had seemed so simple. Maybe now if she started again

144

things would be different but she had neither the energy or spirit to do so. She lost so much of herself to the Earth she was not prepared to risk it again.

As she left the observation tower for the last time she again thought back to the beginning when she had flooded the world to rid it of all evil saving only those she thought the most virtuous of creatures to re-populate the Earth. She had given them a second chance then but now there would be no more. As the tears came she realised with a bitter relief that her last job had been saved. She would not have to flood the Earth or do anything likewise for she knew without the need of her mother's intuition that as the seconds ticked by for her and the years went by on Earth through one way or another the Earth would destroy itself.

The Habit

by

John Harrison

Some people have simply awful habits. Like kissing the neighbour's wife. But not me. she is nearly seven foot tall, anyway. And I am certainly not going to take up pole vaulting for one brief moment of madness.

No, I decided against that long ago. I am like that - honest, upright - and very much a coward.

There are all kinds of things I could give up doing. But I don't have to because I don't do them anyway.

I make a definite rule to only indulge in those things which are not habit-forming. Like visiting Russia, kissing babies and eating at the Ritz. Many things will not permit myself to do, because one day I know I would want to stop. I find that an excellent habit to adopt.

And I am not prepared to waste my time on things which are not worth starting.

Oh yes, I can give up most things I do - or may do. But I have one quite uncontrollable habit. Silly, silly me - I blush with shame. But, that's enough of that as the hen said to the ostrich.

I cannot stop myself from going to a certain shop. It sells sweets, tobacco, newspapers, and other things which are not good for you. It is an unbelievably horrid shop. Untidy, smelly. Opens late. Closes early. And it goes off to lunch for half the day. Quite a cosmic disaster in its own small way.

And I just cannot stay away. Like gravity, I seem to be magnetized towards it.

It isn't as if I had a particular fondness for the hovel. In fact it depresses me, and my nervous rash flares up like a sunspot every time I go there. And it really isn't convenient for me to get to. I have to catch two buses. Not at the same time, I should add. One after the other.

A soul destroying journey. almost as bad as visiting Russia. It just goes to show how much of a grip it has on me.

The married couple who own it are not at all pleasant. You wouldn't like them. They certainly wouldn't like you.

146

I have never yet been in there without him asking me if I had the right change. And feeling like a criminal if I said no. These days I take two whole pockets of coins to be on the safe side.

And oft-times he's given me my gardening magazine minus the free gift. The number of sweet pea seeds and pruning guides I have been deprived of must be quite phenomenal.

He's a fellow who takes things personally, and he has favourites. Like taking my free gifts and giving them to his relatives. It certainly wouldn't be to other customers - because they don't like customers. And that's certainly all right with us customers, because we are not madly in love with those two, either.

And the wife! Oh dear, oh dear! Nobody deserves to be married to her. Not even him. Talk about a booming voice. She can't even whisper without things falling off the shelves.

At first, I thought she was deaf. You know how you do.

She was awfully rude. Even tried to pick up the counter and shake it at me. I am sure she would have become quite physical if her husband had not had the presence of mind to heave me out through the door.

And still I go there. In spite of always feeling unwelcome. You see, you have to behave yourself. You really do. There is a notice on the door saying 'no smoking no dogs'. Which I consider to be both bad English and an insult to one's intelligence. You may be able to smoke a kipper. But a dog? Never!.

Underneath that is 'no ice creams, lollies prams and chips to be brought onto these premises'.

They sell birthday cards, but heaven help you if you touch one. I do believe that if a fly should settle on a wish-you-were-here, they would swat it with a what-you-damage-you-pay-for notice.

It goes without saying that shop-lifters will be prosecuted. Which, at least, consoles the shop-lifters with the thought that the safety of police protection is not too far away.

And you must close the door behind you. That is quite obligatory. Many an offender has been hauled back to the scene of the crime for that offence.

And still I go there. It really is an awful habit, I know. I should make the difficult effort to break it.

If only I could find the courage, I should march boldly in there with an un-smoked dog sitting in a pram. Chomping away extrovertly on my ice lolly and chips, and shouting wildly whilst I handled the cards.

I should then take something without paying - such as my sweet pea seeds and pruning guides, and depart the place forever - leaving the door wide open behind me.

That's what I should do.

But, as I have said - I am not given to starting what I may wish to stop one day. That is really not the sort of habit that I would care to have.

I shall just have to put up with it that's all!

A Right To Life

by

Pam Ellis

The problem now confronting her was one which she had not anticipated. Not
that she had had the time to anticipate anything really. Everything had happened so quickly. It had all been such a muddle. So much to think about. One
moment her husband was there, the next, he was not. There had been such a lot
to organise, to re-organise. Looking back, she was surprised at how well she
had coped over the last few months considering. . . well, considering that she
had had to manage alone. She had no close relatives and knew very few people
in the small village where they had retired. Her ability to manage had increased
her self-confidence and she was no longer quite so shy and nervous. More able
to make decisions, take action. She must take action now.

She looked around her at the garden that had slowly changed into a jungle.
Her husband had always done the garden and as she surveyed the tangled
weeds and long grass, she was made aware of her own ignorance of horticul-
ture. She really had no idea how to distinguish a flower from a weed, or what
to do with an annual or a perennial, even had she been able to tell the difference. She was sure that trees and hedges should be pruned. She did not even
know how to start up the mower. Something would have to be done, and quickly.

Her reverie was interrupted by a black cat which cleared the garden wall and
scuttled past her feet, closely followed by a large dog. They both disappeared
into the undergrowth. A few seconds later, a head appeared over the wall.

'I'm sorry Missus. It was the cat you see. She usually does what I tell 'er but
when she sees a cat she just goes berserk. She won't hurt you.'

Mrs Powell had not been at all frightened by the dog, but looking at the head,
she felt distinctly nervous and unsure. The sides of the head had been shaved
and the top hair, which stood up in spikes had been tinted a delicate shade of
purple. Mrs Powell had led a sheltered life. She knew that young men nowadays often wore ear rings but this was the first time she had seen a nose ring.
Unable to tear her gaze away from this terrifying apparition, she was even
more disconcerted to discover that the nose ring was in fact, a safety pin.

She clutched her cardigan tightly round her suddenly shivery body and looked down at the dog. Unable to locate the cat in the dense foliage of the garden, it lay panting a few feet away.

'Well I suppose you'd better come and get her,' Mrs Powell took a few paces backwards. The head immediately disappeared and a slim body clad in black leather vaulted over the wall. As he walked to the dog and attached a lead to its collar, she was dazzled by the chains and studs adorning his jacket as they glistened in the sunshine. His jeans looked as though they had been shrink wrapped round his legs and the large gashes in the knees could have been either for ventilation or because he was unable to afford a new pair. He approached Mrs Powell and waved an arm around vaguely.

'You look as if you've got a bit of a problem 'ere.' He slouched beside her, both hands in his pockets, the dog at his feet, 'The gardener run off with the cleaning woman has he?.' He chuckled to himself. Mrs Powell felt that politeness necessitated a reply.

'Well actually, my husband used to do the garden but he is. . . no longer here.'

The youth shrugged. There was a silence between them that Mrs Powell, try as she might was unable to fill.

'I could do a bit.'

'I'm sorry?'

'I could do a bit. Cut the grass and that. If you like.'

Mrs Powell hesitated.

'Do you know anything about gardening?'

'Nope. But it doesn't look as if you do either. Not meaning to be rude. I could chop the hedges down. Tidy it up a bit. I could make you a pond. I helped my uncle make one once. Lovely it looked. All goldfish and water-lilies in it.'

Mrs Powell took a deep breath.

'It's very kind of you but no thank you.'

Looking at the young man, she suddenly felt mean. She had been worrying about the garden and here, leaping over the wall as if in answer to a prayer, the solution had presented itself and she had rejected it. He looked rejected too. Shoulders hunched, staring at the ground; perhaps his whole life had been full of rejection.

Desperately hoping that she was doing the right thing, she said, 'I don't really like ponds but perhaps you could tidy up a bit. I couldn't afford to pay you much though,' she added hastily.

The boy looked at her eagerly, 'No well, I wouldn't want much. It'd give me something to do. Not much to do here.'

Mrs Powell smiled sympathetically, 'No, I don't suppose there is.'

He stuck out a not too clean hand and grinned, 'I'm Gary by the way.'

'Oh, Louisa Powell,' she took his hand.

'I think you've got moles.'

'I beg your pardon?'

'There, those heaps on the grass, they're moles they are.'

'Oh yes, well, perhaps you could catch them or something.'

Gary took a pace backwards, 'I couldn't do that. I'm a vegetarian.'

Mrs Powell stared at him. Perhaps the boy was simple.

'Gary,' she said slowly, 'I wouldn't expect you to serve them up for dinner. Just get rid of them.'

'No, I can't. I don't believe in killing things see. Moles have a right to life just as much as you do. I love animals I do. I couldn't kill any.'

Mrs Powell sighed. Perhaps she should have advertised for a proper gardener. Perhaps she would live to regret allowing charity to overrule sound judgement and making such a hasty decision.

'Well forget about the moles then. Just. . . do what you can.'

'Right. I'll start Saturday then shall I?'

'Yes, that'll be fine.'

They soon fell into a routine that pleased them both. Gary would arrive at 8.00 am and start work straight away. After about an hour, she would take him out a drink and they would chat about the garden. He really did seem to be interested and in Mrs Powell's unprofessional eyes, appeared to be doing a good job. Even the mole hills did not look too bad now that the grass was cut. From time to time, Gary would bring up the subject of a pond again.

'Right there, near those trees. A pond would look lovely there. My uncle's was done in no time.'

Mrs Powell shivered suddenly, even thought the sun was warm.

'No Gary, no pond. Thank you.'

'Well I'll get some bedding plants then shall I? Build a rockery?'

Mrs Powell had no idea what bedding plants were or where the rocks were to come from but she did not want to be too negative. She smiled as she took back the empty cup.

'Yes, all right then.'

In the evenings now, she would sit outside and contentedly think of what a pleasant life she had. Now that the garden was taken care of, she hardly missed her husband at all. Just occasionally, something would remind her. She would read something in the newspaper about a battered wife and her heart would go out to the unknown victim. She knew so well how it felt. But, for the most part, she never thought about him. She only counted her blessings and continued with her peaceful, uneventful life.

She had been on the waiting list for the operation on her varicose veins for so long that the letter from the hospital came as a surprise. She had almost forgotten that she needed surgery. Strange really. Since her husband's death, her legs had not been so bad. Nothing had been so bad.

She told Gary that she had to go into hospital and that he could just carry on as usual. He was quite worried.

'Is it serious?'

'No, it's just a simple operation.'

'Will you be in long?'

'No, only a few days. A week at the most.'

'I'll come and see you then shall I?'

Mrs Powell was very touched. That he should even think of giving up some of his time to visit her in hospital brought tears to her eyes. She could imagine him clomping down the ward in his big boots and torn jeans, the safety pin swinging gently from his left nostril.

'Well, if you get the time. That would be nice.'

He looked away. She could tell that he had half expected her to make an excuse for him not to visit.

She was dreaming that she had wings. She was flying over her garden looking down from a great height. There were her lawns and flowerbeds and molehills. There, under the trees was the bent figure of Gary digging. His jacket and shirt were hanging from a bush and the dog lay nearby. She could see the sweat glistening on his naked back. She slowly felt herself being dragged back to reality. There was a hand on her shoulder and a gentle shaking. She awoke to find the sweat was on her own body and a cold fear gripped her. A nurse was leaning over.

'Mrs Powell. Wake up dear. You have some visitors.'

Strong hands helped her to sit up. Screens were drawn around her bed and two visitors were admitted. She had never seen either of them before but she knew immediately who they were, or rather, what they represented. As she looked at them she could picture clearly the next scene in her dream. The one that she had been about to enter. Taking advantage of her absence, Gary had decided to surprise her by digging a garden pond.

'Mrs Powell. We're police officers. We'd like to talk to you about your husband.'

Uranus And Company Limited

by

Desmond Tunstall

Two ancients were sitting on a public bench, the evening sun warming their thin backs, before them a promenade, and their gaze lay beyond the protective railings on the wide lapping sea with white menacing sparks of foam spurting out erratically over its greyblue surface tinged with points of gold. There might have been a quarter of a century between the octogenarian and his younger companion. They talked of times past and of their failing powers. The sea, its distant roar a reminder, seemed to reflect the dying sun in their lives.

A young woman coming from the north passed the old philosophers, her brown hair streaming down her back, a few strands caught up in the bag slung from her shoulder. Two pairs of discoloured eyes, never shy, followed her passage. She smiled and walked on. The thin-haired heads housing those atavistic eyes nodded. Nobody spoke.

She passed out of earshot and the older seer, raising the walking stick held in his left hand, pointed it shakily in her direction and said with the melancholy wisdom of years: 'You know, boy, a young woman's hair is like a man's life, so many strands all going in the same general direction; some get caught where we don't want them to be until we brush out the unwanted knots.'

'I was thinking of Yeats's poem,' the other said but he meant to sigh.

'Politics!'

Their gaze remained with the smiling passer-by until she was a speck in the distance like a passed memory, still with them vividly but no longer relevant to this annus domini.

Politics. Their conversation, intermittent and darting like the birds overhead, remained on politics and how it was possible to restore the Golden Age.

Then they reflected on their lives when young, on the great river which led into this sea further south along the coast. But the river and the sea still roll on as powerful and as full of life as they were in youth.

The younger of the two sages had just retired after fifty years working as a seed and fertiliser merchant at Kington on the river Abus. Finally, in a position of managerial responsibility he had enjoyed more power than even the older prophet, his father who sat next to him.

154

His father had been a law unto himself, owning a small business and ruling with vigour. He had had no notions of giving his business up until his son had unsurped the older entrepreneur's powers and the latter had with bad grace abdicated. And now they were both old and the sun was setting behind the sea-front guest houses over their emaciated shoulders.

A bus came down the road breaking the sound of the sea up into an inconsequential hiss. It drove on, a passer-by, a rolling river of time, a fading memory moving south. It carried only two passengers in the quiet August evening in this old seaside village dying like the sun, growing old like the benched philosophers - the bus had passed by.

Seated together on the sea side of the omnibus, a young man and young woman, quiet and for now satisfied with their lot in life, looked out at the old codgers, said nothing and watched the grey-blue immensity of the horizon-touching waters. The bus reached the terminus, an extended layby with shelters for waiting passengers who now were absent. The concrete shelters, the concrete layby, the whiteness sullied by dust, litter, graffiti and time, gave off a stark agedness, bare and hard, calloused into ugliness. The couple alighted and walked over to the concrete steps leading to the beach.

A young woman coming from the north passed the young couple, her brown hair streaming down her back, a few strands caught up in the bag slung from her shoulders. Two pairs of distinct and lively eyes, shy and surreptitious, followed her passage. No acknowledgements. Nobody spoke.

The young couple walked and skipped down the steps. She thought: I wish I wish I had her beauty. He thought: which way will the strands of life lead me next?

They ran across the soft sandy beach, picking their way between, around, over the shingle, drift wood, broken glass and sharpened shells. Along a smooth margin of seacaked sand they danced and skipped, laughed and called, their shouts drowned and muffled by the great ocean divinity, roaring his approval of their obeisance. Yet they took no notice of his power.

With a lull in their excitement they began walking back northwards along the strand until they reached a patch of rock pools amid boulders covered in green-haired wrack, smooth and slippery. The girl went over to them and clambered about nimbly, unconcerned, looking for crabs, starfish and other kinds of life. He, feeling the slipperiness and fearing its power over him, gingerly putting one foot forward and finding a safe base for it before bringing up his back foot, looked for nothing.

155

Beyond the rock pools they strolled hand in hand, lovers, young, ritualistically instinctive. At a moment's notice she broke from him and ran towards the sea, taking up her skirt in front of her, and waded into the shallow lapping waves. He followed after rolling his trousers up carefully. They began a duet of love play, spraying the briny water at each other and running, held back by the oceanic power of the water, their ineffectual attempts to stay dry now carelessly forgotten. They ambled further along the margin arm in arm. He wanted to give her a. . . here a. . . He pulled her around to face him and softly looking at the blue-grey welcoming eyes kissed her softly on her soft protruding lips, blue-grey late evening, soft hued under the iceblue sky. The beach disappeared suddenly.

They climbed the concrete steps, off-white, rough, cracked, back up to the seafront promenade. Silently, their hands lightly touching, they passed two old veterans, sitting side by side on a public bench, gazing at the mighty ocean. Two pairs of discoloured eyes, never shy, followed their passage. Nobody spoke. The thin haired heads housing those atavistic eyes knowingly nodded.

When the young couple were out of earshot, the older seer said:

'How about a drink, boy?'

The agreement led to their rising from the bench. As they made their slow, ponderous way back through the facade of seafront guest houses to the countryside behind, the sky began to darken noticeably and the air grew chilly.

A few days later Moira Destin remembered walking through Carew-on-Sea, a small village a few miles away, and smiling at two elderly gentlemen, sitting on a public bench, gazing out to sea. Since then she had been away from home and had just returned. Picking up the local daily newspaper she was taken aback by one article about the little village. It read:

Wayside Death

An 89 year old man collapsed and died on Saturday evening last whilst walking home with his son along the lonely inland road from Carew-on-Sea.

Charles Fox Lochran had spent the summer evening on the promenade and had been in good health. His son, Albert Fox Lochran, 66, said they had sat on the promenade for a long time before calling in at The Old Father Time public house. Mr Lochran, jr., who was holidaying with his parents, said that on the road back to Abus House, the elder Mr Lochran's home about a mile from

Carew, he had been overcome by a bout of sickness which had resulted in his passing out.

When he came to his father was missing. It transpired that Mr Lochran, sr., concerned at his son's illness, began hurrying back to the village for help. But before he had got more than a few yards he too collapsed. Death was attributed to cardiac arrest.

> Thus the Muse well sings:
> No matter how you rue this
> The melancholy truth is
> Time destroys all things.

Mr Ticket

by

Joseph Andrews

I'm laying on the bed now, dreaming of yesterday when I unthinkingly informed Lucy of my plan.

Her keyboard had fallen into sudden silence as Lucy's fingers froze in mid type, each digit contorted and bent in some grotesque parody of Nosferatu's menacing shadow.

Someone turned a blowtorch against my cheeks and I looked away in an attempt to conceal my rising embarrassment.

'You're going to what?' she'd exclaimed, her chin momentarily threatening the space bar.

Why can't I keep my big mouth shut? I thought, realising too late my mistake. I tried the 'matter-o-fact' approach.

'I'm just going to have them. . . you know, enlarged a bit,' I said in a semi-controlled splutter; inwardly scolding myself for having offered my reputation to the sacrificial alter.

Lucy found her amusement impossible to hide.

'What, your boobs?' She snickered loudly. Without moving a single joint in her stilted claw, Lucy had motioned towards my less than adequate cleavage.

I gave a nod of affirmation, but was then desperate to quieten her.

'Will you keep your voice down!' I pleaded; and then, with a feeling of wasted breath, '*Please,* keep it to yourself.'

'Oh! of course I will, Phillipa darling, you know me!'

That was the problem, I did; and her tone suggested, with alarming certainty, an already burning itch to share her delight. The whole office will know by lunchtime, I thought.

It was alright for Lucy, twenty one, beautiful and engaged, she hadn't a care in the world; especially where men were concerned. Whenever one of the rep's came into the office it was always *her* desk they hovered round, laughing and flirting. For two years I'd had to listen to the telephone conversations with her never ending string of boyfriends, and more recently with Paul, her fiancê. I, on the other hand, could count my own love affairs on one finger; Brendan O'Connor had lasted three days and a single, unaccomplished, grope.

158

But now there's Mr Ticket. I don't know his real name, not yet anyway, but I call him that because of how we met.

As usual the 5.45 was crammed and I had been suspended like an orang-utan from the luggage rack. When I dropped my season ticket he just appeared, picking it up for me and sliding it into my pocket.

'There you are,' he had said, and gave me a smile that etched itself on my retina. They say it can't happen, but I fell in love with him, right there and then.

Never having seen him before, in the last few weeks he has been in the same carriage, at the same time, every evening. I've been reading Papillon and he saw the cover. Now when he see's me he say's, 'Hello, Miss Butterfly,' and allows his lips to part and broaden into one of those delicious smiles; talk about the tingle factor, this guy could put me into orbit by just winking.

And then there's his eyes, those big, deep blue eyes; one of these days I'm going to springboard off the nearest briefcase and plunge right into them.

Then one evening I caught him staring at my chest. An over zealous artist with three buckets of white emulsion couldn't have hidden the scarlet I felt creep quickly over my jowl. Mr Ticket looked up, but instead of turning away he just flashed his brilliant white incisors at me.

Arriving home, I'd cried for an hour. My small chest hadn't really bothered me since being at school; the last one out of vests I had been the centre of shower room humour.

'No-tits Phillipa' they'd called me; originality not being your average school-girls' forte. To discover that Mr Ticket was a boob man was just too much for a bosomless girl to take. That's when I decided on cosmetic surgery,

'If he want's big breasts, then big breasts are what he will get,' I said to myself; love, after all, is worth any sacrifice.

The next night Mr Ticket acknowledged me in his usual fashion, whilst I tried to guess at his marital status. The absence of gold wasn't proof he was certificateless, or that he didn't share a bed, but I felt reassured all the same.

Getting off the train, he glanced at my chest again, and, gently brushing my arm with his hand, said, 'See you, Miss Butterfly.'

All day I had wrestled with my conscience, but his affectionate gesture had set my pulse off at Olympic qualifying speed, extinguishing any doubts that still lingered; I would do anything to snare Mr Ticket.

My savings were reasonable, but a new clinic, no more than a mile from the office, advertised opening offers; I was glad at the supermarket mentality. I phoned, booked an appointment, and went to see them.

It was the surgeon himself that consulted me, not doctor, but Mr Guthrey. He was quite nice really, well he would be wouldn't he. A nurse took measurements and half a dozen photographs. Mr Guthrey insisted that I have a coffee, and then another as he flicked through a brochure of 'before and afters'. There were so many questions and he made me go back to the clinic twice more before allowing me to sign all the papers. With a final, 'Now are you sure, Miss Prentice?' We had eventually agreed on a date.

I booked two weeks holiday and, when the days of waiting had eventually melted into my anxiety, I went in to say cheerio to the boss.

He gave a knowing wink, 'I suppose we'll see a new you when you get back, Phillipa!' he chortled.

I had been right about Lucy, damn her. But on the way home Mr Ticket gave me a smile that seemed even bigger than normal and it all seemed worthwhile again.

And now there's today.

I booked into the clinic at around nine o'clock and a very nice lady showed me to my room. It has an en-suite bathroom and a view into the garden that's breathtaking. Mr Guthrey came in to say hello, followed by a nurse who ran through the agenda for the day. I was to have a bath, put on the gown that she left for me, and wait for them to bring a pre-med. Things would happen quite quickly after that, she had said, with the operation scheduled for around midday.

I am nervous to say the least. The bath has helped to relax me and I'd laid in it for almost an hour, dreaming of Mr Ticket and what the look on his face might be like when next we meet. I don't know what he will do but in my own little fantasy I imagine him sweeping down on one knee and lifting my hand to his lips, pledging his undying love.

Wrinkled from the soak I have put on the robe, and now here I lay. They're going to cut me under my arms and stuff those silicon bags through the holes; I wonder if I'll be able to use deodorant tomorrow?

Minutes seem like hours. A lady had been in once or twice to ask if I'm ok, but as the clock ticks away I am becoming more and more tense. I can't believe I'm actually going through with this. Maybe it'll hurt afterwards, maybe I'll be allergic to the antibiotics, yes, that's it, perhaps I should put it off just now so I can get my G.P. to check my history.

But the nurse has just been back in and told me that the anaesthetist is here.

160

I can feel my body going rigid and the adrenalin pumping fiercely through my veins. Please God, don't let me vomit! I'm digging my fingernails into my palms as I listen to the sound of footsteps outside in the corridor, there are muffled voices, whispering. My surroundings are becoming abstract, a surreal nightmare is beckoning; but then a rivulet of sweat tickles my nose, and once more I concentrate on straining to hear what they are saying outside the door.

Am I having second thoughts? Yes! No! Of course not, it will all be worth it in the end; after all, I'm doing this for . . . but wait, the door's opening now and. . .

Hang on a minute. . . it can't be; I, I . . . No! But it's. . . it's. . .

'Hello, Miss Butterfly. My, it's a small world, isn't it!'

He's giving me that oh so familiar smile and I'm looking into those deep blue eyes, and. . . No wonder he. . . No wonder he looked at. . . Oh, my God! Oh my. . .

Mr Ticket is leaning over me, he has a small plastic medicine cup in one hand and a stethoscope hangs menacingly from his neck. The green gown he is wearing is brushing against my hands as he leans forward, I know he is speaking to me, but I cannot hear for the clamour in my head.

Just now, I think I'm going to be sick.

The Pepper Pot

by

Robert Coulson

'The pepper pot is the Education Department and this is the railway company.'

We all nodded as he placed the tea-cosy in front of my mother.

'Over here,' he continued, 'is me, and this,' screwing up his newly ironed napkin, 'is what we're talking about'.

The Old Man illustrated his tea time talk by using anything handy; it made his dissertation more graphic. My mother who was his intended audience, appeared to be paying close attention as she thoughtfully picked her teeth with the corner of an invoice. I suspected that she was 100% occupied with matters concerning the shop, listing in her mind the thousand and one things to be done before bedtime, and was not hearing any of his lecture. Not that it mattered. The rest of us tried to follow his drift but this was difficult due to the distractions his illustrations caused. While I was trying to reconcile the railway with the tea cosy I lost the thread of his argument on a subject I had brought up.

At the beginning of each school term, we would pick up our free railway pass at the ticket office, but mine hadn't turned up after four days of school. My father was working out what, if anything, he could do about it. An uncle on my mother's side worked in the Education Department, but he was pretty useless according to my father; anyway, he was wowser. It had already cost one and fourpence for my tickets without a pass, and my father was looking at the problem from all angles, starting from the standpoint that the government was bloody useless as were all the civil servants working for it.

'Now if I', he went on, 'supposing if I', he placed my mother's spectacle case alongside the napkin, 'applied to the railway', putting his finger on the ashtray, 'and asked for the money back, what would they say?'

No-one volunteered as answer; we wouldn't have been heard if we had. He went on: 'They would say: Oh well, it's not our fault; you gotta complain to the school'. Here he reached over and picked up the sauce bottle and put it next to the pepperpot. 'Now'. he said looking up to check we were listening. 'Now this would happen.'

Before he disclosed what would happen, my mother got up from the table to go to the lav thereby interrupting his peroration. This was Ok . She always did

162

so; what he had to say could wait. He took the opportunity to open his tin of tobacco and peel off a paper from the little packet he kept in there. It was standard practice amongst roll-your-owners to attach the paper to the bottom lip while proceeding with the ceremony of rubbing the 'ready rubbed' tobacco strands in the palm of the hand. Bits of tobacco always spilled on to the table cloth during this process but after the cigarette was rolled, my father would sweep them back into his tin. In fact, scarcely any went back into the tin, most went on to his lap and the floor. Nevertheless we were accustomed to his cigarette-rolling and the misshapen object he ended up with. The Old Man never spoke when he was rolling a cigarette; it was a contemplative occupation and during my mother's absence it seemed to promote philosophical thought. This lasted through the lighting up phase and the casual spitting out of the loose bits of tobacco. During this break, we children remembered we had things to do, like homework or the clearing of the table, and each of us got up from our chair while, arms folded, he smoked peacefully and silently, all the time staring at some spot on the wall just above the clock.

When she returned from the lav, my mother stopped in the kitchen and began to scrape the dishes. My sisters moved around her bringing more dirty plates or putting things away in cupboards. The noise level discouraged my father from resuming his lecture. He made no objections when the pepper-pot, the tea cosy, and other symbols were removed from the table. He was so used to domestic chores going on around him that he would pick up his tobacco tin, his box of matches and the ash tray and hold them until someone removed the table cloth, even though this might take several minutes.

Only occasionally did I see the absurdly funny side of his lecturing. One afternoon I amused my sister by mimicking him. We were sitting at the table in between meals and I began by taking from the cupboard an object and placing it on the table.

'Now', I was saying, 'if this 'ere toothpick holder came near the fruit bowl, what would this 'ere carving fork do? Would the serviette ring, no, the butter knife, worry the ash tray? Not at all! The mint sauce, 'ere, would join up with the steel and poof!' I made a sweeping gesture which knocked my school bag off the table.

'I disagree', my sister said with a big giggle; 'You've forgotten the Old Man's car-keys. They would immediately get lost with the bottle opener.'

This was too much for me and the pair of us collapsed into uncontrolled and helpless laughter. My mother came in from the kitchen and asked us what was the joke. 'No joke', I told her, 'we were just wondering whether the Old Man's serviette ring would ever shack up with this ink stain.' My sister shrieked and started me laughing again just as my father came in from the backyard with Arthur Poole.

'What's this then?' he asked.

'Mum will tell you', I said feeling as if my rib cage would burst.

'I'm blowed if I know what's got into them', she said; 'I think they're wondering if you want them to set the table.'

'We can't', my sister yelled. 'Not until we know what a table spoon is!'

'Or this ink stain', I said

'You mean, how to remove it?' my father asked.

'What! Move Anzac Park?' More bursts of laughter. 'What about the authorities?' I said, holding up the salt shaker.

'Come on, Arthur', my father said, 'Let's go, it's nearly six o'clock. We'll go to the new pub, it's closer'.

'Where is it, dad?' I asked, 'Near Anzac Park? Here?' I pointed to one edge of the ink stain.

'No, here', said my father and leaning across placed a glass on the table.

I couldn't recover for fully ten minutes and at tea time both my sister and I had to be shushed a hundred times before we started the washing-up. Only once did my mother betray any sympathy with us when she asked us to pass her the League of Nations.

Your Move Partner

by

Bel Bailey

Emily Meredith sighed with satisfaction as she plopped down on the chintz settee. No doubt moving was tiring when you were 65 - but well worth it for a view like this! Her hazel eyes brightened as she gazed over the rolling parkland surrounding Tamarisk Hall and the melting blue hills in the distance towards Shropshire. Under the window a fountain sparkled diamonds in the sun.

How grand it was to return in triumph to their home village, and to the very best mansion in the area as folks agreed. Tom, her husband, newly retired, was a pleased as punch too, she could tell. He'd smiled quietly as she went into raptures and observed humorously to their eldest daughter,

'There'll be no holding your Mum now, Paula. Proper lady of the manor she'll be, mark my words, though it was all my idea really.'

But Emily could sense that Tom's quiet satisfaction was really just as strong as her own pleasure. No wonder the pair of them looked like two Cheshire Cats! And why not? What a long way they'd come since they were childhood sweethearts in this very village over 50 years ago.

In those days they lived next door to each other in the old two-up two-down terrace cottages near St Michael's Church. Their parents were loving but terribly poor - why once Emily's dad had to go out picking wild blackberries to sell in the nearest town, until he could get another regular job. With five children to feed sheer need made him enterprising and Tom's dad had been much the same.

'Wait till the sun shines, Nelly,' he'd tell his wife whenever things looked extra bad. 'If my ship doesn't come in then perhaps young Tom's will instead!'

Another glance around their lovely sitting room assured Emily how right old Mr Meredith had been. Their ship had indeed come home to bring them to port here in this near stately home.

'Thirty bedrooms,' the old butler at Tamarisk Hall, had assured young Emily when she first stepped over the threshold into the servants quarters at the Hall. 'Thirty Bedrooms my girl! What d'you think of that then?' And the others - housekeeper, cook, tweeny maid and ladies' maid had all laughed at her big-eyed stare of amazement as she looked around.

The twelve year old Emily had never been inside such a handsome mansion in her whole life before, but she'd long admired the fine red brick house up the long, winding drive. What a thrill it had been for her to importantly open the wrought iron gates and walk very tall and proud up the drive to deliver the groceries at the back door of the Hall. Even now the 65 year old Emily could shut her eyes and vividly recall that golden day in far off pre-war summer!

As she entered her teens, now grown surprisingly pretty almost overnight with shining brown hair and wistful, attractive smile, Emily still dreamed about the Hall. Suppose ... suppose one day she married a rich man who would *buy* the house for her. *What* a fine thing that would be!

But no rich man came along, even in the war. Emily wrote her usual long and interesting letters to Tom - now in the RAF and stationed far away. How sad it was the see the Hall's fine rose gardens now neglected and the flower beds dug up for vegetables.

'Dig for Victory!' they called it - but how Emily mourned the lost beauty of the Hall's gardens. She poured out all her feelings to Tom who was always glad to hear from her when she was not too busy working as a Land-girl at Farmer Wheeler's. At least she could still live at home and help her mother with the younger children while her father at 48 put in long hours with the Home Guard.

Now Emily broke off from her reverie to lovingly arrange the roses she had picked from the garden that day. Thank goodness the Hall was thriving again - everything blossoming for them especially it seemed.

She and Tom had married soon after the war and now their silver framed wedding photograph stood in place of honour beside the roses. They could never have dreamed then that in retirement days they'd actually live at Tamarisk Hall. How surprising life could be.

When their children were growing up, Emily and Tom had visited the Hall together one summer twenty odd years ago. A charity garden party was being held and how she had envied the glamorous wife of the owner at the time. They had sold up and moved on long ago but even now Emily could remember that pang of envy - not of the lady's husband (she'd rather have darling Tom any day) but envy of her home.

Emily's long time dream castle in the air. It was Fate, she thought, Fate all along had intended to reward them in their golden retirement years - and here was Tamarisk Hall for them to enjoy after all ... Again Emily smiled with joy. How lucky they were.

Entering the room suddenly, Tom, grinning like a boy, put down a tray of drinks on the little table at her elbow.

'I've asked some people in Em,' he said. 'Remember I told you about the Paradines - they're new here just like us - think you'll like them. John plays a decent round of golf and Betty wants to join the WI - she's into wine making, I told her you could introduce her to some kindred spirits in the village.'

It was working out just as Emily had hoped she thought later, as the newcomers joined them at the window of their sitting room, exclaiming at their wonderful views.

'Well,' she replied cheerfully, 'and no wonder, this used to be the master bedroom you know, in the old days. Your flat used to be the Servants Hall where I first delivered the groceries to earn some money.'

And the two couples drank a toast to the 'Good New Days,' now that the Hall was expertly divided up into Older People's Flats. This desirable residence of 30 bedrooms was now a superb retirement haven for many older people even though Emily secretly still thought of it as 'hers'!

Emily had never told Tom of that far off day she had visited the Hall's fountain after delivering the groceries. The butler had given her a silver sixpence as a tip and the child Emily had secretly tossed this into the gushing waters. Today that wish had come true. It was worth half a century's wait! But it was good for Tom to think the move was all his idea.

The Red House

by

Bewick Wilson

The old woman did not want to leave the Red House. She sat by the fire-side, her bony fingers clenched, as she fought her son for the right to keep her own territory.

'This is my home. The fire has never died here in 200 years.' But the son had no wish to keep the old place. He would have his mother come and live with him - and let the fire go out. He had no interest in the past. He tried to make her understand. How could he?

'This house is ancient. It is falling down. You must face the truth mother, and come with me to the new place. It will be warmer, safer and I can look after you.'

'But this is where our family belongs,' said the old woman, fingers white with pain and anger,' Being born and dying here ... for all this time. Why must you be the one to change it! You know I cannot leave.'

'You must,' said the son - stronger, firmer and sure that he was doing right. 'It will soon be winter and I cannot leave you here alone.'

And he left her to think on his words.

And the old woman did so, as she stared into the fire. His words had worn her down.

But then she thought of a way! She would take some burning sticks and embers to the new place, to keep the fire alive!

But when she told this to her son, he shouted at her.

'We have no need of it mother. Don't you understand?'

'But if will bring good luck my son and keep the heart alive inside you home!'

'I am sorry mother,' he said 'but there comes a time when things must die. I know that people have lived and died here for 200 years - but this is the end. When you die, the fire will go out too. For ever. This will happen, because I shall not carry on the old ways. So - you must agree.'

The old woman listened to her son and in the silence then, between them, she made up her mind.

'Very well, so be it. I see I must accept the way of things.'

'Good ... it is best. Do not be sad mother. Collect up your bits and pieces and I shall come for you tomorrow.'

When he had gone, she sat for a long time before the fire, remembering her life and the lives of her family and friends. She thought of the child she had lost - And of the man who had been her husband. She could not bear to think about her son.

Tonight there would be no need to fetch the wood in. Tonight would be the last one in her home.

Slowly she began gathering together all the totems and trinkets that had helped to bring meaning to her life; her rings, a picture, a scarf, the pipes, some letters and an old broken box full of memories - mostly forgotten. With love, she began to surrender them all into the heart of the fire; while she whispered a strange poetry, learned long ago.

For the fire had not only kept them warm and cooked their food throughout the coming and going of generations, it had also kept away ghosts. The old woman knew that. Now, she would go to them.

'We'll go out together,' she sang to the flames. 'The time is right.'

When the son arrived early next morning, the fire still raged with a passion, burning his face in an intense glow. There was nothing, only fire.

Later, he would grow frightened in the night and wonder if he should have carried the red hot ashes to his hearth. Instead, he let the fire burn in his mind - so that his sons called him crazy.

Journey's End

by

Charlotte Robertson

Doris checked the time on the grandfather clock which stood grandly in the narrow hallway leading to the kitchen. It was exactly ten minutes before nine o'clock, which meant it was shortly time to catch the bus. Having been previously unaware of how late it was, Doris now started rushing around like a mouse, scurrying here and there but leaving no mess behind her. She filled her old shopping trolley with the usual assortment of bizarre objects - a pair of pink, rubber gloves which had holes in the fingers, an old cloth, some silver polish, and lastly, but most importantly a large bunch of Azaleas freshly cut from her small back garden wrapped in yesterday's newspaper. All she needed now was some money for the bus. She delved deeply into her bone china teapot, which now served as her savings account and counted out the exact amount she would need - not a penny more. Without having time to replace the old teapot to its place of safety behind the cooker, she ambled to the door, pulling her tartan coloured shopping trolley behind her. Wednesday had come round again.

As Doris slowly approached the bus stop, the familiar red and yellow coach pulled over to let the other passengers get on. The driver of the bus knew to wait for her, he was quite used to doing so now. Eventually, Doris reached the bus, a little out of breath, and after paying her fare in coppers, she went to sit down amongst the regular sprinkling of passengers.

'Morning Doris - nearly didn't make it this morning, eh?'

'I haven't missed this bus in seven years Maud, and I'm not about to now - you should know that as well as anyone' was her reply, as she eased herself down gently on the seat next to Maud. Maud was a stout lady, who always had a friendly word to say to everyone, especially Doris.

'You know Doris, it really wouldn't do you any harm if you didn't see Albert every Wednesday, I'm sure he'd understand considering all the effort you make.'

'No harm? Wouldn't do any harm, you say? Of course it would - Albert relies on me visiting him every week without fail, and I'm not about to let him down now, I couldn't ever live with myself if I did.'

170

Maud understood how much seeing Albert meant to Doris, and decided to change the subject a little, so as not to cause any upset.

'What have you got for him today, then? Daffodils? I noticed some lovely daffs in your garden the other week.'

'He had daffs last week; poor man will be growing them out of his ears if I give him any more! No, I've got him some beautiful azaleas - cut them this morning I did.'

'Lovely, I've always liked azaleas'.

'Well let's hope he does, I know better than anyone what a fussy, old devil he can be.'

Maud just smiled. She worried about Doris; she always appeared so brisk and lively, but she was nearly eighty now and wasn't in any real condition to be making such a long journey to see Albert every week. The bus stop that Doris had to get off at was a good mile away from where Albert was, and yet in all weathers she walked it, her creaky little trolley following behind her like a stray dog.

As the bus struggled up the hill, rain started to beat hard against the windows, It wasn't just a shower but a real torrent of water. Doris looked out as she cheerfully remarked 'And there's me forgetting my brolly, this will teach me to be so unprepared won't it?'

'Here look, I've got one, take mine - you'll be needing it more than me.'

'Don't you be so daft, Maud, I've got my raincoat, I'll be alright. A bit of rain won't hurt me.'

And with that, Doris started to get up from her seat; the next stop was hers. Maud knew that she would be wasting her time trying to make Doris take her umbrella. Once Doris made her mind up, that was it, there was no changing her - not in anything she did. Maud had never quite been able to decide whether she had always been so stubborn, or whether it was that she was older, her foolish pride made Her that way. Whatever the case, Doris' strict insistence about everything cause Maud a great deal of concern.

'You take care now Doris, it'll be slippery out there. Just take your time now, won't you.'

'Oh, stop fussing girl, I'll be just fine.' She called, as she stepped off the bus taking one step at a time; and holding up the people behind her who waited patiently to get off. Doris waved goodbye to Maud and the driver, and then began her long walk to see Albert.

Sometimes, the walk was a real pleasure; in the summer when it was warm and the trees were in blossom, Doris would savour the countryside around her, and almost forget the drone of traffic which filtered past her along the busy main road. Today, though, was a little different. The rain beat down heavily against her tatty, brown raincoat, and it wasn't long before she was soaked through to the skin. Doris didn't let the weather get her down' she had a way of dealing with every occasion, and the way in which she dealt with the walk when it was particularly miserable, was to break the journey up into little stages. She had walked the first stage - along the main road and now, as she turned the corner into a quieter street, she could comfort herself with the knowledge that she had now reached the second part of her struggle.

She walked slowly now; the trolley started to feel heavier with every step, and the wet clothes against her skin sent a chill right through her frail body. A car sped down the road through the deep puddles, sending a spray of muddy rainwater straight into Doris' path, By this point though, she was so wet that she didn't notice the sudden addition of water which made her coat drip onto the pavement. The end of the walk was in sight now, Doris tried to quicken her pace, realising that because of the rain she was later than usual. if there was one thing she hated it was to be late. She could never excuse other people not being punctual, and had always prided herself in keeping good time. Every Wednesday she would visit Albert at ten o'clock - that was how it had always been, and the thought of being late now, filled her with anxiety.

The black iron garden gate creaked as Doris let herself through, still pulling her trolley behind her. The distinct smell of freshly cut grass, and the birds chirping in the trees, welcomed her as they always did.

She loved to see the many shrubs and rose bushes which lined the pathway on every side. She stopped, before she got to Albert, to get the azaleas out of her trolley; she always liked to welcome him with the flowers - she liked to think that the splash of colour would instantly cheer him up. The azaleas were drooping a bit now, and the newspaper they were wrapped in was all smudged and soggy. They were a sorry sight, but still they were fresh from her garden, and that's what really mattered.

Doris stopped at where Albert was and put her rubber gloves on, ready for the cleaning that she always did whilst she was there. She bent down stiffly, and pulled out last week's flowers from their silver-plate holder. Carefully, she arranged the drooping azaleas as best she could.

'Sorry about these, Albert, I'm afraid they didn't survive the journey as well as they might have. I'll bring some better ones next week though - don't you worry. Now then, how have we been? I hope the rain isn't getting you down too much - I just think the good it must be doing the garden, I mean that's one way of looking at it - isn't it?' As she chatted away cheerfully about anything that occurred to her, she began to scrub at the marble grave stone, until it was so clean that you could almost see your reflection in it. The carefully engraved letters stood out bodily: 'Albert Hunter, Died 17th February, 1985. Rest in peace'.

'There, you look a bit more respectable now, although I can't get this flower holder as clean as I might. Perhaps it's this new silver polish, I thought I'd give it a try but I think I'll go back to my old brand - this one's not up to scratch by any means.

There wasn't a moment's silence as Doris did everything possible to tidy up Albert's grave. it was by far the best kept patch in the whole cemetery, and she knew this and felt proud to think it. Albert had given her everything she needed for fifty-four years; surely it was the least she do now to make sure he looked his best? She wasn't just going to forget the only man she ever loved, the only man who ever met her every need to the best of his ability - even when times were desperately hard. No, she had a duty to, an honour to keep, and come rain or shine, sickness or health, she would do it till death do her part.

A Walk in the Country

by

Tony Steene

The constriction in her throat made breathing difficult. Her heart beat quick-ened, the sound pounded in her head. He had ducked down among the ferns and she couldn't see him. She stood in the clearing like a frightened animal, all her senses straining to locate his position. Trying to detect which direction the menace would come from. Ready to flee, but too terrified to move.

The early morning rain dripped from the trees. The carpet of leaves, acted like a taut drum skin, amplifying the sound. The insistent, muted drone from the distant motorway added to the blanket of noise, making it difficult to hear any other sounds. The strident alarm call of a nearby blackbird startled her, she was near to breaking point. It was only fear that kept her rooted to the spot.

Had he disturbed the bird? But it was to the left, not where she last saw him.

All she could hear was the pounding of her heart to the accompaniment of the drumming raindrops. No sound of help. No comforting sounds of other people, of dogs barking, no children playing.

There's just the two of us. *He's somewhere in the undergrowth. But where?* And where's my dog? She's supposed to be protecting me. I could call her, but he'll hear me. Keep quiet, but he knows I'm here. Listen. Where is he?

He's over there behind that tree, I can see his breath! There's someone be-hind the next tree! Oh! God! There's two of them!

No! Wait, my eyes are playing tricks with me. Yes, all the trees are steaming, it's just the warming sun drying the trunks. Stop imagining things. Keep control of yourself. This is the last time I take the dog for a walk on my own. When John goes away in future he can take the dog with him.

Oh God! He's still there in that undergrowth! I can hear him! He's not trying to be quiet! He knows there's only us here! *What shall I do? Run?* Run like a frightened child with some imagined horror snapping at my heels, not daring to look back. *Run where?* I won't get to the car before he catches me. There's no houses nearby.

Don't be silly, keep calm, deep breaths. Control yourself! Now, *think, think,* you're a grown woman, not a child. Where's that damn dog? *Think!* What did you learn at that self defence class. I can't remember. It's OK in the school hall, but in the middle of these woods it's a nightmare.

Think! Think! Hit him where it hurts. But he'll be stronger than me and I'll just freeze. What would I do for a hat pin or something? *Find a stick! That's it!* That's no good, too small and I won't be able to lift that one. Here's one, this'll make him think twice. *Damn, it's rotten. Where is he? I can't hear him.* Maybe he's gone, seen someone coming or had second thoughts.

Listen! Can't hear anything. Maybe he's creeping up behind me. *Oh My God! I can't look round. I can feel him getting closer.* Use the keys, scratch him, scream and shout. Maybe he'll run away.

Beasts like him should be all locked away. Why should I be afraid to walk the dog? It's not fair. I enjoy walking. Why should I need protection? Women should be able to go out alone without fear of being attacked?

Where's that damn dog? I can feel the back of my neck crawling. I'm going to have to look round. Do it quick, take him by surprise. Grip the keys. *Turn!* No one! Nothing! I was sure he was there.

Is that someone staring out of the bracken! Or just my imagination? Certainly looks like someone, but they're not moving. Must be my imagination. Yes, it's no one. You fool, don't make things worse, try to keep in control.

I can hear him. Over there in those tall ferns. He's coming, crashing through the undergrowth. Come on you swine, I'm ready. Here he comes. Ready! Ready!

Oh! It's only the bloody dog! Thank God!

'Come here, there's a good girl. Good protection you are, now stay here. Shush! Be quiet! Stay!

'Have a dog,' he said, 'It'll be company when I'm away.' More trouble than it's worth. Look at the state of it. I'll have to bath it when I get home, if I get home.

'Stay here Bonnie. Try to look vicious.

'Why are you looking at those bushes, can you hear him? I thought he'd gone.'

If only someone else were here. Where's the old lady with the Yorkshire Terrier or that man with the Border Collie? Still tucked up in bed I suppose. Stupid to come out so early, won't do it again. Thought I'd be safe, no one about. What do these men do? Lurk in deserted places waiting for unsuspecting women. Why have we got the police? What are they doing? Why are these people free? It's not fair. I should be able to do what I want. Go where I please.

The dog's still looking at those bushes. That's where he is.

'Can you see him, Bonnie?'

I can't see properly, the sun's still low and right in my eyes. Just dark silhouettes and the sun shining on the steam makes it difficult. Can't see any details. Everything just a uniform grey.

There he is, I can see him. He's coming straight towards me. What's he got in his hand? It's a stick. Oh My God! He's going to hit me with it. I can't look.

What's he saying? Good morning?

'Good morning. Have you seen my collie? I was in the bushes picking some fungi when my dog ran off. I think it went after your dog. Oh! There she is. I reckon they've both been in the pond. Two dirty dogs for a bath, eh! Quite nice now it's stopped raining, isn't it. Enjoy your walk. Bye.'

Doreen's Cuppa

by

Dick Tracey

Heather looked up into Tony's face.

'Do you think Doreen knows?' She asked.

Tony didn't reply immediately, his interest was in the television. In the few seconds that elapsed Heather moved up the settee so that her head was more comfortable in his lap. He pressed the remote control and the screen blanked into nothingness.

'How many times do I have to tell you, she hasn't got a clue.'

'But doesn't she question where you've been 'till all hours of the night?' Came the retort.

'What time is it?' He asked.

'Five and twenty to eight.'

'Then she'll be stuck in front of that tele' watching Coronation Street, nothing on earth would get her away from that box when there's one of her favourite programmes on. She is a creature of habit as well as being bloody boring.' He reached for his cigarettes and placing two in his mouth lighted both, offering one to Heather. She blew the smoke into the air, the trails making swirling patterns as they ascended towards the single light immediately above.

'I feel a bit guilty really, she's my best workmate and we've known each other for years and specially as we only live three doors apart, you at number sixteen and me at number ten.' She looked into his eyes trying to see if there was any show of emotion to that statement.

'Look sweetheart, Doreen doesn't want children, she's got no desire to have a family and as far as sex goes, she thinks it's something Southerners have their coal delivered in,' he smiled to himself, rather good that pun.

'She won't give me a divorce so the only thing we can do is carry on the way we are.'

'What if I want a family, have you considered that?' She asked.

Tony didn't reply, but, drifted into his own thoughts. The situation was becoming stalemate. Any love he had for Doreen had long gone, his new love was Heather, they were good together, both had the same sense of humour, their likes and dislikes were on a par. Things seemed to click when they were

177

together. The only thing to do was to get rid of Doreen, but how? That was the question.

'We could always up sticks and go and live somewhere else.' He said. Doreen was a creature of habit, he'd watch her for the next few days and surely he could think of a way.

It only took him three days to get the idea and he prayed that it would work. A packet of that 'paraquat' weed killer from the garden centre where he worked, that could do the trick. He had access to those sort of things and nobody would notice if he went about it carefully.

'I've packed your lunch. Don't forget I want to get down to the supermarket straight after we've had our dinner tonight so don't be late,' she said.

'I'll try not to be late, especially Fridays, I might go down the club for a pint while you watch your bloody Coronation Street.'

'No need to swear, I get a lot of enjoyment watching that,' she replied.

Tony looked at his watch, he had just made his last delivery from his garden centre van. Time now to nip home and put his plan to work.

The first snag came as he drew to the end of the street where he lived, Reg Birstall his next door neighbour was out leaning on the front door jamb.

Tony pulled a little further along the road and parked by the rear alley. 'Hope I don't meet anyone I know,' He thought.

Down the passage and into the small backyard, so far so good. He let himself in through the back door and crossed immediately to the kitchen worktop. As he thought, one mug, tea-bag already placed in the bottom waiting so that when she came in it would be straight on with the kettle so it boiled whilst she changed out of her overall.

Tony lifted the tea-bag out of the mug, placing it on a piece of kitchen towel he gently slit the tea-bag open with a razor blade. Gingerly he fed the paraquat into the bag and superglued the edges together. Making sure he had disturbed nothing he quickly replaced everything and let himself out of the house.

Half way down the passage he started to have reservations, 'I'm not that kind of animal,' he thought. Then his thoughts went to what it would be like to have a life with Heather. By the time his mind had settled down and before he realized it he was parking the van in the garden centre car-park.

Heather and Doreen sat opposite each other in the factory canteen.

'These chips taste funny to me,' said Heather.

Doreen didn't reply, her mind seemed to be on other things.

'Will you come in for a chin wag when we get home? She asked.

'Why?' Came Heather's response.

'I've been thinking, I want to change, I think I want to start a family. Tony has always wanted kids, but it's been me who hasn't fancied the idea. I've been a bit of a stick in the mud. I must change for his sake. What do you say, will you pop in?' She asked.

'Don't know why you're asking me, I'm six years younger than you and I've no experience with that sort of thing,' replied Heather.

She thought of what Tony had said about moving and starting a new life together.

'You've got a lovely figure, you know how to use make up and you look lovely when you dress to go out. You can probably give me some tips on how to transform myself for Tony's sake.'

'Alright, but I can't stay long.' She knew Tony would be round as soon as Coronation Street started and she wanted to know what would have been said.

For the rest of the day Tony was on tenterhooks, he had two near misses in traffic. His mind had not been on his driving. Several other drivers had leaned out of their car windows questioning his ability to drive and the doubts to his mental state and his parentage.

He inserted the key and opened the front door quietly.

'Hallo love, had a busy day?' The voice came from the stairs.

He looked up to see Doreen descending.

'What's the matter?' She said. 'It looks as if you've seen a ghost.'

Tony's mind flew in tangents firing questions and trying to answer them at the same time.

'Bloody hassle I've had with deliveries and I've got guts ache,' he responded hastily.

'Go and sit down I'll get you a cuppa,' she ordered.

Tony sat down in a lounge chair, his mind all awash, different images coursing in and out.

Doreen gabbled on, talking to the kitchen wall as she prepared the evening meal. Tony wasn't really listening, until she came into the lounge.

'There must be a bug going around, Heather came in for a chat and a cuppa when we finished work. She wasn't here long, I had to take her home. She said she felt really poorly, it's a good job she only lives a couple of doors away, I

179

don't think I could have coped. It was either them chips she had at work, or it could have been the coffee we had when we came in. I had one too, it made a change from tea. No it couldn't have been the coffee otherwise I'd have been bad as well.'

Tony looked wild eyed into the empty mug he was holding, he had just finished the remains of the tea. It was then he started to sweat, the restrictions in his chest beginning to take control of his breathing. The light from the lounge window was beginning to dim.

It was a week later. Doreen being supported by her brother on one side and Heather on the other. The funeral had been a simple affair, the death certificate had said cardiac arrest, in other words heart attack.

The vicar sprinkled earth on to the lowered coffin and was finishing his mandatory eulogy.

'It could have been so different if he'd lived,' sobbed Doreen.

'I know what you mean,' thought Heather staring into space.

Return Journey

by

Mary Park

Last Winter I fell wildly, deeply, recklessly in love. Not with my husband, who is my dearest friend. No, I had left George standing at the baggage retrieval rotunda at Gatwick Airport. He awaited our cases with his usual quiet patience, while I went off in search of a luggage trolley.

It always seems that our bags are twice as heavy at the end of a holiday, even though the sun oil and shampoo is all used up and the bottles discarded. Perhaps it is the heavy heart, dreading the return to tedium and dullness, that makes the weight seem to increase.

It was late at night. The airport teemed with tired, heavily-laden travellers. The trolleys were all in use and I had to search high and low until I found one. I seized it triumphantly and guided it in the direction of my George. I could just see his head above the crowds. He was watching the long stream of suitcases snaking their way around the hall: each of the passengers poised, heron-like, waiting to snatch away their prize.

I was aware of being watched. As I slowly wheeled the trolley towards the crowd, I felt a gaze burning into me. I turned and the most amazingly handsome man I have ever seen was moving slowly towards me. Our eyes met and he greeted me with a shy half-smile.

His eyes were glistening, smouldering black like those of an Indian Prince. He reminded me a little of Omar Sharif when he was a younger man. His hair was thick and black, swept back away from his face. His skin was creamy and golden. His lips parted ever so slightly as he smiled. The flash of his teeth as he smiled, took my breath away.

He was tall, nearly as tall as George, though some twenty years younger, I guessed. He was wearing a calf-length creamy-tan cashmere coat. He seemed to glide towards me rather than walk. As he moved, the coat floated around him and I could see that his suit was expensively cut, French-looking.

It seemed impossible he should single me out in the crowd - but his face was searching mine, as if he sought some kind of reaction.

I was lost in his gaze, swept up in his nearness. I could only smile gently, reassuringly back at him.

He was coming for me, bearing down on me and I knew that I ought to be strong. I should thrust him aside and shout: 'No! I love George. I am a married woman. Be off with you!'

But he was coming for me, to sweep me into his arms and carry me off, I knew it. I didn't know where and I didn't care. I would go with him to the ends of the earth, leaving husband, family and home just a past and distant memory and I would never give them a second thought. My prince had come!

My expression changed with this realization, to a knowing, intuitive welcome and I closed my eyes as I leaned forward, for his kiss to warm my cheek. The time for passion could wait until we were alone.

Just then, at that wondrous, breath-taking, exquisite moment I heard a voice say:

'Where do you get those trolleys?'

I opened my eyes to glare at the interloper, intruding in this most magical moment of my entire life. But no-one else was there. We were isolated. Alone. Two islands in a sea of moving bodies, blissfully unaware of the occasion.

The voice was coming from my own Sweet Prince. I stared at him, puzzled. Try as I might, I could not connect the words to the moment. They seemed so remote, out of context. What could they mean? For what seemed like hours I puzzled the possibilities around in my head. He smiled with a tolerant - playful smile as I gradually re-emerged into the world around me.

He leaned towards me, repeating the words. His voice was as silken as the fabric of his suit.

'Where..., ' he asked, in the softest tones, '...where do you get those trolleys?'

'Oh... I see... ' I stammered, the words tumbling over themselves on the journey from my mind to my lips. I was in shock. 'You want a trolley, is that it?'

I could not bear to say it, though I knew in my heart it was true.

'Yes,' came his reply.

I did not know whether to laugh or cry. How could I return to my poor George, whom I had, in my heart, betrayed so bitterly. I felt as if I had spent a lifetime in this beautiful man's embrace. I was sure I could confide in him and I found myself confessing:

'I thought for one moment you were going... to take me away from all this.'

He started to laugh and then stopped in an instant, when he saw the pain in my eyes.

'I'm sorry,' he said, 'I just need a trolley.'

I felt a blush, flooding my face and the funny side of my tragic situation suddenly hit me. We both erupted into giggles.

'You're sure?' I said.

'Yes, I'm sorry. My cases are over there; look,' and he pointed to a half-dozen matching cases stacked neatly by the door. He was grinning now and I punched him playfully.

'Here,' I said, 'you'd better take mine.' I stood watching him as he wheeled it away into the night.

I searched around, found another and rejoined George. I was sure he would see the shame I felt. I had let him down so badly, but he was only pleased to see me, as ever. He deserves so much better than me.

I never told George why I had taken so long with the trolley. I never mentioned the handsome stranger. I have broken his heart many times in our years together, with a thoughtless word, an irritable jibe. His tender heart is easily bruised, it would be cruel to do it knowingly.

We drove home, the light rain smearing the windscreen and the wipers squeaking as they ran out of moisture to ease their path. I was glad of the dark.

Dead Lucky

by

Janette Osang

Sarah was always the lucky one. Sarah is my younger sister by eighteen months, all her life things have fallen into place without effort. She's the one you can see by the trees with the (naturally) blonde hair casually falling over her face as she cries. She even cries beautifully. Me, if I cry, I get red, swollen eyes and look terrible - not a pretty sight on a wet Sunday morning I can tell you. But then, that's Sarah. Lucky. Let me explain.

When we were small children, we were given the choice of guinea-pigs for pets. I chose a handsome brute with thick glossy chestnut colouring, strong and virile. Sarah, because she felt sorry for her, picked the smallest, a tiny brown and white thing that looked as if a strong gust of wind would carry her off. What happened? Alexander (The Great) contracted some awful wasting disease and died only two weeks later. Mopsie (I ask you!) never looked back. She lived to bear countless children - courtesy of next door's pride and joy - until peacefully joining Alexander some seven years on. See what I mean. Lucky.

Father Christmas singled her out it seemed. He went out of his way to give her the gorgeous baby dolls I wanted, the delicate china tea set I coveted in the toy shop window and most of all the frilly night-dress case that I'd have killed for. How I longed for a doll to dress, but all I ever got were colouring books or monopoly sets! All her toys are still in the loft, I saw them the other day when I left. Mine were the ones that seemed to get broken, lost or thrown away. Why did Mother never throw Sarah's away? I suppose some of her things must be quite valuable now, as curios.

The seeds we both planted as budding Percy Throwers, ran true to form. Hers inevitably came up in abundance, growing on to cause comment and admiration from visitors. Mine made spasmodic appearances, finally rotting as if the effort of germination was too much for them. Her sunflowers were always two feet taller than mine, her cress, thicker, more tasty. Even the apple pips from the same apple we potted, favoured Sarah. Mine, still growing admittedly, is a spindly cankerous specimen with the odd leaf here and there. Hers, a fine bushy tree, bore fruit within three years! Lucky!

As we grew older and reached adolescence, my sister sailed through with nary a spot to her face. I didn't dare go out the house for fear of being labelled a plague carrier! She didn't go through the agonising self doubt, the Who Am I? What Do I Want? Stage. She didn't have to suffer the platitudes of: 'It's only puppy fat, dear, you'll grow out of it.' I never grew out of anything. Sarah's hair always shone with health, never seeming greasy or out of place. Mother said it was because Sarah took more care, ate the right things, exercised. I called it luck.

When it came to end of term reports, I'll admit, luck didn't really come into it. I was never much good at sitting still and concentrating. I wanted to be outside, climbing trees, looking for frog spawn, throwing stones in the pond. Sarah was a natural for study, she adored learning, excelling at English and History. Boring I reckoned, who wants to know about the past when the future is much more exciting.

Taking exams was an even more separating time. I could never learn more than a token amount of any one subject. Typically, the bits I did know didn't ever come up in the exam. I was very unlucky. I failed every exam I took at school, except Art (all those colouring books had made their mark you see). Sarah, on the other hand, apparently had access to the papers, for the subjects she revised all came up. She passed everything. Lucky.

You might think, by all this griping that I dislike my sister. Not so. I love her dearly, she is so pretty and so good. Look, you can see her hair better now that she has stood up, see how pretty she is? Her eyes are stunning don't you think? If I'd had eyes like that I'd have stopped eating long ago. Lucky old Sarah, she hasn't a sweet tooth in her head, so her figure, as you can see, is still as trim as when we were young. Looking at my revolting body, I don't wonder they've all been so concerned lately.

You see, all my life I've had to fight my craving for chocolate, in all forms, but mainly boxes. Boxes and boxes. I was very careful not to actually let anyone know how many I'd eaten. How I prayed for the strength to stop even as I was opening the next box. It's funny though, after all this time, I have finally overcome my desire to eat constantly. Sarah, of course, is one of those irritating people who can make a box last for a couple of months, taking one every now and then. I hated her for that and longed to scoff hers as well, but my severely depleted pride hadn't sunk quite that low.

That man there, the one with the black suit and red socks with his arm round Sarah. He's Alan, Sarah's husband. He used to take me out, before he met Sarah that is. I didn't like him much anyway. Although in all fairness, he has made

Sarah a good husband. He still cherishes her, relieves her of the more sordid details of life, like bills. They live comfortably, not sumptuous luxury you understand, but comfortable. I have been staying there myself until recently.

I never married, you know. Never seemed to meet anyone. Sarah was forever surrounded by fresh faced young men, eager to have the privilege of taking her out. I usually ended up making a four with her current boyfriend's best mate. Whilst Sarah and John, or Trevor, or Mark canoodled, giggling in the back row of the cinema, Norman, or Gerald or Julian and I would sit silently eating peanuts as dutiful chaperones. Mother would have had a fit if she'd known. She thought I was the flighty one, Sarah could do no wrong.

She was even lucky when we took our driving tests. We took them on the same day, when I was nineteen and she just over seventeen. Her examiner was a young, good looking bachelor, anxious to please. Dishy? You've not seen anything like it! Mine was a crusty old curmudgeon, ninety, if a day, who thought that women shouldn't be allowed - at all, let alone on the roads. I failed. She passed. Lucky.

Consequently, Sarah could always find a parking spot in the busiest of places. I used to travel with her whenever I could for that reason. The car parks I went in (when I did finally pass my test - at the fourth attempt) were always full, or I hadn't the correct change for those rotten machines. Besides, people were forever giving Sarah their unexpired portion of tickets, it was much easier shopping with Sarah!

We used to meet for coffee every Friday, when I was well. Whoever got there last, paid. Needless to say, I paid most of the time, if Sarah had to on the odd occasion, it was odds on that she would meet an old flame who would offer to pay instead. It was like that, shopping with Sarah, people would open doors for her. I think I must have been invisible. Even if I was right behind, the door closed in my face. One day, my luck would change, of that I was certain.

If we both sent back faulty goods to the manufacturers, I'd get an, albeit polite, letter apologising for my inconvenience and the postage refunded. Sarah would get an invitation to visit the works and innumerable free samples. That's how it is, Sarah is lucky.

Even today, of all days, when I should be uppermost in people's minds, I can say with total certainty, that it will be Sarah they will be concerned for. I don't begrudge her, she is a good sister, willing to help out whenever things got rough. Why, she was the first to offer me a bed when I was ill, even though it meant she and Alan had to sleep on the sofa-bed.

Watch all those people milling about outside, gawping. They're only here out of curiosity. The local newspaper reporter is hiding behind the old split oak, see? I suppose it's fair enough, it's not every day the village had a notable happening. They are all wondering how on earth Sarah is going to manage. The man looking glum with the tatty briefcase, he's the family solicitor. He came to see me yesterday. I was overjoyed. You see, Great Aunt Amy has died at last. Guess who is next of kin? She left no will, thought she could take it with her, so as her oldest great niece, there being no male issue, as they say, I inherit! Rolling in it I heard. I couldn't believe it, me - Pamela Hartford - rich!

I laughed so much, they got worried and sent for the doctor. I heard them talking in the hall, in low voices, about the risk to my heart. Well, you can understand their worry, I did weigh twenty-two stones at the last count. I was still laughing when it happened. It wasn't nearly as painful as I thought. What? Oh! The heart attack. Sorry, didn't I explain? I died laughing last night, so now Sarah inherits the fortune. I told you she was lucky. Dead lucky!

Just What You've Always Wanted

by

F R Watt

It was a long nerve-racking walk, not helped by the fact that Thomas Rift felt nauseous. The heat on that cramped terminal bus had been stifling, all those sweating bodies squashing him into the corner causing the atmosphere to have an oppressive feel which made his legs physically tremble. Then panic had brought about the irrational thought that the fat man standing next to him would roll over onto him forcing the air from his insignificant body, a fear difficult to dispel in spite of the relief he'd felt when he burst out through the concertina doors as they slowly hissed open, to stumble like a new-born foal onto the runway. The tarmac shimmered in a heat haze as he plodded along finding it impossible to lift his gaze from the almost molten surface; Thomas had no wish to look any of his fellow passengers in the eye let alone make their acquaintance, he burned with the need to carry on with his intentions and yet took no pleasure from them. Climbing the steps to the aeroplane was horrendous; his legs felt numb, almost redundant, as he willed them on; scaling a mountain couldn't possibly have been harder. Then when he reached the top thinking the worst was over, Thomas came face to face with the stewardess, almost crying when he looked at her young beautiful face, innocent of all the wrongs he'd been dealt throughout his life.

Moving slowly along the aisle, trying desperately to avoid eye contact with the passengers already seated, Thomas Rift was causing an effect opposite to that which he desired. Almost without exception everyone on the plane had noticed the timid little man whose gaunt face jerked constantly around, only surpassed for activity by his squirrel-like eyes flicking from one inanimate object to another. At last he was in his seat, his pulse beginning to ease, its racy pace almost dropping to a normal rate when suddenly a sickening feeling of guilt sent it rampaging up again as his gaze came to a shuddering halt.

She confronted him, freckles lightly scattered over her nose before disappearing in a gradual way around the contours of her shiny pink cheeks. Lauren's almost perfect smile was made only more engaging by its flaw; the black hole located in the centre of otherwise straight gleaming teeth gave the five year old girl a look which promised to melt the heart of any casual observer - it was impossible to see that smile without feeling the urge to protect her from a cruel and uncertain world. Thomas fought down that urge which threatened to send him running hysterically towards the flight deck in search of the Captain. He closed his eyes and willed the girl to stop leaning over the back of her seat. It was too late now, the dye was cast. The timer was set and out of his reach, by now it was sealed in the cargo hold. It was difficult but he focused his mind on the reasons for this once in a lifetime extravagant gesture.

Thomas was the man who people talked around, looked over and failed to hear but at least they would notice him die. They wouldn't be able to ignore that! The aeroplane roared into life, its movement sudden and vigorous as it careered down the runway to lift majestically into the air. Apart from a general chit-chat everything was quiet and he tried to sense if the girl was still there, but his head was pulsating making it difficult to concentrate as the constant tension began to take its toll. God, he needed a whisky! But that would involve ringing for the stewardess, a thing which would have defied Thomas's courage under normal circumstances let alone with him possessing the knowledge that in two hours time a bomb, which he'd planted, would go off killing every man, woman and child aboard. Oh no! His thoughts went back to the girl, his eyes opening before he could stop them. She was still there!

Lauren looked at the funny man and came to the conclusion that he was scared of flying. She thought this was a little bit strange for a grown man, after all she was only five and not at all scared, even though her daddy had warned her that she might be. Well, there was only one thing for it, she would have to explain to him how it was only like being on a bus, just as daddy had told her. Of course, Lauren knew it wasn't at all like that but that didn't seem to matter.

Everything had gone blank; Thomas could see the girl's mouth moving but he couldn't make out what she was saying, all he could hear was a buzzing. He was so hot it felt as if someone had built a fire in his stomach. The aeroplane walls seemed to be closing in on the periphery of his focus, forcing him to look at the girl with tunnel vision. He was no longer able to lower his eyelids. Then it began to register that the girl was acknowledging him. Wasn't that what he'd wanted? To be involved, brought in from the outside and accepted? Suddenly she was snatched away from the seat by her father and tucked into the corner by his legs. That wasn't fair, he hadn't done anything to her and never would have, what were they implying? Were they trying to make out that he was some kind of pervert? He almost cringed at the thought as tears filled his eyes. Then the scene began to unfold in front of Thomas - it hadn't been him at all. The plane was being hijacked!

It was ludicrous but, although Thomas had planned suicide, he now found himself absolutely terrified as the Mediterranean looking man came storming up the aisle, pistol in hand, occasionally crashing the butt into a passenger's head on the way. As the hijacker passed him by Thomas Rift quickly but fully analysed for the first time why he was on this plane. His own actions, although more subtle, were no different than this sadist, as he callously went about beating up defenceless people. He'd always avoided thinking about the consequences of his actions in favour of that strange dream world in which he went out in a blaze of publicity, never again to be forgotten.

The female hijacker stood with the barrel of her gun only inches away from the Captain's head, the pretty stewardess who had caused Thomas so much anguish lay in a crumpled heap by the cabin door, her unconscious body deliberately dumped there in order to prevent anyone gaining entrance to the flight deck. The hijacker's accomplice back in the passenger section of the plane had stopped hitting people and was informing them with a ridiculously over dramatic performance that, should anyone manage to overpower him, his partner would instantly kill the pilot. Almost as if it were taken from a sketch, some low budget sit-com, on ending his speech the hijacker instantly returned to hitting and kicking passengers while shouting incomprehensible threats at them in a foreign language. Spanish - Thomas recognised it immediately - as the terrorist came menacingly towards him. This was it, the only time in his life he hadn't wanted to be noticed! Then to his surprise and the father's absolute horror Lauren stepped out in front of the gun-wielding madman to be kicked aside like a rag doll. Lauren watched through tear glazed eyes as the gun fell in a wide arc knocking her father to the floor, then there was pain as a back-hand stung the side of her face almost rendering her senseless. This was too much for Thomas; without conscious thought he leapt up, catching the hijacker with his right fist under the chin. The blow was more surprising than painful but the terrorist hesitated long enough for the other passengers to grab him and wrestle him to the ground.

They stood around looking accusingly at Thomas - what had been an heroic act could result in them losing their lives. He tried the handle; it was no good, the door wouldn't move. From the flight deck came a foreign voice asking what he wanted. Thomas replied, also in Spanish, that he needed covering while he used the toilet.

She opened the door to be confronted by an insipid looking young man pointing a hand gun at her face. She let the gun slip slowly through her fingers made numb with fear, then raised her hands nervously in a gesture of submission.

190

Now that the plane had turned around and landed Thomas was getting more attention than he could ever have hoped for. He was a hero surrounded by adoring pressmen and television people, all eager for a word from the man who had saved an aeroplane full to capacity with passengers. Then without warning a big man stepped through the crowd, took hold of Thomas's arm and marched him towards a room marked 'Private'. As they passed through the doorway the man was saying something about anti-terrorist squad and wanting a word about Mr Rift's suitcase. Thomas's knees gave way beneath him. In the excitement he had forgotten all about the bomb!

The Kids who Rent are Having a Party

by

Candyce Lange

It's late Saturday afternoon at the seaside. At the kitchen window I stand on tip-toe, pretending to look over our fence out at the sea, but really I'm spying on our neighbouring chalet. I'm watching the kids next door getting ready to party. She's up on a chair, twisting crepe paper. He's blowing up a balloon. Silhouettes preparing to celebrate. I know them by now, the end of the summer. He washes his own clothes and hangs them out to dry. And I've wondered why she doesn't tell him to hang his T-shirts upside down because clothes pins make marks in the shoulders.

Where's the other girl? The one who owns the car, whose short hair - when she dances by herself - moves with her. Constant music from over there, just the right side of politeness. And once in a while they play the Pink Floyd and I imagine I hear the boy's mock-DJ voice: *This one's for the old folks next door.*

The hottest hours are over; this is our favourite time of day. Outside, you're twisting up newspaper for the barbecue, gathering bits of wood. I finish washing the lettuce and wrap it in a towel. Our friends think we own two sets of everything, but we don't have a lettuce twirler. It's on a list somewhere, but very low. It's the kind of thing you don't think about when you're swimming laps in the pool or walking on the beach at midnight. And there are so many more important things to think about: electricity bills, insurance, mortgage payments. Plural.

I sigh and go outside to tilt the umbrella, wipe off the table. You've just oiled the lock on the front gate, now you're whistling, wandering around with the oil can: What else can you make work more smoothly?

I sit down and watch the butterflies and feel like a tourist. 'They spend more time here than I do,' I say.

You grin, not at me exactly, as you build a tidy little fire in the barbecue, so I sit with our statue, she's as naked as anything and dips her feet in a little pool. It's my job to make sure the birds have water and sometimes I chill the wine in there as well.

We dress for dinner. Inside our high fence, we wear what we like. You in your old track suit, with a hole in the bum. I'm in a pair of second-hand striped men's pyjamas, which I bought in town for a song. Someone, sometime, scrawled on the label in indelible ink: *S Crow,* so we call them *'the Scare-crows'*. I like our language and the way we talk in code: it's a bonus of marriage I didn't expect.

We sit for a long time before we light the fire; the summer goes so fast, we like to stretch out the evenings. Then we settle down to wait for the slow hot coals, that's what we want. I count the cobwebs on our statue and pour the sherry which I buy from a big keg at the post office.

Next door the music gets louder, then softer.

'Maybe they'll invite us.'

You laugh.

So we sit and stare at the ground we own; the weeds grow so fast and my problem is I take them personally. You're going to get the Strimmer out first thing in the morning. And I know you mean it: you have so much energy up here, or is it that you don't want to waste a minute. And I start thinking about the uncivilised work week we have and I remember what my father said when he retired. *They should change it around,* he said. *Have more fun while you're young and go to work when you're old.* And for a moment, I wonder what happened to those carefree days when I just paid rent and took more chances? And for a moment, standing there in my striped pyjamas, I'm a prisoner and this property is my ball and chain. Then I remember those old movies where the men doing time refuse to see their wives on visiting day - it only makes them want what they can't have.

'Hey,' you say, bringing me back. 'This party won't start until midnight. Hear the car? They're going to the pub first.' And you look happy, throwing the chicken on the grate, helping yourself to a scoop of potato salad.

Dinner tastes wonderful and lasts for hours and the wine relaxes us. I know we're going to sleep like children tonight. We sit on the bench together, our thighs touching. We talk about whatever comes into our minds: we catch up with each other.

Then you say, 'I almost forgot. A present for dessert.' And out of your pocket you take a little flat package.

'What is it?'

'Tattoos. Temporary. Look, Hollywood Style. Matching birds. Bluebirds of happiness.'

Maybe they're Birdseye 'birds of freedom', I want to say, but I don't. Don't want to break the mood.

Matching. It's a private joke because we don't have matching wedding rings. Well, I'd been my usual impatient self, bought what I wanted out of the Argos catalogue - and then when you ordered your hand-made ring with three kinds of gold, I wanted one like that, too. Only you'd laughed and said, 'No, you already made your choice.' So now we have other things that match: hats, and reading lamps over the bed, and chocolate bars side by side in the refrigerator. Which we don't eat very often, but we like to know they're there.

When it's time to go in, we pile everything back on the tray, take it in and dump it on the kitchen counter and make our usual remark about hoping the maid shows up before morning. Then we turn off the light, but neither of us can resist a last look at the kids' chalet. They've left a light on, so the room welcomes them back: the red lampshade with streamers dangling from it, and on the bookcase the greeting cards all in a row - and I think, how I always enjoy the day *after* my birthday more, you don't expect so much. And I think how strange life is: you never see the room waiting to be entered, you never see yourself the way other people see you.

I say, 'I was looking at the word 'mortgage' in the paper today. Really looking at it and remembering how it used to be a scary grown-up word. Today, I took it apart, syllable by syllable; I thought about gauging death, death gauges. Little coffee spoons of life like T S Elliot.'

'What else?'

'Manslaughter is the same as man's laughter.'

'Is it?'

'Same letters.'

I'm staring into the kids' living room and I can't help remembering all those parties in the Sixties, all those mornings waking up with people who didn't even know me. And what I hated most was that everyone said those were the best years of my life. I was afraid they might be right.

Then you touch my arm. 'Come on, I want to search for a good place for a tattoo.'

When I lived at home, my father had a rule: We spent Sundays with the family at home. As we walk to the bedroom I think: That's what making love with your husband is like.

Out in the garden old coals smoulder.

Mr Talbot's Roses

by

Jonathan Magee

Mr Talbot had never looked happier as he passed through the doors of Newman's News. His eyes were bright, his face fresh. A bell sounded as the door opened before him.

'Hallo Mr Talbot.' The rosy faced shopkeeper said as Mr Talbot walked up to the small tidy counter.

'And greetings to you Mr Newman.' Both men exchanged informal handshakes. Mr Talbot, local MP, passed an appraising eye past Mr Newman to the shelf that stocked boxes of finely decorated chocolates.

'Something for the wife Mr Talbot?' The rounded proprietor asked. Looking back, Mr Talbot nodded.

'I thought something a little bit special tonight Mr Newman, maybe something a little bit more expensive,' he returned, and Mr Newman smiled, clasping his hands together. He raised his spectacles to his eyes, turned and pulled across a low step ladder from his side. He climbed up, taking several boxes from the top shelf. He brought them down and placed them on the counter. Pushing a box toward Mr Talbot, he smiled again.

'Now, if it's a good price you're interested in, then you've got to be looking at yer Imperials.' He described their various soft and hard centres, then proceeded with several other boxes, different shapes and sizes. Of them all, Mr Talbot seemed particularly impressed with the Strawberry Petals. Mr Newman sighed in delighted agreement.

'Now, with yer Petals,' he said, 'you've got a good selection of fruit flavoured centres, leaning strongly towards, yer soft centres and yer strawberry creams.' Analysis passed he left a pause in which Mr Talbot interjected.

'Most agreeable Mr Newman, my wife does have rather a 'soft' spot for the cream centres.'

Mr Newman laughed politely and Mr Talbot took his wallet from his coat pocket.

'Very good Mr Talbot, now if you're in agreement with my prognosis, I think you'll find them a very reasonable price.'

Mr Talbot nodded and took notes from his wallet, inquisitively.

'That will be fifteen pounds please Mr Talbot.' As Mr Newman spoke he put the box in a brown paper bag.

Mr Talbot handed over two ten pound notes.

'And buy something for yourself Mr Newman.' Mr Talbot concluded as he turned away.

'Thank you very much Mr Talbot.'

The door closed and Mr Newman placed the money in the till.

Mr Talbot walked happily down the road whistling. He nodded at passing friends and waved at people he knew across the road. He opened the florists door and inhaled deeply. The fragrant aromas filled his head making him feel pleasantly light. A young girl stood back from where she arranged flowers to smile at him. He returned the gesture.

'How can I help you today Mr Talbot?' She asked.

'The usual please Laura,' he returned, the young girl laughed.

'You old romantic, I think it's great that you are still so happy after all these years.' She produced a dozen red roses from beneath the till.

'How is Mrs Talbot?' She asked with a sly wink.

'She is a little tied up at the moment, house work dragging her down a little.'

She smiled and saw the package under his arm. She inquired after it and he answered light-heartedly.

'She's a little gem, Mrs Talbot.' He concluded, there was a proud glint in his eye as he left.

'She works hard, so hard, it's as if you have to tie her down to keep her still these days.' He called back, voice full of concern for his beloved wife. He closed the door, sun bright and alluring in his eyes.

He walked home stopping only at the chemists on the way, as he left he waved goodbye to Mrs Harris, walking her dog on the pavement opposite. She waved back. Nelson barked.

As evening fell, Mr Talbot had dressed in his best suit and had his car keys in hand. He had explained to his wife that he was going out for dinner and explained that in her weakened state it was impractical for her to escort him. He had kissed her goodbye on her cheek, tucked her in and had propped her back comfortably against two pillows. He had felt sad as he walked down the stairs. Placing his wallet in his jacket he opened the door. Just before he left he picked up the flowers he had hidden behind the sofa, he tucked them beneath his jacket.

He drove into the darkness, flowers in the back seat. Parking the car down a dark back alley, he proceeded to cross the dimly lit road and walked along the uneven pavement, then the heavens opened. He pulled up his collar, pushing his hat over his eyes.

The woman stood by the corner, shivering, wet and cold. As they met, they embraced, alone in the silent darkness, their soft words inaudible against the rain swept night. They walked briskly through the park, together, arm in arm, then as they met the cover of a tree's wide branches they stopped.

Ice had formed thinly on the still lake, channels of dark water separated smooth edged shards of cool white. For a while they stood talking together, in oblivious stillness, moonlit lovers. The rain fell painlessly upon them, silhouettes blissfully undaunted by the pelting water. She smiled shyly into his eyes, no more than a girl, he kissed her. He pulled the flowers from his jacket like a cheap magician and she took them with a smile. Her eyes were bright blue, softly damp. Her smile was a heartfelt plea, in desperate, abundant love for this older, wiser man, so unlike any she had ever met. He beckoned to her to take their rich scent and she did so. Her lips rich and alive, she went to kiss a petal in gesture. Her lips touched the flowers and the powerful spray he had added took control, she fell helplessly into his arms. He pulled her tight, moving her frail body into the bushes, tenderly he removed her clothes. She moaned to his body movement, but in weak pain. He kissed her soft lips and explored her soft young flesh. Kissing every inch of forbidden skin. He was gentle and kind, with experience against her own fragile virginity. She was limp and her eyes struggled to focus upon her assailant, her muscles in hopeless resistance.

When he had finished, he pulled the knife from his pocket and cut her slowly, clinically precise, from neck to between her legs, one long, deep incision. She tried to scream, her voice weak, fading completely in stuttering gasps, as the knife made deeper penetration. In the morning the police would find the body free of organs and drained, almost totally, of blood.

He walked slowly to the lake and washed his hands and face in the still, cold waters, separating panes of ice. Taking the flowers he threw them to the still dark waters, finding a gap between the ice. He was surprised when they sunk slowly beneath the surface and turning, he walked from the scene.

Climbing the park gate he dropped to the path below. Before entering his car he removed his jacket and blood stained tie from his collar. He inspected his shirt and removed it, he straightened the replica beneath. Brushing a leaf from his trousers he started the engine.

He dropped his keys on the table, leaving his shoes on the mat. Hanging up his coat he walked up the stairs. He opened the bedroom door, his wife laying still, breathing softly. He picked up the chocolates from the bedside table.

'You haven't touched them.' He said softly, pulling the tape from across her lips. She tried to scream but he pushed a chocolate deep into her mouth, followed by another and another. So as she wouldn't spit them out, he placed a hand over her mouth between insertions. She struggled weakly against the leather straps. There was a knock at the door.

He smiled and walked down the stairs. He straightened his collar before opening the door.

'Hallo, Mrs Brindle.' He said to the stout woman who stood in the doorway. She smiled.

'I just wondered how Mrs Talbot was, Mr Talbot.'

He invited her inside, climbing the stairs, beckoning her to follow.

'I think she's awake, but she really isn't much better.' he replied.

They entered the room together. Mrs Talbot lay still on the bed, her eyes closed, her chest heaving slowly.

'Well, she seems to have fallen asleep.' He said, concern in his voice, he looked at the chocolate that had fallen on the carpet from her outstretched hand.

'Oh dear.' He said picking it up, placing it on the bedside table.

'You really should call the doctor Mr Talbot.' She said with a kind smile.

'Yes,' he replied, 'I will in the morning.' He looked at her, she looked worried and he held her hand.

'Would you like a chocolate Mrs Brindle?' He asked handing her the box.

Bird Love

by

Isabel Empson

There are six of us. The only survivors. The only humans to be left on earth maybe. Six of us. Me, the wife, her two sons, my daughter and one lad's girl-friend. That's it. The lot!

What happened? Nineteen-ninety-three. That's what happened. The end of society. We shouldn't have been surprised really. After Aids, blue pig disease, salmonella in hens and mad cow disease it came as no great shock when the birds started dying of Black-bird disease. But no-one could foresee the conse-quences then, how important those birds really were.

It started last year - nineteen-ninety-three - mid May. According to the BBC news, some kid first spotted half a dozen dead blackbirds on the drive as she left for school. By lunch time the whole playground was covered in dead birds. Dead sparrows, starlings, robins, thrushes and finches. You name them. There they were. By the end of the week the whole country reported dead birds in thousands. By mid June there were no birds to be seen anywhere in Britain. It was eerie waking up in the morning to no dawn chorus. But they were only birds. Nothing too serious. Until the cats started dying! Scientists soon linked the two viruses. Birds had Black-bird. Cats ate birds. Bingo - cats got Black-bird too. It seemed to end there though. No further animals or humans were af-fected.

It was hot and humid in July. Hot, sweaty and itchy! Insects, aphids, flies and caterpillars swarmed everywhere. No birds to eat them. The market gardeners and farmers shouted the loudest. Insecticides couldn't cope with those swarms. The bugs stripped all the crops. Cows got madder. Pigs got bluer. The sale of eggs was banned - that's if you could find any - there weren't many hens or ducks left. The coalition government appealed for food aid for Britain. We got it. Parachuted in. We also got put in quarantine. A whole bloody country in quarantine. That's politics for you. Any bloody excuse!

Overseas trade ceased. The country went into a deep recession. High interest rates. Redundancies everywhere. Families homeless - couldn't pay the mort-gage. The banks refused credit. Loans were called in, so businesses crashed. Unemployment benefit ceased. The social services went down under the strain.

Then the banks collapsed. There were no jobs. Money was useless. Food tickets became the new currency.

Food was distributed from the banks by security guards to ticket holders only. Food tickets were obtained from Town Halls and issued to council tax payers only. Tough on the rest! Supermarkets were empty raided weeks ago. Whole towns queued for food. People standing for hours in apathy. Risking being mugged for a carrier bag of food. Dogs, horses and even rats disappeared as people became more hungry. In the country there was a little more variety. The odd deer, fox, badger and hare to eke out the rabbit to feed a starving family.

In October the oil ran out. There was no more petrol or diesel, so no transport. Crowds stormed parliament. The few MP's remaining in government fled for their lives. Then the electricity was cut off. No TV. No radio. No 'phone. No computers. No schools. No hospitals. No public services. Violence and suicides became the norm. Trees were felled for firewood. Open fires were used to cook the meagre rations. Candles were used for light. Although road accidents ceased almost overnight, there was a huge increase in fire accidents. Houses burned and no fire brigade came to help. The sick and elderly died first. Helpless, hopeless and hungry.

In January the food aid stopped. People fled from the towns, invading the countryside in spite of the snow and ice. They grabbed whatever still grew wild to eat - mainly grass. Others tried to flee the country. Rumours came back as fast as they did. No-one would have them. The birds were dying in other countries too by now.

February. We had to get out. Stay and we'd freeze and starve. There had to be somewhere better than here. We had to do something - anything! When we stumbled across a human barbecue the reeking smell of burning flesh combined with the mad shrieks of the hungry dancing once-human animals forced our decision. Our last hoarded provisions were hidden on our boat, a thirty-six foot yacht. A few tins of milk, stew and veg. Some damp flour, sugar and tea. A bag of moulding potatoes plus fifty gallons of fresh-ish water. No diesel so no engine.

We sailed from Plymouth on the second of March. Straight into a storm. The wind hurled itself on us from the North-East. We ran before it out into the Atlantic. The kids were scared. So were the wife and I. Had we only escaped the cold and hunger to be drowned? For five days we ran under bare poles, battened down below. Praying. Five heaving, lumping, sicky days and nights. At last the wind and rain died down. The seas calmed. The sun shone. And we saw a bird. We did! A real, live, flying bloody bird. The wind still dictated our course but we followed that bird.

So, that's how we found this Island. Don't know where we are. There doesn't seem to be anyone else here. Only we six. There's fresh water in plenty. Bananas, Oranges and Avocados grow in abundance. Fish in the sea. We are not cold. We are not hungry. And - we've got birds. Lots and lots of them. We love 'em!

Mr Macey's Peace

by

Nancy Johnson

It was seeing the bonfire in somebody's garden by the park that put the idea into Alfred Macey's head. He was out there for his usual evening stroll and saw the smoke spiralling upwards in a slow, grey coil. A broad grin spread across his wrinkled face. He set off for home again, not too fast because of his asthma, but he couldn't wait to be back and get on with his plan.

His neighbour had died about a year ago and the Graingers had come to live next door. Pleasant, they seemed at first, with two school-age children and both parents out at work. The children weren't noisy, really, only when they kicked a ball around sometimes after tea and only once had the ball come over the fence. Quite polite, they were. But after a couple of months Mr Grainger had a load of wood delivered and some rolls of wire netting, and the banging began.

Mr Macey had lived alone for quite a long time. It was quiet in the house since his wife died and he lived at the end of the street so he wasn't used to a lot of noise. It began on a Saturday morning and by Sunday evening his head was aching and he had retreated to the kitchen which was the furthest point from next door.

As soon as the Graingers left on Monday morning Mr Macey fetched the step-ladder and climbed up to see what was going on. Quite a big structure it seemed, about eight feet high by ten feet and made of good strong wood, but definitely not just a garden shed. In spite of himself Mr Macey was intrigued and kept watch.

The hammering and sawing went on every evening that week and Mr Macey kept himself shut in the kitchen or went out for a walk, dreading the weekend. But by Saturday teatime it was quiet again and he enjoyed Sunday more than usual because of the peace.

On Monday morning he fetched the step-ladder again and stared at the finished work. Wire netting over most of the top and three quarters of one side. A solid wood back and sides and a door big enough for a man to get in. Animals? Mr Macey shuddered. Was he going to have howling animals next to his precious peaceful garden?

One evening bales of straw were delivered and some bulging sacks. By now Mr Macey's nerves were in shreds, dreading the arrival of the animals he expected to prowl up and down on the other side of his fence.

But at last Saturday came and when a van drew up outside the Grainger's house at last Mr Macey knew who were to be the inhabitants of the structure next door.

Budgerigars. It was an aviary.

The birds were brought out of the van in cages and transferred to their new home and Mr Macey breathed a sigh of relief. Tiny things like that, they'd be no bother at all. Now he could live in peace again.

He hadn't reckoned with the straw. Little pieces of it floated on the breeze and got caught in his rose bushes, on his beautifully mown lawn, even in his hair. Then there were the feathers. Very small, they were, like down; blue, green and yellow. He even found one in the kitchen one day. You never knew with feathers, didn't birds have ticks or lice, or some such parasite? He began to be obsessed by feathers, peering everywhere in the house and garden and putting them carefully in the dustbin. It was no good trying to sweep them off the path, he found, they just blew along out of reach of the broom. He had a bath and washed his hair every day now, just in case a feather should touch him.

Worst of all were the sounds the birds made. They twittered all day long, chattering to one another in a never-ending babel of bird-talk. Sometimes they squawked at each other when they got in one another's way or jostled for a place at the food container. Mr Macey could hear the fluttering as they flew from perch to perch, chasing each other, and the constant tapping sounds as they pecked on the wire netting. Then there was the bell. Only a little thing it was, but the high-pitched ting-a-ling caused a jangle of nerves in Mr Macey's head. His days were spent in battling against the straw, the feathers and the incessant sounds from the aviary. In desperation he even thought of moving.

And then he went for his walk by the park to get away from it all and saw the bonfire.

Of course, that was it, he'd have a fire and make a lot of smoke. It was well known that birds soon died where the air was bad.

For several days Mr Macey went to the park and collected bits of wood for his fire. Not too dry, he didn't want flames, it was smoke he wanted. He brought back quite a big branch off a pine tree one day and some damp cones. He mowed his lawn while the grass was slightly damp. And at last he was ready.

Next morning Mr Macey walked quietly across his lawn to begin building his bonfire. The Grainger family would have gone, all he could hear were the birds.

Not for much longer, though, he smiled secretly.

'Morning, Mr Macey, lovely day!'

He jumped visibly as he heard Mr Grainger's hearty voice.

'N-not at work today?'

'Had to take a day off, got a relative's funeral at eleven. 'Often see you looking towards my aviary,' went on Mr Grainger. 'Like to come over and have a look?'

Shakily Mr Macey went round to his neighbour's garden.

'There you are,' said Mr Grainger proudly. Through the wire netting Mr Macey could see about two dozen brightly-coloured budgerigars, some flying around, two tapping the bell and all twittering noisily. He shuddered, hoping Mr Grainger wouldn't notice.

A small green bird clung to the wire netting near Mr Macey, looking towards him and chattering softly.

'That one seems to like you.' said Mr Grainger. 'He's a young one, you can teach them to talk at that age. You can have him if you like, I'll lend you a cage until you can get one.'

'Oh no, I couldn't trouble you,' protested Mr Macey in horror. But somehow he found himself walking home carrying a small cage containing the little green bird, some seed and water. He sat down with his head in his hands, trembling. Should he let it fly away? Or not feed it?

He opened the cage door and at once the bird flew out and sat on his hand. In spite of himself Mr Macey looked at it closely. How pretty the feathers were, the black spots on either side of the beak, the long iridescent tail. He stretched out a tentative finger and touched the tiny head.

'You're a beauty,' he whispered.

In the afternoon Mr Macey went out tapping along cheerfully with his stick and bought a bright, silvery cage. He hesitated over the bell, but finally bought that too.

Beauty seemed very happy and liked sitting on Mr Macey's hand. Sometimes feathers fluttered about and seed husks fell on the carpet, but they were quite easy to clear up. Mr Macey didn't notice the sounds from next door now.

It was very peaceful here, teaching Beauty to talk.

Sweet Sister Sue

by

Meg Thorndick

It all began when Mrs Purdy, housekeeper at Oaklands Hall, gave me the run of young Sir Robert Markham's room. He was away at his prep school, and his widowed mother was staying in her London house.

Dad was the head gardener, and my mum and Mrs Purdy were bosom friends.

Books I found in that room gave me a taste for reading, and helped me win a place at the local grammar school.

This achieved, I began to ponder on how I was going to acquire some money to go with my education. In the 1930's lucrative jobs were hard to find for even well-qualified girls.

One May morning, as I lay on a slope overlooking the lovely Cotswold mansion, the solution flashed into my mind. I would marry Sir Robert and become lady of the manor.

I saw myself graciously presiding over a strawberry and cream tea arranged for the local populace on Oakland's lawns.

I was determined not to end up like my sad-eyed careworn mother, slaving over a kitchen sink and black-leaded range.

She too wanted something different for me and my younger sister Audrey. 'Use your brains to get on in the world, Sue,' she would say.

What a contrast between poor Mum and Beatrice Markham! They were about the same age, but her ladyship looked much younger.

By that time her son had moved on to his public school. As yet he was hardly aware of my existence.

He was destined to inherit the estate when he came of age. His father, Sir William, had died in 1920, just after the boy was born, and a year after my father came to Oaklands.

Local people said that the baby's conception was a miracle, considering the state Sir William was in when he returned from the Great War.

However, Robert was a healthy boy, strongly resembling his handsome mother, and sharing her passion for horse-riding.

Lady Markham's other passion was her lovely garden. She collected plants from all over the world, and gave them into my father's charge.

It wasn't only a love of plants she and Dad had in common. I discovered this on the morning after she'd returned from a trip to South America.

I'd gone looking for Dad to ask if I might pick some strawberries for my birthday tea - I was fifteen that day.

When I reached the potting shed I froze. Through the half-open door I could see my father with his arms around her ladyship.

'I love you, Beatie,' he was saying huskily. 'I've missed you so.' I'd never heard him speak to Mum so tenderly.

I crept away wondering how long the affair had been going on. Lady Markham often took Dad out in her Bentley to visit shows and nurseries. At least, that's where he said they went. She loved driving, and dispensing with the services of her chauffeur on these occasions.

Well, it was their business, so I didn't breathe a word to anyone.

My chance to work on Robert came the next year in his summer holidays. He'd bought a movie camera, and had enlisted the estate families as cast members in the epic he'd dreamed up.

It was when I acted the part of a serving-wench that he really began to notice me. I'd developed a good figure by then, and I made the most of it.

Our relationship progressed quickly. He was delighted to hear that I was aiming for Oxford. My headmistress believed I could win a state scholarship.

I wanted that less than I wanted Robert and Oaklands, but the knowledge that he was going up to Oxford the next year was an incentive.

Until I knew that he was hooked, I was careful to 'guard my honour', to use my mother's quaint expression.

Then one sultry afternoon when the filming was completed he rowed me across to the island in the middle of Oaklands' lake.

'Oh Sue, sweet Sue, how lovely you are!' he murmured as I lay in his arms. There, in a bower of wild roses, I lost my virginity.

Afterwards, I began to run my fingers through his gorgeous black wavy locks.

'What's the matter?' he asked when he heard me gasp.

'Nothing,' I said. Just a twig scratching my side. I'd better get dressed.'

I could hardly tell him I'd just discovered he was probably my half-brother!

For on the top of his scalp was the same raised whorl pattern I'd inherited from my father. I knew it was very rare.

206

I realised then that there were other things that Robert had in common with Dad that I hadn't noticed before. Though his hair, nose and mouth were his mother's, he had Dad's hands and even his walk.

I blew cool after that. I drew the line at incest. Even Oaklands wasn't worth that. Who could tell what little monster I might produce!

There were other fish in the sea. At University there would be hordes of well-heeled young men. I decided to concentrate on my studies for now.

In the event I went to Cambridge. It was my sister Audrey who went to Oxford, not as an undergraduate, but as a student nurse.

That Christmas she came home starry-eyed.

'Who's the lucky bloke?' I asked.

She wouldn't tell me at first. Then she said 'Oh well, I know you used to like him, but I think that's water under the bridge now. You closed up like a clam about it, and I never did discover what went wrong.'

My blood was running cold.

'You mean... you and Robert?'

She nodded. 'I bumped into him in the High the very first week. I've spent so much time with him I'll probably flunk my nursing exams. But I shan't need to work when we're married, shall I.'

'Audrey,' I said. 'I must tell you something.'

'You look very solemn. Is Robert two-timing me?'

'No, it's not that. I think he's our half-brother.'

Then I told her what I'd discovered.

She was startled. Then she laughed and said, 'Well, well!'

'I should have thought it was no laughing matter if you've fallen for him!'

'What colour are my eyes?' she demanded.

'Brown of course, What's that got to do with it?' Have you gone off your rocker?' It must be the shock, I thought.

'No. Fact is - our mother and father couldn't have had a brown-eyed child. It's genetically impossible if both parents have blue eyes.'

'But you were born in this house, you're not adopted.'

'I was Mum's baby all right. But I can't have been Dad's, so Robert's not my half-brother.'

'How do you know you've got it right? About the eye colour, I mean.'

'I read it in a magazine article. Then I checked it out in a book on genetics in the County Library.'

'But you look like Dad!'

'So does Uncle Mike.'

'What?'

'I'm sure he's my real father.'

I remembered then how depressed Mum had been for many months after Dad's brother had emigrated to Canada some years before.

'I wonder how Dad will react to you engagement if he doesn't know you're not his child,' I said.

'I rather think he does. He's never really liked me. Anyway, we're going to keep it secret till Robert comes into the estate.'

'That's sensible,' I said. 'Whatever her own dallying, I don't think Lady Beatrice is going to be happy about her son marrying into the working class.'

As it happened, Dad never did have to lose any sleep over the match. Five months after Audrey's revelation, he and her ladyship were killed in a road accident when returning from the Chelsea Flower Show.

Robert became lord of the manor and married Audrey. To their sorrow, they had no children.

One summer afternoon when I was staying at Oaklands, I persuaded Robert to row me over to the island for old time's sake. Audrey was in London on yet another visit to a gynaecologist.

The boat, which I'd secretly weakened beforehand, capsized, and Robert was drowned. Unlike me, he couldn't swim.

That's why I sit here today, mistress of Oaklands, awaiting my guests for my annual strawberry and cream tea. You see, at Cambridge I'd met and married Sir William Markham's nephew Hugh, his only surviving relative. It's our Golden Wedding this week.

Europe Isn't There Any More

by

Anne Filkin

Deana hovered unobtrusively, scanning the racks of brochures, and waiting to see which assistant would be free first. It was the young man with horn-rimmed specs at the end counter. She smiled at him as he waved her to the seat so recently vacated.

'How can I help you Ma'am?'

'I'm treating myself to a vacation. A package tour maybe, but not just any El Cheapo deal. Have you any Special Offers, right now?'

' Sure - we'll fix you up with something just right for you. Had you anywhere in particular in mind, Mrs Er...?'

Prendergast. Well, I thought of London to start with, then Florence, and somewhere a bit unusual - like Budapest. Then on to the South of France, a classy resort, to soak up some sun and...'

The young man was frowning a little, now.

'Hold on a minute - d'you mean London, England and Florence, Italy?'

'Why yes, of...'

'But Ma'am, had you forgotten that Europe isn't there any more?'

Deana stared back at him.

'Um, sorry - don't get it.' She peered at his name badge. Carl Miller.

'Ma'am, there isn't any Europe. It sank.' He shrugged apologetically. 'All gone. Sorry!' He leaned back in his chair. 'We've a nice cruise going...'

Deana interrupted him. 'I just don't believe what I'm hearing - is it some sort of Fun Day? What are you telling me?'

She knew she sounded panicky. The boy (well he looked quite young) was signalling to someone behind her.

'Would you like a nice fresh cup of coffee? Laurie, bring Mrs Prendergast a coffee, would you pet.'

She was tearful now. 'I - I don't understand.'

'The Meteorite! You must have heard. There's been nothing else on the News and in the papers, for months.'

She took a sip of coffee. 'I've been ill, very ill - in hospital. I didn't see any papers or tv. I had an accident, you see, and I was unconscious a long time. I'm

209

alright now. They suggested a vacation in Palm Springs to convalesce. But I wanted somewhere more exciting.'

'Yes, of course, and I can suggest the very thing - India! That's the in-place nowadays. Everyone's going there. Kashmir won't be too hot in May.'

Mrs Prendergast started to cry.

'All those people - drowned! Millions and millions of them. England and France and Spain and Portugal...' Her voice was rising; people were looking at them.

'Spain and Portugal are mostly ok. The Meteorite hit the middle of France. Bonk! Just as they said would happen,' he added, a touch complacent. 'Like hitting toffee with a hammer.'

He reached over and patted her hand. 'But no-one's drowned! Everyone had plenty of warning. They all got away - well all except a few people who thought it was a government plot, and refused to budge. Oh, and some British Navy types insisted on going down with the ship.'

Deana swallowed the rest of the coffee in one gulp.

'Halford!' she exclaimed, 'my brother - he was over in Europe! In Winchester, England, visiting my niece and her husband. And they've just had their first baby. Oh, what will have happened to them? Why haven't I heard?'

'Well, things aren't back to normal yet. But they could all be over here; American citizens got priority. Uncle Sam did a huge airlift - we had to take on extra staff.'

Deana stared at him. He sounded quite elated. A great wodge of European culture had disappeared, and it had hardly caused a ripple here. Right opposite was a large, coloured poster of The Parthenon. *Hellenic Discovery*, it was headed. Across the bottom a sticker had been added - 'By Glass-bottomed Sub'. How callous could you get?

She could hear the girl at the next desk on the phone. 'No, Sir, we're not taking bookings for Ireland at the moment. We can't locate it. It floated away. We've had a few sightings - I'll let you know.'

'Fancy the Alps? No problem there.' Her assistant was still shuffling brochures.

She rose abruptly, and somewhat unsteadily. 'I'm sorry, Mr Miller, I just can't concentrate. Best if I come back another day.'

Next moment she found herself being gently propelled across the shop.

'Now, Mrs Prendergast, why don't you sit here at this nice quiet table next to this nice potted palm, while I find you some really nice brochures to look at. Laurie! Laurie'll bring you another cup of coffee. Now, have a little think about

Australia. I think you'd like Cairns - wonderful beaches, and the Barrier Reef as well.'

'No, no coffee - a glass of water will do fine, thank you. Australia! Oh, I suppose, but not the seaside. I can't swim. Anyway, I'd be worried about another meteorite. How high is Ayers Rock?'

'I know you're off duty, Doctor; but we thought you'd want to see her. She's spoken a couple of words. Nurse Lorie heard 'water' and 'rock' quite clearly.'

Dr Muller was still in jogging gear, incongruous against the white sterility of his surroundings.

'You did right to call me, Sister. This is distinctly promising! Frankly, I was prepared for the worst - she's been unconscious so long. She must be recalling the accident.'

The others were watching the monitor. He sat by the bed and took the patient's wrist, to feel the pulse. Deana opened her eyes.

It was hard to know who was most amazed, - Deana at her surroundings; or the three spectators, at her instant recovery. The nurses couldn't help clapping, and almost cheering; which, when explained to a staff nurse glancing in from the corridor, passed around the building as a sigh is borne on the breeze: 'Mrs Prendergast has regained consciousness!'

It was probably a dream. She was in a strange bed, in an ugly nightie. A handsome young man with horn-rimmed specs was holding her hand. A large plump woman and a small thin one dressed as nurses were smiling at her from the foot of the bed. There were flowers on the bedside table. Propped against the vase was a postcard: a photograph - she tried to focus - of a cathedral? Winchester Cathedral.

She remembered. The Meteorite! In fear and doubt, she repeated the words aloud.

The young man answered. He had produced a stethoscope, and was prodding her chest. Surely he couldn't be a real Doctor in that rig.

'Hardly that, Mrs Prendergast - though it must have been a pretty large boulder to knock you into that lake. Luckily it hit the chair, and not your head! Your friends got a nasty shock; they saw the rock falling, but their warning came too late. By the time they got to you, you'd been under a few minutes. I'm afraid your masterpiece is still at the bottom of the lake with all your painting gear.'

A genuine impression that all might be well, flooded through Deana's mind, bringing strength to her body. She would try to make sense of it later. She

211

struggled to sit up; and at a nod from the young man - why *was* he labelled *Sea World?* - the two nurses propped her up against the pillows.

She smiled at the younger woman.

'Y'know, I'd just *love* a nice fresh cup of coffee, Nurse Lorie!'

The Decision

by

Sylvia R Monk

Henry had always been too trusting. Easily taken in. It was not surprising that his friends thought he was heading for a sticky end. Basically it was all down to: should he have put that X on his pools against no publicity or not. Well, he hadn't and look where it had got him. Especially as it was only the third time in his life he had done the pools.

If he had just taken that extra care there would have been no begging letters which really worried him. He had made a point of reading every single one. The tales of horror that came through the post were so bad. A few pounds here and a few pounds there, were religiously sent back much to the delight of the vultures whose tales were mostly made up with vivid imagination.

There would definitely have been no Ida standing on the door step, for all to see, through those twitching curtains. Her plaintive look, haunting eyes taking advantage of his generosity, or so the nosy neighbours thought. Her sense of dress, slightly bohemian in looks, her long hair gave the appearance that a good shampoo and cut wouldn't go amiss. But behind those tatty looks there was something familiar about her.

Henry had lived on his own for more years than he cared to remember. His wife Maud had been a loving scatter-brain. She had met her death in a tragic way as he had always feared. Her life was always very unpredictable. So it had not been a surprise to Henry when she fell from the cliffs while on   holiday. Her foot had gone down a rabbit hole causing her to over balance. All the same he still grieved for the wife he loved so much, for many years.

He realised after a long while that he had started to enjoy this solitary way of life, plodding along at his own pace which even when he was young had been a lot slower than Maud's hectic days bustling about, in and out to different charity events and woman's organisations. She rushed about so much she never really had time to spend on her appearance but that was the way he loved her, never wanting her a dolled up smart figure.

His offspring, two sons and two very money minded daughters-in-law appeared very seldom much to Henry's relief. Once they realised he hadn't got much money to spare they had kept their distance. He didn't get much pleasure out of his grandchildren descending on him, wrecking his home, treading on his vegetable garden throughout their occasional visits. All he longed for was the time the door shut behind them as they drove back to their busy worlds of banking, public schools and parties, leaving him in peace with his cat. So life had really become quite enjoyable in his own little world with nobody interfering. If he ever felt like company he would put his cap on, pick up his stick and go for a walk in the park. He enjoyed the times when he could sit on the bench and have a chat to a stranger who he didn't have to get involved with.

But this was all to alter when the pools man arrived on the doorstep. It was a cold and miserable February day. Henry was quite happy napping by the fire, his feet in the well worn slippers that were beautifully comfortablY moulded to his old feet. His only companion was Ginger the cat who was blissfully lapping at the cream on the top of the milk Henry had forgotten to put away after his morning cup of tea.

All hell was suddenly let loose. As soon as that door opened poor Henry's life changed. Even Ginger couldn't cope with all the commotion and decided to head for a cushion in the garden shed. The photographer's flash light was soon working overtime. The investment genius giving his advice to Henry to make his million pounds work for him. But the worst thing was the relations appearing from all the corners of the country. They nearly drove Henry insane. Should he give the lot away to the cat's home where Ginger had come from and then he could disappear back in his shell. But the decision didn't come easily and those wretched grandchildren were back again, using his runner bean poles as goal posts was more than he could bear.

Peace descended then for a few days, giving him a false sense of security. Until the front door bell was ringing again, making Henry regret the action of ever doing the pools let alone winning them. He was in the middle of daydreaming about Maud and how she would have loved all the activity. She would have know what to do with the new found riches.

The March wind roared through the door as he opened it to the stranger on the doorstep, although she seemed familiar in a strange way. She introduced herself as Ida, with her hand outstretched to him. He let her into the lounge and she sank thankfully down into the chair by the fire. Ginger appeared from nowhere, jumping onto her lap as if he was greeting a long lost friend. Henry could not make this out. He couldn't even make himself out for letting this woman into his house. She sipped the tea he put before her and he sat himself back in the old fireside chair as she told him she had a story to tell him and prepare himself for a shock.

214

She had read about him in the paper when he had his pools money presented she knew immediately as she looked at his face staring out at her. A face she had seen the features of so many times as she looked in the mirror. She had been searching for nearly twenty years since her parents had died and she had been left a letter telling her she was adopted, a secret that had been well kept from her and they had left her with a few clues to trace her real parents. It turned out her mother had been pregnant and unmarried when the war had started, her lover was sent away to fight for his country without being told she was expecting his baby. After the birth at a maiden Aunt's miles away where nobody knew her, her parents decided the best thing was to have the baby adopted. So Ida had been brought up by a childless couple who were sworn to secrecy. After many years of searching the country for her real parents that paper had given her the answer she had wanted to know for so long. Henry was her father. Her mother, Maud, was dead and had been for many years.

Ida's life had been a sad one. She had married but had been unable to have children. Recently her husband had died after her devoted nursing for the past year. He had left her enough money for a very comfortable life but it had not brought her much happiness. She had just decided to buy an old house and grounds where there was a cattery for stray cats. Cats were now her only love. This was certainly why Ginger had taken to her.

Once Henry got over the initial shock of what Maud had done to them both, he realised how typical of her and how it must have hurt her at the time she handed over their daughter. But here she was just wanting him for himself. His money problems were solved, a great burden had been lifted since Ida appeared on the scene. He shared a proportion of his winnings between his two sons, which got them off his back. He would have a nice little bungalow built in the grounds of Ida's home so that he and Ida could see each other whenever they wanted to without being on top of each other. He helped her out financially with the running of the cats home and also gave a very large donation to a local home for unmarried mothers.

At long last he was suddenly very grateful to fate for letting him forget that X, so that he could live the rest of his life in peace with Ginger and his new found daughter.

Striking a Blow

by

Pat Caldwell

'Frightened? No, to tell you the truth I was angry. When I saw him standing there in my home, I was enraged. It's funny but I wasn't even surprised.'

'But you have just told me that he broke into your house. That you didn't know him.'

Mary was aware of a change in the attitude of the young man. To her surprise she saw suspicion in his eyes. He set down his mug of tea and took up his notebook again.

'Let's see - yes, here it is. You stated, 'He broke in, threatened me, and, in the course of a struggle in which I feared for my own safety, I inflicted the wound in his chest.' Do you now wish to change that statement?'

'No of course not. Look - what are you getting at? *He* broke into *my* house. Haven't I the right to defend myself?'

'Not if there was no threat to you.'

'What do you mean? No threat. Doesn't finding someone in my house, in the middle of the night, constitute a threat?'

'Not necessarily - no.'

She felt as if she were caught in a nightmare, where everything was reversed. This wasn't the way it should be. Why had she said that she hadn't been surprised to find the intruder? This powerful, confident young man wouldn't understand. All women are aware that one day they may have to protect themselves, that one day they may become another victim, another statistic. When it happens, when they are confronted with an intruder or an attacker, why should they be surprised? It happens to women everywhere, every day.

The policeman stood up, put on his cap, opened his breast pocket and neatly stowed away his notebook.

'I'm sorry Mrs Tate (it had been Mary just ten minutes ago, she thought) but I'm going to have to ask you to accompany me to the station. Will you go and get dressed please?'

She laughed then. She couldn't help it. His expression hardened.

'I've requested that you accompany me to the station. I don't want to use force but I will if you don't comply with my request immediately.'

216

You know the events which followed. It was in all the national papers. There was a public outcry.

Headlines screamed, *'Woman on Murder Charge For Defending Her Home'*, editorials asked, 'Where is justice for the ordinary law abiding citizen when it is an offence to defend ourselves against attack by criminals?' and, 'Shouldn't this woman be applauded for her courage, rather than pilloried for doing no more than striking a blow for every frightened, victimized woman in this country?'

Months later Mary walked from the court, free and exonerated. After all, when it came to light that the deceased had been a known criminal and had spent ten of his twenty-eight years of life in prison for crimes which included breaking and entering, petty theft, and even, on one occasion, manslaughter, the jury had no option but to find Mary Tate innocent.

She had no living relatives. The woman who drove her home from the court was a social worker who also happened to be President of W.A.G.O.F.F.F. or Women's Action Group Offers Freedom From Fear. She was very kind. She was also, or so it seemed to Mary, indecently, ecstatically, triumphant.

She treated Mary as if she were a heroine. As if, when Mary had plunged her knife into the heart of that pathetic little lout, she had freed women everywhere from the chains of fear forever.

At last, the woman left. Mary put the kettle on, relishing the silence of her small kitchen. The last months had been an enormous strain, mainly because of the total absence of solitude. She supposed she had become too used to being alone, but if she couldn't be with the ones she loved she'd rather be alone.

The kettle boiled. She warmed the pot, swirling the water around carefully before tipping it into the sink. A small spider ran out from beneath the bread crock beside the draining board, she watched it while she measured tea into the pot and poured the boiling water onto the leaves. From a small cupboard above the stove she took a blue knitted tea cosy and as she pulled it into place her fingers lingered upon the red, woollen pompom which decorated the top...

'Look, look, Mummy, I made it. I made it for you.'

She sighed, her movements were slow and heavy now as she assembled the tea things upon a tray and carried it through to the lounge. She sat down thankfully.

As she raised the cup to her lips, her eyes met those of her husband in the picture above the mantelpiece.

'It's over, George,' she whispered. 'I kept my promise. He has paid for what he did to us.'

217

It had all been so easy. There had been nothing to connect her with her victim.

Gerald, her daughter's husband, had died that dreadful night two years ago as he went to the aid of a neighbour. It had been a knife wound in the heart. A wound that had destroyed not only Gerald but all of Mary's family. For, just two months later, Sarah had taken a massive overdose of sleeping pills and followed her husband. It had been too much for George. He had had a heart condition for years and on the day of Sarah's funeral, he had died as well. Mary had promised him then, as she looked down on his poor dead face, that Peter Chipton would pay.

From the first shock of recognition in the street, to the planning of her strategy, it had all happened just as she meant it to. She had followed Peter that day. He had led her to his flat, a shabby, run down place, with dirty windows and a pile of empty bottles stacked outside the door. She had watched him then, for weeks. Following him to the sleazy pub and snooker hall where he spent the greater part of every day. Waiting, watching for her chance. It had come on the night she had bumped into him.

'Oh, you startled me.' She had looked back, nervously, over her shoulder. 'I think someone is following me. I only live a short distance away... could I ask you? No... No... it doesn't matter...'

'Do you want me to walk you home?' She saw the gleam in his eyes as he took her bait.

'Would you? I would feel so much safer. I really must get secure locks put on my doors and on those dreadful flimsy sliding windows too. You know, even when they're closed I'm sure they can be lifted from the frame. I realise that a woman living on her own has to be more careful. I haven't lived here long though.'

That night she had made her preparations. She had taken a large kitchen knife and placed it on the table by the side of her bed. Then she had undressed, put on her dressing gown and sat, waiting, in the darkness.

He had made quite a noise. She wasn't surprised he had spent so many years in prison, he wasn't even good at what he did.

She thought she had seen recognition in his face, at the end, as if he realised who she was. It didn't matter now. Nothing mattered. She was very tired.

'I think I'll take a little nap dear,' she smiled at George's picture, put her feet up on the sofa, laid back against the cushions and closed her eyes.

Scales of Justice

by

Sheila Barker

Maria raced down the hill on her bright, red bicycle singing at the top of her voice, her long black hair bounding on her shoulders underneath her pink, bowler hat that had large Daisies on it.

'There she goes again,' her next door neighbour spoke shaking her head, 'Mad as a hatter she is, how her husband puts up with her I'll never know.' Her companion nodded in agreement as they both watched till Maria was out of sight.

Maria having reached the bottom of the hill turned off the main road until she came to a country lane. Standing her bicycle up against a tree she threw her hat off beside it, then turned and ran into her lover's arms kissing him passionately with a hunger she never thought existed within herself.

The rustling of the trees made them quickly draw apart and David went to investigate, 'It's okay,' he said, looking relieved, 'it's only a rabbit.'

Maria tossed her long hair over her shoulders and laughed.

'You are as white as a ghost. Don't worry no one followed me, I'm sure of that, they all think I've gone quite mad and avoid me, I should have taken up acting as my profession. Now to put plan B into action.'

David was completely under Maria's spell. He found her quite fascinating and had never met anyone quite like her, he would even kill Martin, her husband, if she had asked him, but Maria wanted that pleasure for herself.

David, being only twenty, was ten years younger than Maria, but strain was already showing around his pale blue eyes, which were looking directly at Maria. Clasping her hands tightly, his voice was hoarse as he spoke.

'Please be careful Maria, I just could not stand it if things were to go wrong, I love you so much.'

'Don't worry David, I didn't study car mechanics for nothing, now I'm going to put my knowledge to good use.'

'It's going to be agony darling not seeing you for a few days, but we had better stick to the arrangements.' Maria gave David one more lingering kiss before they went their separate ways.

Maria was sick of her boring husband and had only married him because he was so rich. Putting on her sweet innocent act certainly fooled him and within two months they were married, but, after a year looking at his bulging stomach and bald head over the breakfast table she found it very hard to hide her revulsion. She didn't want all the bother of a divorce either. Having tasted the good life she wasn't going to accept half measures. She wanted it all and was determined to get it.

Maria was confident of all her plans, but still slept uneasily. She looked at the luminous clock on her bedside table. Three a.m. Better now or never she thought to herself. Slipping on her black ski pants and baggy green jumper, she checked on Martin, just to make sure he was sound asleep, the sleeping tablet was definitely working. Making her way outside to the garage, she set to work on the brake cable. When she was sure everything was in order she went back to bed.

Eight a.m. Maria decided she would play the dutiful wife act and take her husband's breakfast upstairs to him on a tray.

'Maria darling what would I do without you? You're such a dear. I feel quite groggy this morning, I must have slept rather heavily last night, but I won't let it dampen my appetite.'

No, nothing could ever do that Maria thought despondently.

Maria busied herself downstairs if only to keep her mind occupied. Having daily help there was never much that needed doing. She thought she heard Martin shout, but ignored it, he was probably only playing with that ugly old dog Brutus as he usually did.

A few minutes later the dog came down whimpering, he jumped up at her, claws catching the legs of her tights, it was obvious to Maria the dog was trying to tell her something.

Brutus rushed up to his master's bedroom with Maria in pursuit. From the doorway Maria saw Brutus licking the face of his dead Master, the dog snarled at Maria as she went near her husband. She hurried to 'phone for an ambulance. Maria's thoughts were racing, it seemed in no time the ambulance had arrived.

'Heart attack I'm afraid Mrs Williams.'

It was arranged that Maria would go to stay with Martin's family till after the funeral. She felt relieved when everything was all over and could not wait to be with her lover, she had not been able to speak to David for eight whole days and was desperate to see him. At last she was on her own and was able to 'phone.

'David, David,' but it wasn't David who answered.

'David has been in an accident,' replied his mother in a quivering voice. 'He's still in a coma, he is in the City General.'

Maria left the 'phone dangling off the hook to race to the Hospital. In top gear she sped down the motorway. It was the first time since the day Martin died she had used the car. She put her foot down on the brake. Her blood went cold.

Her piercing screams could not be heard as her car plunged over the bridge and somersaulted down the trail of darkness into the depths of beyond.